THE EVANGELIST IN HELL

JIMMY LEONARD

eLectio Publishing
Little Elm, TX
www.eLectioPublishing.com

The Evangelist in Hell
By Jimmy Leonard

Copyright 2017 by Jimmy Leonard. All rights reserved.
Cover Design by eLectio Publishing.

ISBN-13: 978-1-63213-386-1

Published by eLectio Publishing, LLC
Little Elm, Texas
http://www.eLectioPublishing.com

Printed in the United States of America

5 4 3 2 1 eLP 21 20 19 18 17

The eLectio Publishing creative team is comprised of: Kaitlyn Campbell, Emily Certain, Lori Draft, Court Dudek, Jim Eccles, Sheldon James, and Christine LePorte.

Publisher's Note

The publisher does not have any control over and does not assume any responsibility for author or third-party websites or their content.

For Emily

ACKNOWLEDGMENTS

Thank you to Christopher Dixon, Jesse Greever, and the entire team at eLectio for making this book possible. It's been such a privilege to work with you.

I'm grateful to the early readers who challenged my thinking, offered brilliant insights, and encouraged me along the way, including Tim and Jess Courtois, Jack Duiven, Julie Leonard, Melanie Leonard, Andrew Mast, Scott Osdras, and Shepherd Smith, among so many others. Chris Mann and GJ Frye were some of the first to spur me on, and I appreciate your support from even before I had words on a page. Thank you especially to Kyle Chase. You've helped me see not only the story I'm writing but also the story I'm living, and both are better because of you.

I'm also indebted to J.F. Spieles and Michael Leonard, who paved the way before me and showed me what was possible in writing a novel. It might have taken me longer if I hadn't watched you do it first.

Finally, thank you to Emily, who not only endured more drafts than anyone but also endured me while I wrote them. I love you, and I can't wait to share more adventures with you.

"The mind is its own place, and in itself
Can make a Heav'n of Hell, a Hell of Heav'n.
What matter where, if I be still the same . . .

Here we may reign secure, and in my choice
To reign is worth ambition though in Hell:
Better to reign in Hell, than serve in Heav'n."

— John Milton
Paradise Lost

"Hell is a state of mind—
ye never said a truer word . . .

But Heaven is not a state of mind. Heaven is reality
itself. All that is fully real is Heavenly. For all that can
be shaken will be shaken and only the unshakeable
remains."

— C. S. Lewis
The Great Divorce

ONE
KNIGHT'S QUEST

JOE PLATT HAD BEEN practicing all day. On the treadmill before work, in the shower, at lunch, again in the elevator as he descended the nine floors from the office to the lobby. He rehearsed the demonstration once more as he drove toward Midtown, repeating his talking points while sitting in traffic, highlighting the software's intuitive interface as he turned left onto Woodward.

Two weeks till Christmas, and the sun set early, joining the great exodus from the city on its own afternoon commute. Gray slush lined the sidewalks, and car exhaust formed like exhales in the frigid air. Joe found a street spot a block from the restaurant and slid his car in parallel to the curb. A glance at the clock: T minus one hour. Months of stress and trial and error and countless overtime had all come down to a single evening. Time to launch or scrub the mission completely. It was hardly an overstatement to say the fate of the company now rested on Joe.

Lord, help us all, he thought as the car door shut behind him.

At twenty-four, Joe was part of the new class of entrepreneurs seizing Detroit's cheap real estate and revitalized downtown, riding on dreams and venture capital, in it less for the money and more for the love of the game. And while many startups crashed and burned in their first two years, UrbanCalc was still going strong at eighteen months, boasting positive feedback from three schools' worth of beta testers and serious interest from multiple districts across the state.

"I want to revolutionize education," Garrett Elson had said when they first met, back at the CS department spring showcase a year and a half ago. "You know, make it accessible. Make it fun."

He was only four years older than Joe, a diehard Tigers fan, and remarkably industrious despite his privileged pedigree. Indeed, most of their early backers had been relatives and wealthy friends of the Elson family, but with good press and the right word of mouth, Garrett had since caught the eyes of some particularly well-resourced investors and potential advertising partners—and it was a good thing, too. Product reviews aside, Joe knew their nascent company still dangled precariously over the great churning sea of startup oblivion. They'd need a big financial push to reach the national market, and for that, they'd decided to host an event.

The place was Sri Bagha, Midtown's newly opened and highly reviewed pan-Asian eatery. Joe could personally recommend the curry pad thai, having ordered it for takeout on more than one occasion to break up a long night of coding. They had a private room in the back—red and gold color scheme, dim lighting, almost uncomfortably warm on such an otherwise bleak and wintry night. Joe and his few coworkers helped set up the projector and equipment and an hour later found themselves joined by twenty-five potential investors and their various significant others, all well-dressed and seated at tables with elaborate centerpieces, like a wedding reception without the bride.

"You nervous?" Ted asked, balancing a sushi roll with chopsticks and carefully dunking it in soy sauce before taking a noisy bite.

"A little," Joe admitted.

It'd been Garrett's idea to mix it up, saying it'd be good for the investors to hear a voice other than his own. More likely, Joe suspected, the boss wanted to avoid stumbling over a technical question, making Joe the obvious choice. Either way, in classic Tigers metaphor, Garrett had promised, "I'll pitch it. You hit the home run."

Or swing and miss, Joe mused.

"And I am proud to say," Garrett spoke confidently from the front of the room, "that this fall we saw a hundred and fifty students using *Sir Lanceplot* both in the classroom and at home, and not only do the kids love it, but our teachers are saying that test scores are already higher."

The portable projector screen displayed screenshots of UrbanCalc's groundbreaking achievement: *Sir Lanceplot*, a customizable graphing app creatively embedded into a medieval-themed role-playing game. The latest version even included a Knight's Quest feature, allowing advanced students to take on enrichment opportunities—one of Joe's own special projects from the past year.

Joe loosened his tie just slightly, trying to calm his stage fright. An ironic situation, he knew, for the designer of a game about valiant mathematician-knights riding into battle, but hey, what could he do?

"Fear is a warning sign," had been the sermon at St. Peter's just last week. "It's our instinct to protect what matters. But the Lord tells us to not be afraid because he is with us. He will uphold us in his righteous hand."

Great in theory, Joe thought, *but God's not about to give this demo.*

Garrett began his introduction. "Now enough of me talking. You're all here to see this thing in action."

Joe double-checked that his phone was on silent. When he pulled it out of his pocket, however, the screen caught his eye.

New text from David.

Of course—just what Joe needed right now. He swiped to ignore it and set his phone face down on the table. No time for that. Certainly no time for that.

" . . . we're lucky to have one of UrbanCalc's extremely talented programmers . . ."

Deep breath. Just a quick demonstration and a few questions at the end. Nothing he hadn't prepared for. Nothing he wouldn't know how to answer.

" . . . who's put in countless hours toward the success of this project . . ."

Smile. Be personal. Make it engaging. Have fun.

" . . . give it up for Joe Platt!"

He stood. Their applause came louder than expected.

"If you remember," Ted argued, hoisting his glass to drain the final sip, "the name was my idea."

The party had officially ended an hour ago, and although Garrett himself had left after a few minutes of investor chit-chat, the rest of the squad had stayed for another round and a collective exhale. The private room's door was propped open: Rollicking shouts erupted from the bar as downed *sake* bombs hit the counter, and the overhead music had subtly switched from instrumental to electronic. Joe checked the time on his watch. Not even ten o'clock.

"It was back before UrbanCalc even started. Garrett and I were out in Seattle for a conference, and he pitched me the idea. You know what he wanted to call it, though? *The Coordinate Realm.* Still with the whole castle and dungeon theme, but I mean"—Ted unleashed a massive belch—"how lame is that?" Ted had rowed in college and still had the build for it, although deep down he was as geeky as the rest of them.

"Anyway, I had a whole bunch of 'em. *King Arthogonal. Merliner Equations. The Hyperbolic Grail.* Then one morning it just came to me in the shower, like divine inspiration, man. *Sir Lanceplot.*"

4

Lena, their marketing and social media coordinator, groaned from the across the table. "You're such a nerd. No wonder Jordan always wants to hang out with you."

Ted smirked. "Where is your beau tonight, anyway? Thought he was coming."

"Canada, actually. He's at Caesar's with his brother."

"Decided to cross the river for a little sports gambling, eh?"

She rolled her eyes. "I wouldn't know. He only tells me when he wins."

"Wouldn't wait up, then, if I were you. Besides, they might get snowed in if we actually get what they're predicting. Wouldn't be shocked if they shut down the border."

"Yeah, seriously," said Lena, flicking a strand of loose blond hair behind her ear. "Everyone's acting like it's the freaking apocalypse. Like, we live in Michigan, people."

A waiter stopped by the table, offering Joe another Sprite. He politely refused.

"Sure you don't want a real drink?" Lena asked. "I think you've earned it."

"Agreed," Ted chimed in. "If I haven't said it already, you killed it tonight."

Indeed, Joe had survived the presentation and even managed to enjoy it, garnering a number of oohs and ahhs in all the right places. If the investor handshakes and animated conversations were any indication, they should have enough funding to keep *Lanceplot* on the battlefield for the foreseeable future. After a big success, he should be kicking back and enjoying his Friday night. Plenty of reason to celebrate, right?

"I'm okay," Joe said, referring to the drink. "I should probably get going soon anyway."

Actually, he felt exhausted enough to have left an hour ago. It'd been a long few months, and he wasn't quite on break yet. He still had work next week and an early start tomorrow with the St. Peter's monthly men's breakfast, for which he'd agreed to bring donuts, provided that the pending Snowpocalypse didn't lead them to cancel it. No, he'd stayed out and awake tonight for one reason and one reason only: David.

The text he'd received earlier had said, *Call me ASAP. Kind of an emergency.* Typical David—high on the drama and vague on the details. Joe had called as soon as he could, but of course there'd been no answer. Last time, the word *emergency* had meant David was sitting in a jail cell following a DUI. The time before that, David had wanted to borrow six hundred bucks but was too embarrassed to ask Grandpa. Yet he'd had no problem asking Joe.

To be fair, Joe's brother was making strides. David had just finished a court-ordered rehab program and decided to move in with a friend who could hook him up with a job. A family hardware store or something like that—Grandma had told him, but Joe couldn't remember exactly. Still, it was a better situation, better opportunity, etcetera, etcetera. In other words, no more trouble with the law, and no more aimless drifting.

If only it were the first time David had said that.

Another round of shouts from the bar. Ted was cracking up, although Joe had missed the joke.

It felt so much later than it was.

Well, he'd waited up for David long enough. If it really were an emergency, he'd have called back by now. After a few quick goodnights and see-you-Mondays around the room, Joe grabbed his coat and ventured out into the tundra. An icy wind slapped his bare cheek, and he could already feel the snot freezing inside his nose. Joe speed-walked to his car and was scraping snow off his windshield when he finally heard the ringtone in his pocket.

Impeccable timing, as always. Perhaps against his better judgment, Joe answered it.

"Hello?"

"Hey, man," David said. "What's up?"

Way too cold for small talk, Joe thought.

"How about you tell me," he replied, his tone about as frosty as the car. "I got your text."

"Oh, um . . . yeah, okay. Sure. Thanks for calling me back by the way." David's voice was muffled, and traffic noises sounded in the background. Joe opened his car door and climbed in to finish the call.

"So, actually, I kind of need a favor."

No surprise there. Joe adjusted the heat to warm the interior of the car instead of the windshield, wondering what kind of trouble it was this time. Couldn't be jail—he would have noticed the strange caller ID. Money was always a possibility, although Joe steeled himself to say no. He had to draw a line somewhere, didn't he?

When his brother failed to elaborate, Joe pressed, "What favor, David?"

"I need a ride. That's it."

Yeah right, Joe thought. Nothing was ever *that's it* with David.

"I'm at a work thing right now, David. We had this big presentation tonight and . . ."

"I can wait," David interrupted. "If you need to finish up or whatever, I don't mind."

Joe sighed. "Can't you call a cab or something? I mean, it's late, David."

"I could, but there's a little bit of a situation right now, and I just . . . it's not what you think. I'm getting back on track, Joe, I just . . . I can explain when you get here."

Potential responses swirled in a tempest. *I'm sorry, David. I can't always do this. Not tonight. Not right now. This time, David, call someone else.*

Snow had already covered the windshield again, entombing Joe in the car. He flipped on the wipers and turned up the setting. He'd be home in ten minutes if he left now. Home and upstairs to his apartment with a nice hot shower and a nice warm bed. He was perfectly within his rights to say no, wasn't he? And who knew? It might actually be good for David to figure this out on his own for a change. As anyone with an addict in the family knew too well, rescuing and enabling were two sides of the same dirty coin.

The silence lingered, and Joe realized his brother was waiting for a response. He opened his lips to say no, but stopped, catching his eyes in the rearview mirror. His bloodshot, tired eyes. But what was the point of waiting up for David just to ignore him now?

He's your brother, reminded Joe's conscience. *Who's he supposed to call if not you?*

For crying out loud—of course it had to be the middle of the night, and freezing, and a blizzard. Might as well make it Christmas Eve, just to add a little more guilt.

I knew this would happen, Joe realized, *as soon as I answered the phone.*

"So much for drawing the line," he muttered.

"I missed that," David said. "Did you say something?"

Despite the mind's best intentions, the heart could be a real sucker.

"Tell me where to go," Joe replied as he put the car into drive.

TWO
NO CONTEST

BY ALL ACCOUNTS, the Platt brothers had shared a tragic childhood.

Their home was broken in the classic sense—parents married young but separated shortly after David was born, and even before that their father was more of a recurring houseguest than a permanent resident. Joe did remember some things about their first house. It was yellow, one-story, and had a tree swing where Mom used to push him in the backyard. He and David shared a room, and at night, Joe could hear the trains whistle as they raced over the tracks and the shouts carry from the bedroom across the hall. They moved into Grandma's house in Livonia not long after Mom accidentally broke a flower vase while cleaning one night—a story that, even at his young age, Joe knew better than to believe.

By the time Joe finished kindergarten, his dad was completely out of his life—no phone calls, no birthday cards, and certainly no weekend visits. In a way, it was like missing a ghost. Even though he was gone, life actually felt more real. Grandpa had already become the de facto father figure, a role he naturally stepped into. It was Grandpa who had taught Joe how to shoot a basketball, flip a pancake, bait a fishing line, and do a cannonball off the dock at Duck Lake.

Then, on a warm September afternoon when Joe had just started second grade, everything shattered. Like an invisible bomb with no noise, no flash, no shrapnel lodged in his side—but an explosion just the same. Joe knew emotions more than facts: shock, confusion, pain, anguish. He felt an emptiness in his stomach when he wasn't hungry, and he felt a tiredness in his limbs while he lay wide awake. Hours blurred together, but yet the moments themselves held a striking vividness, small details seared into his memory like burns on the skin. Flipping through *Where's Waldo* with David in the waiting room, not caring to look. Doctors standing in white coats and nurses faceless in their dark blue scrubs. Grandma in tears and Grandpa crying too, noiselessly, his silent grief confirming what Joe already knew but couldn't possibly understand.

Aneurysm was the word he learned to explain it.

"Nobody knows why it happens," Grandma told him gently.

Every day for weeks, it seemed that something else would rupture too. The fuel line at the gas station. The pipes in the basement. The showerhead in the bathroom. The blood vessels inside Joe's own brain, throbbing as he lay sleepless on the pillow each night.

Joe thought she would look peaceful or maybe just asleep at the viewing, but her actual appearance caught him off guard. Who was this person with stiff and sallow skin but the face of his mother? That was her brown hair, and those were her thin lips, but something was off all the same, as if they'd hired an artist to make a dummy, and he hadn't quite gotten it right.

Uncle Russ drove in from Chicago. He talked to Joe for a long time before the service, telling him again and again how courageous he was. How lucky David was to have such a brave big brother. How his mom was so proud of him—was still so proud of him.

"You know a lot of people are sad today," Russ said. "But I'll tell you something. Your mom is up in Heaven right now, having a big old party with Jesus. I bet you she's singing and dancing up there just like she used to."

Joe tried to imagine it but couldn't. Truth be told, he'd never seen Mom dance.

At the church service, they played a song Joe liked about flying up on an angel's wings. He decided that he'd keep it in her honor, that he would remember it and sing it again and again, each day and each night, maybe forever. But when he tried to recall it a few hours later, at home and lying on his bed, he couldn't think of the tune or the verses or a single word from the chorus. Everything washed off like watercolors, and there was nothing to keep it from fading. Reality became no more than a dream, and dreams themselves became nothing.

Of course, everyone knew. Joe didn't have to tell them—they already knew. The bus driver, the lunch lady, the recess monitor—somehow they all sensed it, as if her spirit were following Joe around the school, always just where his eyes weren't looking, visible to everyone else except for him. The principal stopped him in the hallway just to ask about his day. Mrs. Rollins, his teacher, gave him pencils and extra stickers and asked him first if he wanted to hand back papers to the class. He never did. Ten math problems on the board, but she whispered to Joe that he only had to do five. Later, she slipped him a bag of Skittles for doing all ten anyway.

It was the same at home. In the evenings, strange people came to the front door with baked goods and fruit baskets and, once, a fully cooked ham. There were cards in the mail and phone calls from extended relatives and close friends and half the church. That Christmas, the boys received a mountain of presents—sweaters and T-shirts and tennis shoes and chapter books and Disney movies and baseball bats and LEGO sets and a pair of remote-controlled cars with stripes like lightning bolts on the sides. For these, Grandpa helped them build a racetrack in the basement using boards for the walls and folded pieces of cardboard to bank the curves. Joe beat David every time, but Grandpa owned the track record. After all, what couldn't he do?

And—Joe couldn't help it—there were times he cried. He could go all day at school alert and smiling, and then be just fine with his math homework and playing catch in the backyard with Grandpa. Then, on those nights when he lay restless in bed, warm tears would drip down onto his pillowcase. He imagined her dark hair and tight hugs and warm eyes that sometimes looked sad, even when she was laughing. He felt her hands on his cheeks and her lips planting a kiss. He heard her whispered *I love you* resonating deep inside his ears.

And so the echoes lingered and lulled him to sleep, and days rolled into weeks, and acceptance came gradually but noticeably, like color to the sky just before sunrise.

For David, however, things were different.

Even the simplest requests became monstrous ordeals. He soon progressed from temper tantrums to willful defiance. Grandma received frequent complaints from the kindergarten teacher—David didn't listen today, refused to share the blocks, pushed another student. At home they tried spanking, timeouts, no TV for a week. Then, the opposite approach. They put a sticker chart on the refrigerator, one star for every good deed. Ten stars earned a cone at Dairy Queen. Progress hit a wall around star number four.

Joe, for his part, usually stayed out of it. David was trying, he knew, and just needed some time to adjust. He wasn't really a bad kid. Sometimes he just made mistakes. The two of them played together well enough anyway. They raced their cars on the track in the basement, shot baskets in the driveway, joined neighbor boys for kickball in the Nelsons' backyard. When they did fight, it was only words. Joe would retreat to his room to read, fantasy and adventure stories being his favorites. Several chapters and an hour or two were usually all he needed to forgive. Besides, he knew how David felt, even if they expressed it in different ways. And he knew he had to look out for his brother.

In the springtime, Joe painted a picture of his family in art class. He was quite proud of it. The white paper warped slightly from the dried watercolors—green for the grass and red for their house and brown for the stick figures, all four of them side by side.

"And who's this?" asked Grandma when he showed her the picture, indicating a fifth figure standing on a cloud.

"Mom," Joe explained. "And this"—he pointed to the rose-colored blob floating over her head—"is her new brain."

"I see," Grandma said cautiously. "And what gave you that idea?"

"God gave it to her. It's her new one because her old one broke."

Grandma placed a hand on his shoulder and looked him directly in the eyes. "Yes, he did, Joe. I believe that he did."

She hung the picture on the refrigerator, partially covering the sticker chart.

When David was in sixth grade, the gym teacher caught him smoking cigarettes in the boys' locker room. David was with another student at the time, the notoriously delinquent Ronnie Jones. The pair of them were suspended a full ten days—the district citing its highly publicized zero-tolerance policy to justify the maximum sentence.

Joe's first reaction was to downplay the whole situation. Risky activities like smoking and drinking were atypical of the suburban Firestone Middle School, or at least they were among students of Joe's academic caliber. Lacking the expertise and vocabulary to discuss such matters, Joe fielded questions like a politician on campaign. Why wasn't David on the bus today? *He didn't come, that's all.* Why do you have all of David's homework? *My grandma made me get it.* Is David in trouble? *You'll have to ask him.*

But, of course, nothing stayed secret in middle school. Before long, it was the scandal of the month. Even though Joe personally had done nothing wrong, it seemed that now all of his classmates saw him differently, as if he were carrying some rare disease, fascinating some and terrifying others. He caught their glances in the hallways, and he heard their gossip in the cafeteria. Can you believe it? Isn't it strange? Who would have thought that Joe Platt the honors student would have such a troublesome little brother?

The bolder ones asked him directly.

"Are you mad that he did it, or do you not care?"

"Do you think they'll kick him out for good?"

"Why didn't they just go outside and not get caught?"

And, from Max Yearling, one day at lunch, "Did you even know David smoked?"

"He doesn't smoke," Joe replied matter-of-factly.

"Dude, how can you say he doesn't smoke when he got suspended for smoking?"

Well, it was hard to argue that. Joe wondered how long he could continue defending his brother's reputation. Or how long he *should* continue defending it. But it was like when they were younger, wasn't it? David just made a mistake. A big mistake, but a mistake nonetheless. Joe chewed a bite of his sandwich and found the peanut butter stickier than usual.

"Like, I don't get why it's that big of a deal anyway," Max said. "It's just cigarettes."

Joe seized the opportunity. "Yeah, I know. Everyone's freaking out for no reason."

"Like, it's technically not even illegal."

Joe questioned the veracity of this assessment but allowed his silence to concede the point. The more to David's credit, the better.

Max shotgunned a chocolate milk and wiped his mouth with his shirt sleeve. "But you have to watch out, though. Ronnie Jones does all kinds of stuff way worse than that. That kid's messed up in the head, man. You better tell David to stay away."

Joe frowned. "It's not like he listens to me." Max was the youngest in his family with two older brothers. He should know how this worked.

"You gotta take charge, man. Tell David what's up. Make him listen."

"Yeah, right." Joe zipped his lunch box shut and anticipated the bell. "It's not like you do what your brothers say."

"True," Max replied. "But I'm a good kid."

At home was no better. Grounding a child was only so effective. Grandpa invented new chores—scrub the bathroom tile, clean inside the oven. His lectures were long, repetitive discourses on the dangers of smoking and how to choose friends wisely and consequences being like dominos hitting one after the other after the other.

Joe, meanwhile, was tasked with helping David with his homework, as Grandma fussed about it too much and admittedly provided more of a distraction than any useful assistance.

"Just sit with him," she said, "and make sure he stays focused. He's got no excuse with all this time to work."

All of the assignments David would miss during the suspension were neatly arranged on the computer desk in separate folders, one for each subject, along with a stack of textbooks. Joe checked in every so often, but David didn't need much help. He was smarter than most people gave him credit for, Joe knew.

About five days into the suspension, David did ask for help on a science worksheet. He had to explain how the scientific method could be used to answer various questions, filling in a chart with short answers for each step of the process.

"I forget what a hypothesis is."

"It's like a guess," Joe explained, "but a good guess based on other things you know."

"Just any guess?"

Joe considered this. "Not any guess. It's kind of like common sense, you know? Like for this first one here about the guy with the fruit flies in his kitchen, a hypothesis would be that throwing the fruit out will make them go away."

"So I write that?"

"Yeah, I think so."

"What about the next one?"

Joe pulled his chair closer so they could examine the questions together.

Problem: A woman wants her plants to grow quickly.

Hypothesis: They'll grow faster if she sets them in the sun.

Problem: A man doesn't want his bread to get moldy.

Hypothesis: It'll last longer in the freezer.

"It's not too hard," David said, "once you know how to do it."

They worked for half an hour, designing experiments for these real-world situations with obvious outcomes, easily imagined, so very unlike the real world.

"You know," David continued, "school really wouldn't be that bad if you didn't actually have to go there all the time."

Joe understood, sort of. He thought about how much he loved conducting experiments in class and working in the computer lab after school and going to Science Olympiad tournaments on the weekends. He thought about Max and his other friends he saw every day. But what happened if you didn't like science, or your closest friend was Ronnie Jones?

Problem: David is smart but hates school.

Hypothesis: A ten-day suspension won't change anything.

"Hey, David," Joe said after a while. "Can I ask you something?"

He shrugged a yes.

"Why did you . . . I mean, it's not like it matters, but why did you do it?"

"Do what?"

"C'mon, David. You know what I mean."

Joe's brother glared at him. "Alright, fine. I just wanted to try it, okay? It was stupid, I know. You don't have to tell me. Are you turning into Grandpa now or something?" David's demeanor became tense and catlike, ready to pounce—or flee.

"You know I'm not," Joe said, doing his best to ease the hostility. "I just want to know."

"Why do you care?" David sneered, although his wary brown eyes betrayed the facade. Deep down, it was indeed a question.

"You're my brother," Joe replied. It seemed so obvious. "Why wouldn't I care?"

For almost a minute, neither boy spoke. David colored in the margins of his paper while Joe watched the pencil tip move back and forth in tight, unequal lines, like a seismograph.

"It's just that . . ." Joe hesitated. "I don't know. Lately you've just been different, I guess. That's all."

David lifted his pencil. "Different from what?"

In the kitchen, Grandma started dinner. They could hear the pots clanking. The squeak of the cupboard door. The whine of the faucet.

Neither of them knew it yet, but in three years, Joe would win a scholarship for a summer-long computer camp at MIT, all expenses paid. It would be the first time he'd ever flown on an airplane, the longest he'd ever been away from home. Joe would learn about macros and code, and he'd design his first video game with the help of a team. He'd go on to graduate at the top of his class and attend the University of Michigan, where he'd learn even more about programming and fly on even more airplanes—a conference in Houston, an internship in San Francisco. He'd finish *summa cum laude* with honors and would be considering a job offer at the same company in California when one night, at the department's spring showcase, his program advisor would introduce him to a clean-shaven man wearing a T-shirt and suit jacket, who would talk about microbrews, the Detroit Tigers, and innovating education.

"The system's broken," Garrett Elson would say. "We're about reaching the kids it spits out." Joe would sip his drink and imagine the kind of kid who smoked in the locker room.

And in the same way, neither of the brothers knew that in the summer Joe went to computer camp, just three years away, David would be arrested for the first time on charges of juvenile drug possession. He would receive six months' probation and court-ordered counseling. Thankfully, the program would help. David would ditch his old friends, get clean, move to the district's alternative high school, date a girl named Kendra with a lip ring and purple hair, and by no shortage of miracles survive through graduation. David's first job bolting parts together on the assembly line would bring stability and decent pay, enough to get his own place, until he'd stroll in late on one too many mornings and find his services no longer required. Not long after, under credit card debt and the threat of eviction, heartbroken from his recent breakup,

David would find that people really are creatures of habit. For his second arrest, he'd no longer be a juvenile.

Still sitting at the computer desk, Joe said, "I guess we're both different."

"They were Ronnie's," David confessed. "Just so you know. He stole them from his dad." His voice trembled with longing that extended back across the years.

And perhaps for the first time since David had been caught, Joe himself felt confronted with the truth. Naming a wrong was more than simply admitting it. Responsible meant culpable. A child denied, but to own the facts was distressingly adult. Without realizing it, Joe's question had been his own experiment, and now he had the results.

Upstairs, Joe flopped on his bed and reached for *The Hobbit*, continuing where he'd left off—Bilbo slashing the dwarfs free from giant spiderwebs. Joe half-wondered if there really was such a thing as a ring that turned you invisible. If he had one, he thought, he could slip it on right now. He'd sneak downstairs to the kitchen, grab some chips and energy bars from the pantry—and maybe some apples, just to be healthy—then slip out the back door and walk for miles. He'd go up to Seven Mile and cross the park, taking back roads away from the suburbs, straight on for hours and hours, long past dark and well into the morning, until his feet hurt too much to stand. Then he'd find a patch of woods and build a tent out of branches and leaves, like the tepees he'd seen at camp. He could stay there for days if he had to, all the while invisible, sleeping soundly, knowing he'd never be found.

Problem: David and I are growing apart.

Hypothesis: Nothing I do will stop it.

No—that wasn't right. He had to. If Joe didn't look out for David, who would? Certainly not the school, and Grandpa just lectured, and Grandma was too snippy, and . . .

"You're my brother," Joe whispered. "Why wouldn't I care?"

He put his book down and lay back, staring at the ceiling until finally Grandma called him for dinner.

THREE
BLACK ICE

THIRTY MINUTES AFTER he'd received David's phone call, Joe pulled his black Honda Accord into the gas station where they had agreed to meet. The snowstorm had turned ugly. Sheets of heavy flakes cascaded from the sky. It was the kind of weather nobody drove in on purpose, but Joe couldn't bail on David now. Not after he'd committed to doing this. Between every song, the radio DJ reminded listeners of the winter storm warning. As if they couldn't just look outside.

Meanwhile, David stood inside the gas station, hunched against the front window in a faded hunting jacket, a few days of stubble visible on his chin and a black duffel bag hanging from his shoulder. When they were younger, almost everyone who met the brothers commented that they looked alike, with the same pale freckled skin, brown hair and oval faces. Now one might say they looked in every way the opposite. Joe, with his neat haircut and trim build, exited the car still wearing his shirt and tie from the workday. David, with his gauged ears and paunchy stomach, held open the convenience store door as his brother approached.

"Hey," said David, raising his right hand to shake. Joe took it. The gesture felt oddly formal and a little bit awkward. They could have embraced, shared a laugh, a jolly clap on the back—too late now. It occurred to Joe that this was the first time they'd seen each other in person since David had been released from rehab. That had been, what, a month ago? Certainly better than a lot of families could say, especially with Joe's work schedule, but . . . still.

"You want anything? You drove out here, so can I get you a pop or something?" David offered, nodding toward the coolers lining the back wall.

"No. I just want to get going. I do need gas, though."

"Cool. I can chip in. You think like five bucks is enough?" David already had his wallet open, counting the bills.

"No, David. I got it."

"Seriously, man, I owe you something. I mean, I know it's last minute and—"

"I got it," Joe said, loudly, rudely, surprising himself even. Great. They'd been talking for two minutes, and he was already frustrated. Why was this always so hard?

"Well, thanks," David said meekly. They went in silence to the fuel pump. David slid into the passenger seat while Joe paid with his credit card.

Despite the cold, Joe waited outside for the tank to fill. He needed a minute to clear his mind. The open structure provided little shelter from the wind, and snow raced sideways in the exterior lights, white lines streaking almost horizontal to the ground. There were only two other vehicles Joe could see. A car probably belonging to the cashier was parked near the store, and a red minivan was fueling at the pump behind him. The minivan driver was an absolute ringer for Santa Claus, complete with the beard and everything, only missing the red coat. On a different day, Joe might have made a joke about it to David, but right now he wasn't in the mood. It was all the little things adding up—stressful work week, icy roads, lack of sleep, the fact that David had made him come all the way out here in the middle of a blizzard and still hadn't exactly told him why. That last one was the kicker. Joe had every right to be annoyed, didn't he? So why did he feel like he was the one who owed an apology?

"Let me guess," Joe muttered in Santa's direction. "You're watching."

The man glanced up at Joe, and for a second, Joe wondered if he'd actually heard him.

Finally, Joe got in and started the engine.

"Alright, David. You'll have to tell me how to get there."

"Actually, I was thinking . . . maybe we shouldn't go back to my apartment."

Warning bells sounded in Joe's head. "David, what's wrong?"

David clenched his teeth in a pleading smile. "Well, I was sort of hoping I could stay with you. You know, just for a little while."

It took a few seconds to register. His reluctance to call a cab. Meeting at a gas station. The black duffel bag on David's lap. *I just need a ride*, he'd said. *That's it.*

Joe had been duped.

"David, what?" he exclaimed.

"Just like a few days. Maybe till Christmas. At most."

"Till Christmas?" Joe started forward and banged his arm on the steering wheel. "What do you mean, *till Christmas*?" He knew David's license had been suspended after his last DUI—not that he had a car now anyway. It had made sense that he'd need a ride, but a ride back to his own apartment. Joe would have a nice chat on the ride over, drop him off, then be on his way. Now the real reason for the phone call was obvious.

"You said a *ride*, David. You said you needed a ride, not a place to stay."

"What's the big deal? I promise, you won't even notice I'm there."

"Of course I will!" Joe blurted. "And I have things to do. I have work, and I have this breakfast thing at church tomorrow. I can't be driving you all over the place."

"I'm not asking you to drive me all over the place."

"Not yet, you're not."

"What's that supposed to mean?"

"This, David!" Joe snapped. "This whole thing. You can't just spring stuff like this on people. If you wanted to stay with me, you should have asked. You should have been upfront. This is why people can't trust you, David. You never tell the whole story, and it's deceitful and hurtful and selfish. You just assume I'm going to come out here and get you."

"Yeah, well, would you have come if I told you all that? Or would you have just said, 'Screw you. Figure it out?'"

"How can you even ask me that? I'm your brother."

David threw up his hands in defeat and turned toward the window. "Then why are we even fighting about this?"

Joe had been annoyed earlier. Now he was enraged. He felt the blood rush to his cheeks. He squeezed the steering wheel to keep from screaming and lashing out. He was not about to be blamed for this. To think, all this time he'd been believing that David was staying with a friend, getting a job, getting his life back on track. Isn't that what David himself had told him earlier that same evening, using those exact words, *back on track*? But no, nothing had changed at all.

For nearly a minute, they heard only the hum of the engine, the screech of the wind, Joe's own heavy breathing. He was supposed to be the bigger person, wasn't he? Well, David certainly put that to the test. David could be so immature and selfish—yet Joe was haunted by his question. *Would you have come if I told you earlier?* Did David really think Joe would've abandoned him? Was that truly the reason for his deception? After all the other times Joe had come to his aid, did David seriously doubt he would do it again?

As his heart rate settled down, Joe stared into the driver's side mirror. Santa Claus and his minivan were gone. All he could see were blankets of snow surrounding them on all sides. The gas station was in the eye of a wintry hurricane, an outpost at the end of the world.

"Look," Joe began, "I'm sorry for overreacting. I'm just a little stressed from work, maybe. But I just want to know you're doing alright, David. And I haven't seen you since you got out, and then finally you call me up and ask to stay—it just caught me off guard, that's all."

"I'm sorry too," David admitted, his tone surprisingly genuine. "I was just scared to tell you everything, I guess. I know you don't believe me yet, but I really am not the person I used to be. I just need a chance to prove it to you."

Joe exhaled for a long count to ten. They were still brothers. What could he do?

"You said it's a temporary thing?"

"Just a few nights, at most."

Joe nodded. "Fine. But you owe me an explanation."

David's face lit up. "For real?"

"For real. Besides, I can't just leave you in a snowstorm all night."

"Thank you so much, man. You're seriously a lifesaver."

At this point, Joe mused, *I'm used to it.*

David talked the whole way home, as if Joe's decision to let him stay had unclogged a backlog of rants and news items and random factoids about his daily life. Mostly it was about his job—his ever-expanding knowledge of bathroom vanities and interior stains, the quirks of picky customers, the rickety ladder he thought would collapse every time he put away stock. He also described the ups and downs of working with his roommate, an individual named Kent who, it turned out, was really more of an acquaintance than an actual friend. They'd managed to peaceably coexist from David's move-in until just that afternoon, but now the two had finally reached an impasse.

"Gary, this guy at work, messed up his back really bad—something with a nerve, I guess," David explained. "Anyway, the doctor gave him a script for painkillers, and of course Kent found out about it. All he saw was the chance for an easy score—not that I wanted to," he added, anticipating Joe's question. "But Kent's dad owns the place, and I thought it'd be pretty messed up to put Gary in that position, you know, thinking his job's on the line unless he said yes. So I told Kent that. You know, just having a conversation about what I thought. But then all of a sudden, he freaked. He's yelling I'm a hypocrite and ungrateful and all that, and I was just like, forget that."

"So you left?" Joe asked.

"Nah, I just said I was visiting you for the weekend. I don't think he really believed me, but whatever. He'll calm down. Besides, I need the job."

Joe glanced over. "You could've just told me."

"Yeah, well, now you know."

They drove on, cautiously. Snow pelted the windshield as Joe merged onto the highway. There weren't many cars at this hour, but he didn't dare drive the speed limit. Salt trucks likely wouldn't have made their rounds yet, and Joe wasn't one to tempt fate.

"You know," Joe began. "There's this guy I know at my church. His name's Anthony. He runs a construction company, and I know they do snow removal in the winter too. If you're looking to make a change, I could talk to him tomorrow and . . ."

David laughed. "Are you trying to hook me up?"

"Hey, you're the one who said you're in a bad situation."

"I'm fine, Joe. This whole thing will blow over. I just have to give it some time."

Joe sighed. Few things ever blew over with David. More often they blew up.

And when they do, Joe thought, *I end up driving out in a blizzard.*

Indeed, the storm had suddenly intensified. They faced a complete whiteout now, and Joe's wiper blades couldn't stop the onslaught. If it weren't for the speedometer showing fifty, he'd have no idea how fast they were going—or if they were even going at all. Instead of the car moving forward into the world, they appeared to be stationary while the world moved backward against the car. The blizzard had been strong when they'd started the drive, but now it was ferocious.

"I'd pull over, but I think it's only gonna get worse. We're almost home."

"Dang, it's like a wall," David said.

True, Joe couldn't see the shoulder, or the lane boundaries, or anything. Flicking on the high beams made it worse, so he quickly switched them back off. He turned on the hazard lights and worked to mentally calm his nerves.

Slow down. Take it easy. Nice and careful. Don't slam on the brakes. Gradually slow.

Then a small bump—not a rumble strip, but in front of him—and again on the back tires. Were they on a bridge? He might as well have been blindfolded. He heard the wind howling now, louder than before. There was a high-pitched screeching noise too, different from the wind and somewhere ahead of them, very close to them.

As if the hand of God had pulled back a curtain, visibility returned, and Joe realized two things at once. One, they were on an overpass with only concrete barriers on each side and no shoulder to speak of, and, two, ahead of him was a string of vehicles bashed together in a pileup. The last car in line was a sedan that had somehow spun ninety degrees before colliding, leaving it completely horizontal and blocking both lanes.

The road was a slight downhill, and Joe was still going forward. Too fast.

All caution to the wind, he slammed on the brakes.

His tires met ice.

Skidding, drifting, sliding uncontrollably as the road sloped downward beyond the overpass. *Small adjustments,* he told himself. But then there was a car right in front of them, and Joe panicked and turned the wheel hard, and then they were spinning, a full 180, 270. Time slowed, or maybe Joe moved faster, his senses keener and more alert than they'd ever been before. Joe's knuckles were white on top of the steering wheel. David swore loudly and braced himself with both hands. They fishtailed toward the cars and then around them, sliding down into the ditch on the left side of the road, teetering at its edge, leaning back before finally coming to rest on top of the freshly fallen snow.

Somehow, they'd missed the collision.

Joe swore. "That came out of nowhere."

"Yeah, man. Good driving."

The blizzard continued but with enough visibility now to survey the damage. There were five cars piled up, black shapes of twisted metal and broken headlights, standing motionless as if they were junk in a scrapyard. Two drivers at the front were standing outside to inspect their vehicles, but the others were still seated, dazed behind their wheels. Although Joe had managed to avoid hitting another car, he was now facing the road at a right angle and halfway into the ditch.

"I'll see if I can pull forward."

The tires spun, and when Joe let off the accelerator, the car moved farther down. Joe and David saw the world at an angle as if they were in an IMAX theater with their seats reclined. Only this wasn't a movie.

"Should I get out and push?" David asked.

"Yeah, we might have to. Here, I'll try again . . ."

But suddenly Joe's attention was on something else.

Over the same overpass that they'd just crossed came a semi-truck, an eighteen-wheeler, its blue cab emerging from the snow like a whale surfacing from the ocean depths. Had it been behind them this entire time? Joe hadn't noticed it. Of course, how would he have seen it with all the snow? Again, it came on too fast. Again, the screeching. Again, the brakes proved no match for the ice.

Before it even began to happen, Joe knew that it would. Despite all of his caution, all of his knowledge about how to avoid it. Was it strange that he thought of his friends at UrbanCalc and *Sir Lanceplot*, wondering who would take over his projects that following Monday? And the men at the breakfast tomorrow at St. Peter's, and his grandparents—who would call to let them know? And was it strange that in that final breathless moment, Joe wondered if he could have done something differently to not drive them off the road, or if it had already begun when he'd crossed the overpass, or merged onto the highway, or answered the phone call outside the restaurant in Detroit? Maybe it had begun long before that even, stretching back months and years, a multitude of decisions now piled up like the cars in front of him, irrevocably leading to a single moment: this moment.

The truck driver turned to avoid the pileup just as Joe had and faced the ditch. A natural instinct, a professional driver, a skillful maneuver to escape T-boning a much smaller vehicle. Only too late did the driver realize that in dodging one car, he'd positioned himself—horrifically, impossibly—to hit another head on.

Joe was vaguely aware of the door to his left. An exit? He fumbled for the handle. But he couldn't lean forward—his seatbelt strapped him to his chair. He needed to release it, and yet suddenly his limbs were filled with lead. So much effort was required just to reach the latch. It was stuck or jammed or too far away. No—his arms hung flaccid at his sides. What did it matter? It was too late. He already knew it was far too late.

His headlights, still functioning perfectly, cast a ghastly luminesce over their impending doom. An eerie quiet, as if Earth itself forgot to breathe. The truck cab descended on them like a blue avalanche, like a tidal wave, like a monster from the worst of nightmares.

Time became an invaluable commodity, and Joe had nothing to barter with. All that was left—a few seconds, five heartbeats, maybe a single breath. David to his right, his brother, the one he'd come out here to rescue, to help get back on track. And now . . .

Joe closed his eyes as the whole world went dark.

FOUR
WHITE LIGHTS

HE WAS IN FIFTH GRADE at church camp on the west side of Michigan, a densely wooded property surrounding a dark blue lake. They'd spent all afternoon out on the high ropes course, and now inside the chapel, the pastor was referencing it as part of his message.

"And raise your hand if you were scared to go up the first time like I was."

The air inside was stifling—summer heat and about a hundred sweaty bodies packed together on wooden pews. A simple cross hung on the back wall, and in front of that was the raised platform making the stage, and on it a long table covered in a white cloth. The setting sun through the upper windows provided the only light, tinting the sanctuary a reddish-orange.

"That's what faith is," the pastor continued. "We have faith that the ropes are going to save us when we fall on the course, and we have faith that Jesus is going to save us when we fall in life. In fact, Jesus already saved us from what was the original Fall, with Adam and Eve." Sweat beads formed on his bald head as he spoke passionately into the handheld microphone. His audience was young and fidgety, but for the most part, he held their attention. He stepped forward and scanned the room.

"Now, boys and girls, I'm betting that there are some of you here today who haven't put your trust in Jesus to be your personal savior. Maybe you've prayed before, maybe you've been to church a few times—you might have done all that. But if you're sitting here tonight with any uncertainty about whether or not you'd go to Heaven if you died tomorrow, maybe it's because you've never actually asked Jesus to come into your heart.

"So in a minute I'm going to invite those of you who want to do that tonight to come up here with me right in front of the cross and we're going to ask Jesus together."

And there in the middle of the third row was a boy who, even at his young age, already knew someone who'd left this world. *Your mom is up in Heaven right now, having a big old party with Jesus.* And this boy did pray earnestly, and go to church, and try to be good, because he'd heard the promise that someday he would be there too, and that they could be reunited in that paradise. So when the pastor said to the children that they could be absolutely sure about where they were going and made his call for them to come forward, Joe Platt rose from his seat. He shuffled up to the stage and knelt down facing the cross, the rays of evening sunlight on his face like a direct line to Heaven. As the pastor prayed, he repeated every word.

"Jesus, I trust you as my only lord and savior, to catch me every time I fall."

Later, as a camp counselor led them back to the bunkhouse, under a moon so bright they didn't need to use their flashlights, a breeze came over the lake and gently prickled Joe's skin. His core was as peaceful as the water beside him. Once inside, he brushed his teeth quickly and climbed into bed, listening to a few other boys still talk about the high ropes until, not long after, sleep came as a welcome visitor.

In the morning, Joe woke to the spirited chatter of birds outside the cabin window, and he knew at once that everything was new.

Joe had a dream once in which he was flying above a city. His experience now was quite similar—the sensations, the perspective, the casual acceptance of something that was anything but normal. He was flying. Joe felt weightless and unrestrained moving through the air, but not entirely autonomous, as if he were an avatar in someone else's video game, waiting for direction. It was still night, he knew, but somehow the darkness was lifted so that he could see with total clarity the devastation below. There was the pileup and the icy overpass, and there in the distance were the flashing lights of an ambulance.

An ambulance—that reminded him. Joe turned his floating body so that he could see the ditch with the semi-truck protruding out of it. Beneath the truck was a familiar-looking black Honda Accord, the front end of which was pressed flat like how he'd seen aluminum pop cans crushed for recycling. It was the kind of horrible image he'd expect to see on the news, not in real life. Was any of this real? It couldn't be. He was still in the car, wasn't he? He must be severely injured, unconscious from the accident. But up in the sky, his body was unscathed. There was no pain, not an ounce of anxiety or concern for himself. Even his curiosity to see inside the car was somehow detached. Surely knowing more about the wreckage couldn't possibly make him feel better or worse than he did right now, drifting free along with the wind.

And indeed, he was *drifting*. Currents in the air slowly carried him away from the highway and above the snowy rooftops in the wide suburban sprawl. He was going higher now. In the distance, Joe could see the city skyline, and beyond that the Detroit River, as if he were looking out the window in an airplane as it made its ascent. Except there was no airplane. There was nothing around him at all. He might have had the sense of an alien abduction were it not for his uncanny awareness that there was some purpose to this flight. The knowledge of what was happening flitted at the edge of his consciousness, like a name he was trying to remember to match a familiar face.

As he went higher, he noticed the ground below was fading. Roofs and roadways became darker, and at first, he thought the snow was melting until he realized that the color was simply blackening. It wasn't a shadowy or inky sort of black, but more of a nothing sort of black, like the television turned off. Little pixels of color, snuffed out. Joe would have expected the houses and buildings and highways to shrink and perhaps blur together as he rose, but instead they were simply disappearing.

31

And it wasn't just the ground. The snow in the air, and the clouds too, and then the stars behind them vanished as if the whole world were an illusion. Next his own clothing began to dim. The edges grew faint around his shoes, and then his pants and coat dissolved. What on earth was happening? Still, Joe's mind told him not to panic. He floated on while an unseen brush painted over everything he used to know.

It didn't stop there, however. After a few languid moments of nothing at all, light crept over a new horizon, and the dark sky gave way to a glorious sunrise. A spectacular display, only it wasn't the sun as Joe had known it. Whatever this new phenomenon was, it was ten times as brilliant as any time he'd ever seen the sun. Yet instead of burning his eyes, it greeted them. This new sun was an invitation to come forward as everything around it faded away. A powerful and welcoming radiance, beckoning him to its center.

Ah, yes. The proverbial light at the end of the tunnel.

He was dead.

Of course.

Joe should have guessed it from the beginning—no other explanation made sense. And what should he do, now that he knew it? He supposed he could try to deny it, protest it, swim against the current back to his lifeless body below. He could at least mourn his circumstances, grieve for his tragic and sudden departure from the world in which he still might have done so much. But somehow, he knew those thoughts weren't appropriate for the occasion. This was no time for sorrow. Joe gazed into the light expectantly and felt the rays dance across his face, like they had that summer evening in the chapel almost fifteen years before. As he floated up, a Bible verse came to mind.

Where, O death, is your victory?

Where, O death, is your sting?

He was at peace.

He was going home.

First were the trumpets. Their sound was distant but clear. Joe heard their bold proclamations, their crisp and triumphant notes. Fanfare made for a royal entrance, but as Joe alighted on a hard surface, he knew that he himself was not the one they played for. He felt this not as a disappointment, but as an honor. The closest comparison was the gladness he'd felt attending a good friend's wedding last summer—absolute joy to be in the presence of another. He was on his way to be in the presence of a king.

The brightness dimmed, or perhaps his eyes adjusted, and Joe gasped as he took in his surroundings. Having been in church since a young age, of course he'd imagined what Heaven would look like. He'd seen artists' depictions of clouds and beams of light and rainbows. He'd even heard a sermon preached on the topic at St. Peter's. Still, nothing had prepared him for this.

Joe stood barefoot in the center of a wide road made of stone. Overlaying the rocks, however, was what looked like pure gold. The metal was cool and malleable under his toes, and its surface was as smooth and reflective as glass. The bare stones at the edges of the road were weathered and sunken into the ground as if the path had been there for centuries, and yet the layer of gold shone as if it had been polished that very morning.

On either side of the road were not fluffy white clouds as he might have expected but rather fields upon fields of wildflowers. Blossoms of every size and color—yellow-orange marigolds and red poppies and pink orchids and a thousand other varieties Joe couldn't begin to name. The landscape stretched out in rolling hills for what looked like miles in either direction, eventually reaching forests of dense and impenetrable green. Joe could find no signs of cultivation or labor, no carefully planned rows, stakes, or irrigation systems, yet it was more varied and splendid than any botanical garden he had ever seen.

Perhaps what caught Joe's attention most, however, was the fact that he was not alone. Other people, maybe a dozen in front of him and a dozen more behind him, all stood as perfectly still as he did, spaced at even intervals along the golden road. From the look of it, they were also recent arrivals, awestruck and captivated by the beauty of this new world. There were both men and women, mostly older than Joe but some younger, including a few children. They were ethnically diverse, too, appearing to represent every continent on Earth. Each person, including Joe, wore a plain white robe tied at the waist with a single cord. The fabric was cool and lightweight, like linen.

So this was it, then. Heaven. The atmosphere itself announced it. Beyond the trumpet sounds and the sweet fragrance of the flowers, there was a certain vitality in the air, an aliveness like the kind that Joe felt when he stepped outside on a beautiful summer morning. In fact, the feeling could only be partially compared to what he'd known on Earth, because certainly Joe had never experienced this exact sensation before. It was bizarre in the way of a dream, but opposite. Where a dream was mere fantasy, Heaven was realer than anything he'd ever known.

Joe opened his mouth to say something to David, and only then did he realize that his brother wasn't with him. He glanced around the white-robed figures, still as statues, although clearly alive. David was nowhere among them.

He must have survived, Joe realized. It was possible, wasn't it? Slowly, Joe recalled the details of their car in the ditch and the truck speeding toward them, but the memory felt distant, as if tragic and frightening thoughts had no business here at all. Indeed, the thought fell away from him soon enough as the shock of his glorious arrival finally faded, and he became aware that the man next to him was speaking.

"Glory to God," he said, over and over in a joyful and trembling voice. The man appeared to be in his eighties, with wispy white hair and sepia-brown skin.

"Yes," Joe replied before realizing it was more of a private prayer than an actual conversation starter. He moved to turn away when suddenly the man collapsed.

The smack of his body against the road broke whatever trance had lingered from their arrival, and now the whole group of heavenly newcomers leaped forward at the drama. Joe, being the closest to him, knelt down by the man. It wasn't a heart attack or some kind stroke—he might have fainted were it not for the vehement cries emitting from his chest. The man's fingers clawed at the road, and he wept fiercely, moaning in what sounded like great pain, his thin body heaving with each sob. Joe cautiously put a hand on the man's shoulder.

"Sir, are you okay?" No response. After a moment, Joe repeated the question. What else could he do? The growing crowd of onlookers stared with wide eyes. If any of them had an idea about how to help, they kept silent about it.

After what must have been a full five minutes, the man controlled his breathing and looked up. "I want you to see something," he said, gazing at Joe. He gently brushed the hand off his shoulder. Carefully, the man rose to his feet.

"For most of my life I was bound to a wheelchair, and now I stand in this blessed place. I *stand* here. Don't you see? I've only ever dreamed of this."

Another moment of silence passed while they all took it in. All things considered, the man appeared healthy and strong. The kind of man who, even at his age, would still be ably shoveling snow off his driveway, Joe thought. There was no indication he'd ever needed a crutch or a brace, let alone a wheelchair. But he spoke with conviction, and not a single person doubted. This once-disabled man was now standing tall.

Then he did the strangest of things. He laughed. A joyful and hearty roar erupted from deep within his chest. "I'm standing," he bellowed high into the air. The man grabbed Joe's shoulders and shook him, shouting again and again, "I'm standing!" Most people just stood open-mouthed and confused, but then a young boy with thick black curls, peeking out from the crowd, started laughing too. Sweet, high-pitched giggles, and suddenly it was contagious. The few other children joined in, and the delight spread, and soon the whole crowd was laughing and jumping together like they were the best of friends, finally reuniting after years away.

And now that the first man had started it off, several others rejoiced and shouted praises of their own. A man who'd been deaf in one ear now heard clearly in both. A woman who'd needed glasses now saw each individual tree in the forest beyond the fields. Another woman beside her, who'd suffered from Alzheimer's disease and had felt her mental capacities deteriorate, now remembered everything about who she was. Joe considered his own body that should have showed cuts and broken bones from the car crash but was instead without a scratch. He remembered again how terrifying it'd been to see that truck descend upon him, and yet here he was, having never felt better. So, with the threat gone, Joe laughed too.

As this new group of people in white robes danced about and celebrated together, several of them drew attention to the fact that they could all understand each other. One man observed that of course this was true—they were all speaking English. But then another person heard French from the exact same words, and another Portuguese, and another Korean, and another Swahili. Joe thought of the story of Pentecost, when each person in Jerusalem heard the disciples speak in his or her own native language. Perhaps it was the same sort of mystery at work here.

"What do we do now?" asked one of the children, the same curly-haired boy from before.

"I vote we go toward the music," said one woman. "It looks like there's a fort or something that way." Joe saw it too—a massive gray structure farther along the road, definitely the source of the trumpets. The details were indistinct from where they were. It would be three or four hours' walking, at least. But seeing as everyone was miraculously invigorated, the group quickly agreed. The man celebrating his new legs led the way.

Joe walked in front with Sahil—that was their leader's name, he learned—and they set a steady pace. Sahil talked for most of the journey, telling stories of his grandnieces and grandnephews, and his church, and the many places he'd visited and the people he'd met.

"I know quite a few of them have traveled ahead of us here," he said. "I'll be glad to see them again."

For the first time, Joe considered that they were likely to meet others in Heaven. And, it stood to reason, if he could walk and talk with Sahil, he'd be able to walk and talk with them too. Surely there would be all kinds of great heroes and leaders from every age and civilization. He could think of so many to talk to and so many questions to ask about history and the world. And several people Joe had known personally would be there too, and they could . . .

Mom.

The thought entered his head of its own accord, even before his consciousness put it all together. It made sense, didn't it? If everyone else from history would be there, why wouldn't she? Hadn't Joe believed his whole life that she'd gone ahead of him to Heaven? But somehow the idea of it still seemed ridiculous. Besides, from what he could see, this place was absolutely enormous. Too big, really. The forests stretched for miles, and the city loomed before them, still far off in the distance. And Joe didn't have internet access or even a phone, so it wasn't exactly like he could just call her. How did people communicate up here, anyway? Was there some kind of directory? Joe wondered how he would ever find her—and what he'd say if he did.

As they walked, the group occasionally stopped to admire the scenery, but never because they were tired. Their energy was boundless and increased with every step, as if their muscles had been half-asleep on Earth and were only now fully awake. At every bend in the road, they'd run or frolic or dance through the flowers, laughing with childlike delight. While on Earth, Joe might have felt too self-conscious or perhaps too preoccupied with thoughts of meeting his mother, but here the joy was enough to capture him in the moment and trump all concerns. Joe joined in with Olympic sprints through the flowers, cartwheels over the road, and even a set of fifty perfect push-ups—clapping his hands between each one. Sahil especially was playful and goofy with the children. For a good chunk of the journey, he carried the curly-haired Luiz on his shoulders—a feat of strength he could have never managed on Earth. Luiz, for his part, loved every second of it, never growing bored with the attention.

Up ahead, the flowers on the side of the road gave way to small groves of trees bearing apples and oranges and olives, fruits that normally couldn't grow side by side but somehow in this climate all thrived together. Just as before, the spacing was uneven with no signs of planting or cultivation. These orchards were simply part of the natural landscape.

It seemed right to stop again, so the group gathered in the shade of the grove.

"Can I have one?" asked Luiz, eyeing the apples.

"Why, of course," said Sahil, reaching up to pick one of the succulent fruits.

Something about this caught Joe's attention, although he couldn't quite explain why. He watched as Sahil's fingers gripped the red fruit and pulled it from the tree. It was an innocent and gentle act, but all the same, it felt off to Joe, off in a way he hadn't felt all day. Everything about this place was so good and joyous and full of wonder, but somehow this was different. Even with the shock of Sahil's initial tears and Joe's lingering questions about his mother, this was distinctly the first time since arriving in this extraordinary land that something felt *not* good.

Then it occurred to him. Eating from the tree in the garden.

Definitely not good.

It made sense now. This couldn't be Heaven proper—that must be the gate they were walking toward. This must be a purgatory of sorts, a weigh station to examine the new arrivals. Of course! They wouldn't just let everyone in, would they? Surely there would be some sort of test. How else would the new arrivals prove their faith was genuine? He had to say something. He had to convince the group.

"Stop!" Joe called, holding up his arms. "Don't eat it."

Sahil paused, and everyone looked at Joe.

"It's just," he went on, "I don't actually feel hungry. And you know, eating fruit, and the Garden of Eden and all that. It just doesn't seem like something we should do."

"What, do you suppose we'll be kicked out?" Sahil asked playfully, the same goofy smile still on his face.

"Well," Joe stammered, "I don't know. Maybe. It's just, we all showed up at once and don't really know a whole lot yet, so it just seems like we should think about it, you know, and not act so rashly."

"I see," replied Sahil, more serious now but still not concerned, at least not in the way Joe was. If anything, his concern appeared to be *for* Joe, not because of him.

"But before," voiced a short woman from the back of the group, the one who had recovered from Alzheimer's, "in Eden, that was from a tree God had expressly forbidden. They were free to eat from the rest of the trees in the garden."

"Plus the Bible speaks of our inheritance," said a second woman. "This is our true home, so shouldn't we act in light of that truth?"

"And after the Resurrection, Jesus ate fish," Sahil added. "So perhaps in these bodies we don't need the sustenance, but we're still able to partake of creation. Besides, nothing about this land so far has felt prohibited to me." Others nodded in agreement.

Am I the only one who thinks this is a bad idea? Joe wondered. It certainly seemed that way. Joe's cheeks flushed, and part of him regretted saying anything at all.

"But," Sahil continued, "it also seems that by some divine appointment, we're here as a group. If you, Joe, have a concern, I say we hear your reasons. Shall we discuss it?"

But it was soon apparent that Joe was the lone dissenter. Several others spoke in turn about freedom and grace and good gifts from the Father, each argument well-articulated and amply supported with various passages from the Scriptures. Joe had never claimed to be much of a theologian, but it was still embarrassing to be so quickly corrected in his biblical knowledge. At last they reached a decision, and, even more assured than he'd been the first time, Sahil handed down a large apple to the boy. Luiz chomped into it, streaming juice down his chin.

No alarms went off. No trap doors opened to swallow them into the earth. Luiz took another bite and calmly chewed, his eyes wide and innocent.

Joe lifted his hands sheepishly. *If that had been a test,* he thought, *I would have failed.*

Someone offered Joe an orange to try, and, begrudgingly, he accepted. Of course, it was deliciously sweet—in fact, he'd never had one better. He still wasn't hungry, though, and the group discussion had done little to build his appetite. He couldn't finish the orange, delectable as it was. He gave the rest to Luiz.

They could still hear the trumpets, and now singing voices too, so after their snack, the group set out again for the fort—although they'd covered enough distance now to see it wasn't so much of a fort as it was a walled city, immense and magnificent. As they left the groves, they could see that there were other roads too, stretching out from what appeared to be every cardinal direction to all converge at the city gates. Sahil led the way, more certain than before of their destination. Joe walked in the middle of the group this time, slower than before, speaking little.

As they marched, Joe gazed above the distant city to study the sky. It was redder than when they'd arrived, as if the sun were setting. Only there was no sun—not in the normal sense, at least, of a single source of light and heat in the sky. Rather, the whole sky itself was light and heat. Curiously, the colors appeared to be changing not in spite of the group's movement along the road but rather *because* of their movement. Time, then, was not something that passed independently of their progress but rather something that marked their progress. The realization brought Joe out of his funk, similarly to how running through the field had captured his attention earlier. Joe sincerely hoped that whatever welcome tour they went on inside the great city would include an explanation of the mechanics of this world. He had so many questions—it was hard to know where to start. They walked for another hour or two—that is, if the very concept of hours even existed at all.

Well, whatever amount of time elapsed, they did move forward. The music grew louder, and the towering structure intimidated the group enough to make them think better about shouting their conversations to be heard. Eventually they reached a point of walking on in reverent silence. The experience was mesmerizing. Joe could see only the towering walls of the city and could feel only his barefoot steps on the cool golden road. Finally, they stopped.

The great pilgrimage was over. They had arrived at the gate.

FIVE
RIVER AND REUNION

THE CITY WALLS DAZZLED. Constructed from stone, each block was inlaid with precious gems at the center—deep blue sapphires and sparkling emeralds and russet-colored jasper. The patterns were elaborate and luxurious but in no way opulent or wasteful. It was like visiting a magnificent home that an architect had designed and helped build himself, a beautiful expression of sincere passion. Unlike the gardens the group had passed alongside the road, these walls bore elements of careful planning, and Joe wondered at the craftsmanship. In comparison, the greatest castles of medieval Europe were like tiny toy cabins.

The rampart facing them was high like a skyscraper, but wide enough to contain three separate gates spaced apart by at least several miles. Joe's group stood at the middle gate, and he could see two other roads ending at the two other gates, with what looked like two other groups of travelers about the same number as their own. The gates themselves were about a hundred feet high and made of white pearl. They were wide open.

And there, beside the open gates, Joe at last discovered the source of the music. A dozen angels, six on each side, hovered effortlessly above the ground. These, however, were not the gentle, halo-wearing angels that topped Christmas trees. These fearsome beings had six wings each: a pair extending up toward their faces, a pair extending down toward their feet, and a pair powerfully beating to keep them in flight. The angels were human in form, but taller, and with a radiant aura surrounding them that exuded strength and intelligence. They appeared wise and self-assured, a mix of male and female, and all unclothed—the word *naked* would imply a shame or indignity that these creatures bore none of. Joe had never seen a creature more powerful or majestic.

The two in front played trumpets like heralds while the rest sang songs of glory to God. "Holy, holy, holy, is the Lord Almighty" was their continuous refrain. While the word *angelic* was already correct in a technical sense, its earthly connotations applied just as easily. Joe had never heard a melody so pure and harmonious, as if the words themselves could lift him off the ground too. The music continued for several more minutes, and then at the conclusion of their song, the angels lowered their trumpets and spoke.

"Greetings. We are *seraphim*, and you are travelers on the long road." The angels spoke in unison as they made this declaration, their voices rich with vitality.

"These gates are never shut, for there is no night here. This city is the glory of the all the nations, and nothing impure may cross the threshold."

The seraphim stared down at the group with penetrating eyes, and Joe trembled at their gaze. These were mighty beings who could just as easily lift him in their arms as they could hurl him to the ground. With twelve of them, he had no idea where to look, so his eyes flitted from face to face. The angels all seemed to be looking directly at him. When he'd first arrived at the gate, Joe had felt he was a lucky visitor to this gigantic palace, but suddenly he felt like a trespasser caught in the floodlights. *Nothing impure,* the angels had said. Surely this was the moment of judgment, when they would separate the wheat from the chaff, welcoming some members of the group and turning the rest away. Perhaps the fruit had been a test after all—was this where it mattered? Joe looked nervously at the others in his group. Some had their heads bowed in respect, while some stood tall and confident. Only Joe appeared to be shaking.

My whole life I've tried to be good, he thought. *And I prayed, and I went to church.* But was there something else? Something he missed? Something more he'd needed to do?

As if they'd heard the question voiced in his mind, the angels spoke again.

"By grace, you have been saved. All glory to God. The Lamb has made his sacrifice and overcome the grave. Death has no hold. Your guilt is taken away, and your sin atoned for." They paused dramatically and maintained their gaze. How ironic that the angels wore nothing and yet Joe was the one who felt utterly exposed.

Finally, the seraphim spoke.

"Your names are written in the book of life. You may enter these gates." With that, they beat their mighty wings and parted as much as they had room for. That was it. The arrivals were allowed to pass.

Joe's relief was audible. He felt his new heart pound against his chest.

They certainly could have saved the theatrics, he thought.

But, strangely, now that the angels had welcomed them and cleared the way, nobody moved. Joe and his companions looked back and forth at each other expectantly, each wanting to go forward but not wanting to go alone. Before they could say anything, however, they heard a shout from inside the city gates.

"Sahil!" The voice was more familiar—a human's, not an angel's. Sahil's face lit up in recognition.

"Rohan?" he whispered in disbelief. "Rohan, my brother!"

Then other shouts came too, and to their astonishment, each person heard his or her own name called in the voice of a loved one. Friends and grandparents and aunts and uncles and siblings, all hailing the new arrivals and inviting them to enter the city.

And of course, Joe heard his name too. He couldn't possibly mistake it. Although it had been seventeen years, he knew her voice immediately.

Mom.

She was here. She was calling his name.

Next, they were running, all of them, like sprinters on the home stretch and those shouting their names like cheerleaders at the finish line. As he zoomed past the gates, Joe recognized other people he'd known in life, whooping and hollering and clapping for him. There was Mrs. Ritter, his Sunday school teacher from when he was young, and there was Great-Uncle Bob, Grandpa's brother who'd lived in Ohio. People he'd barely known, people he hadn't thought about in years were now familiar faces overjoyed to see him.

Then he saw her. Her short brown hair and warm eyes were everything like the pictures they still had at home. But as Joe got closer, he noticed her face had aged, and there were more gray streaks than he remembered. She appeared to be in her late forties now, exactly how she would have looked if she were still alive on Earth. It was some time, however, before the strangeness of her physical appearance occurred to Joe. For the time being, he was content with her tight embrace, like a child again in how glad and unashamed he was to be with his mother. She kissed him softly on the forehead and smiled in pure delight.

"I'm so proud of you, Joe. I love you so much."

At last, Joe stepped back. Even though he'd had all day to imagine this meeting—all of his life, really—he still was caught completely off guard. All this time on Earth to think about what he'd say to his mom if they could have just one more conversation, and now they had an eternity in which to talk, and he found himself speechless.

"I . . . wasn't expecting this," was all he could stammer.

"You'll have to get used to that," she replied cheerfully. "There are some who've been here a thousand years and are still discovering more all the time. You know, as a girl, I used to wonder what we'd do all day in Heaven. But there's always something or someone new to know and understand and love here. Certainly not the kind of place you'll ever get bored."

"So is this Heaven, then? This . . . city?"

His mom smiled in response. "Come on. I want to show you around."

The city, it turned out, had nothing urban or industrial about it. Inside the great walls were mighty trees and flowing streams and towering mountains with cascading waterfalls at the center. It was a true Eden, a lush and pristine landscape. Tolkien's Rivendell was reminiscent, but as they moved along, Joe was soon struck by the paucity of his own vocabulary. How could one truly describe the Grand Canyon or the Pacific Ocean with words alone? And yet this new realm was incomparably more breathtaking.

And there were people everywhere, all engaged in some activity or another. Beside a juniper tree, a woman painted a magnificent landscape. On a stone bench, a man lightly sang and played guitar. Across from him, children gathered in a circle to hear two women tell a story with puppets and dramatic voices for the characters, much to their amusement.

"I feel like I'm at an art fair," Joe said.

"In a way, you are. Everyone here is full of talent and passion, and there's no reason to hide it. Drawing, building, writing, teaching, directing—really anything you can imagine that comes from the spirit and glorifies God."

"Right." Joe looked at her. "So, um, what's your talent then?"

His mother placed her arm around his shoulder and leaned in to whisper. "Would you believe I've taken up dancing?"

He met her eyes, uncertain. "I can't tell if you're joking."

She laughed. "What might be undignified on Earth is a celebration here when it's done for the Lord. But there are so many things, Joe. Everything I loved on Earth was just a glimpse of what I love here. It's the difference between seeing a picture of food on a menu and actually tasting it. You'll find things come naturally even if they're strange at first, because, after all, you were created for this. But come on. There's more I want to show you."

The golden street continued, lined with thick vegetation and more groves of fruit trees, this time with a few people tending them, although not as some labor or exertion but with the kind of serene joy Joe had seen Grandma have while working in her garden. As they walked, the street was occasionally bisected by other gilded pathways or gave way to a footbridge to cross the winding river, the water fast and perfectly transparent. The air was warm and still, and the sky a pinkish-orange. It was the perfect summer evening.

They came upon a small waterfall, and Joe noticed a group of children swimming in the pool beneath it, two boys and two girls. Their white robes were cast aside on the bank, and they splashed around unclothed, just as the angels were at the gate. Again, however, Joe sensed no impropriety or shame. They were so joyous and carefree it was hard to imagine they'd have any room to feel embarrassed.

As Joe and his mother came closer, he saw a playful little retriever in the water with the children , dog-paddling alongside them.

"Well, look at that. I guess dogs do go to Heaven after all."

His mom laughed. "You mean Boomer? Yes, he'll get to know you later, I'm sure. He's very friendly."

They paused to watch near the pool. The water itself was clear as crystal. Joe could see straight down to the riverbed as if he were staring out a window. There were little fish too, and Joe thought of the *ichthus* symbol he used to see people display as car ornaments and tattoos.

"Go ahead," his mother offered. "Take a drink."

Curious, Joe bent down and scooped a handful of water to bring to his mouth. He expected it to taste like filtered bottled water, pure and plain, but instead it was deliciously rich with a sweetness and flavor unlike anything he'd had before.

"That's amazing," he said, savoring the taste before he took another sip.

"The stream is living water," she explained. "It's free and plentiful, flowing directly from the throne on the mountaintop. We're never thirsty here, at least not in the physical sense, but you are able to take it as an act of worship."

46

"Did you say the throne? Like, God's throne?"

"Oh yes. You'll see that too, soon enough."

Joe stood up and dried his hand on his robe. "I have so many questions. I don't know where to start."

She laughed. "There's no rush. Why not start at the beginning?"

So he did. Joe picked up right where she'd left off in his life, recounting his school classes and church retreats and science experiments and the first time he went away to computer camp. He shared about his senior design project in college and his work at UrbanCalc. He described his favorite restaurants in Detroit and the Midtown neighborhood where he'd lived and the view from his apartment, and everything else he might have told his mom had she been around to tell it to. She listened with motherly pride, showing plenty of interest but no surprise, as if she knew the details already but wanted nothing other than to hear them again. As his stories got closer to the present, however, Joe was solemnly reminded that his earthly life was no more. He stopped just before telling about the car crash and decided to venture a question.

"Can I ask something else about Heaven?"

"Of course."

"Now that I'm here, am I, you know, done with everything? I mean, I know people here can paint or sing or whatever, but all of my projects and programming—you know, my whole career—was on the computer. And I wanted to help change education for kids who struggled and things like that, but I don't see any schools around here. We're out in the middle of nature where people have all they need and, well, I guess I just don't know what's next."

His mom lifted her arm to rub his back as they walked. "I know it's different. But you're far from being done with everything just because you're here."

"But does anything change at all here? I know you said people don't get bored, but if nothing changes, then what does anyone work toward? And what about all the kids? Can they still grow up? I mean,

47

if they come here as children, do they have to stay that way?" He thought of the curly-haired Luiz eagerly biting into the apple.

"My son, your thinking has it all backward," she teased. "You're asking about growing up, but the Lord says unless we become like children, we will never enter the Kingdom of Heaven."

Joe frowned. "I always thought that was a metaphor."

"And yet this place is full of children who might tell you otherwise."

He stopped and turned to face her. "Seriously, Mom. I want to know."

Her eyes twinkled as she wandered over to a fig tree, reaching up to run her fingers along the bark. "Even the trees here grow and bear fruit. Why should we not do the same?" She plucked a green fig from a low branch and tossed it to him. It clearly wasn't ripe yet, but perhaps that was her point.

"There isn't age here as you're used to thinking about it. All of our souls are meant to have both the maturity of growing wisdom and the excitement of youth, just as our heavenly father is eternally both ancient and new. I'll admit, it takes a little getting used to. Right now you still see and hear others largely as you expect to. It takes a while to break the habit. That's why you hear everyone speaking English and see me as you imagine I should look like with respect to your own age."

"So . . . wait, you don't really look like this?"

"Any gray hairs are purely your imagination."

Joe stood speechless, running his fingers over the fig in his hand. It sure felt real enough. Actually, it felt more real than anything he could recall on Earth, if it were possible to say such a thing, like his old life were the dream and this were his waking state. But there was even more than this?

"Anyway," she continued, "you asked if everything was done. The answer is that your work is not yet finished, Joe, and neither is mine. Heaven is life, and life is never static. As the Lord's ever-increasing glory transforms you, you will learn and grow and understand and see others more and more as he does, truly and completely, without a veil over your mind."

Joe wrinkled his brow in confusion. He supposed it was his fault for asking, but this was all getting a little too metaphysical. For some reason, he'd always thought he'd figure it all out once he got to Heaven. He'd imagined God would meet him at the door and hand over some kind of cosmic answer key. Physics, biology, history, the human mind—all would be revealed with simple explanations, stuff he'd be kicking himself for never realizing before. *Understanding the Universe for Dummies*. But now he was more mystified than he'd ever felt on Earth.

Something occurred to him, and he asked, "How'd you know I'd be at the gate? How'd you know I was coming today?"

"At every step of your life, you were surrounded by a great cloud of witnesses. I was one of many."

So people in Heaven could see those on Earth. Joe considered this carefully. Her response reminded him of something else, something that had been bothering him all day, really since he'd first set foot on the road outside, but had been shoved to the back of his mind because everything else was so overwhelming and strange. But after talking so long with his mother, now he was safe and familiar enough to wonder about it out loud.

"Do you think I can check on David, then? We were in a car crash together—you probably know that already—and I just want to make sure he's not too badly hurt or anything. I mean, it has to be scary with me…not there anymore. And then Grandma and Grandpa will just be wrecks when they find out. So I should probably tell them I'm okay somehow and then…" Joe's voice trailed off as he studied his mom's face. Her expression had changed, and now her eyes were glistening with tears. He'd seen plenty of happy tears so far today, but these were different. For the first time since arriving in Heaven, Joe saw tears of sadness.

"I knew you'd ask this eventually, but I still don't know how best to tell you."

"Tell me what?"

"Neither of you survived the crash," she said quietly.

"Really?" Joe felt a surge of excitement. "Is he close by then? Did he come in one of the other gates?"

His mother shook her head.

Now this was just annoying. Clearly she wasn't telling him something. Joe hated these games, when people used euphemistic and roundabout expressions all to avoid sharing the bad news that he actually needed to hear. There had been plenty of this when his dad left and his mom died, but Joe wasn't a child anymore.

"Mom, tell me where David is."

She nodded, then gripped both of Joe's arms and looked directly into his eyes.

"He made a choice, Joe. He's gone to the place of spiritual death, the land of outer darkness, where there is weeping and gnashing of teeth."

A pause. A moment to process this new information.

"You mean Hell," Joe stated.

At the mention of the word, Joe's mother buried her face in the chest of one son and wept for the absence of the other.

It was a good thing the citizens of Heaven had inexhaustible supplies of energy, because yet again Joe found himself running. His bare feet sank into the lush grass, and he pumped his arms furiously. He took a shortcut, following a tributary of the river against its current. Mom had given him directions, allowing him to go ahead while she stayed back. She wasn't against the idea of his mission. She just didn't think it would work.

It's not the kind of decision we can change, she'd told him.

50

But it had to be. There had to be a way. David wasn't a bad person, really, he'd just made some mistakes. And that very night he'd said he was making changes in his life. He'd said he was done with his old ways. Joe was helping him get off to a new start. If it weren't for the car crash . . .

And now Joe was supposed to casually accept the fact that his only brother was suffering in a land of perpetual fire and punishment while he was up here frolicking through paradise? The very thought repulsed him. He'd heard the charge enough times while he was on Earth. Religion couldn't promise a God who was both all-loving and fire-and-brimstone. It was an inherent contradiction. While Joe had never doubted God existed, he had to admit he was uncomfortable with the whole wrath-for-the-wicked part of it.

But now he'd found out it was true. There was suffering for the unrighteous.

There would be suffering for David.

Joe pushed aside a low-hanging tree branch and increased his pace. There had to be a way to fix this, and he thought he knew what it was.

"They said it at the gate," he'd told his mother. "We're here only by God's grace. Our mistakes are forgiven, and Jesus let us in."

The logic was simple. *If Jesus let me in, he can let David in too.* That was Sunday School 101, wasn't it? The Son of God came to save the world? Every Bible study he'd ever been to had preached the message that Jesus saves. It had to work. Joe had only needed to ask his mom one question.

"Where do I find Jesus?"

Joe emerged from an olive grove on top of a steep grassy hill. At the base was an enormous plaza laid out with the same gold-covered stones as the road. The square was bustling with people, all moving among each other like a crowded marketplace. Only instead of trading wares and produce, they traded words, speaking to each other with affirmation and encouragement. Even in Joe's desperation, the sight was powerfully transfixing. He thought of all the times he'd walked through a crowd with his head down, hoping not to be noticed. Here was the opposite. People entered the square desiring to know and be known.

At the center of the square was a great fountain with a circular ledge large enough to sit on, spouting the same crystal-clear water as the river. The majority of the crowd was surrounding the fountain in anticipation, as if they were about to watch a street performer. In fact, one man in particular appeared to be the center of their attention. He stood on the fountain ledge and addressed the crowd. It was too far away to make out his facial features, but from what Joe could tell, the man wasn't exceptionally tall or strong or even an animated orator. On the contrary, the first word to come to mind in describing him was *ordinary*.

But Joe knew this man was anything but ordinary.

This man was fully God, and he alone had the power to save David's soul.

SIX
KING OF KINGS

REACHING THE FOUNTAIN was more difficult than Joe had anticipated. The square was quite crowded, and he had to slip between groups of people and cut his own path to the center. Simply saying *excuse me*, however, wasn't very effective in Heaven. Every time he said it, instead of moving out of his way, somebody would turn toward him and try to start a conversation. "Joe, I'm so glad you're here," or "Joe, it's great to see you." They all knew his name— not in a creepy horror-movie sort of way, but more as if they were all old friends, welcoming him home after a long absence. Well, he wasn't quite ready to settle down yet. Not while David was still out there.

It was amazing how quickly Joe's opinion of this place had changed. Sure, the mountains were spectacular and the food was delicious and the streets were literally paved with gold, but it was all just an escape. It was a wonderful diversion from the reality that actual souls of real men and women were burning in Hell. He suddenly detested the way people chatted and laughed so merrily. Who could do such a thing while others were tortured far below?

Closer in toward the fountain, people were shoulder to shoulder, and Joe used both his arms to swim through them. He didn't care who he had to shove aside. Although he didn't pay much attention to it at the time, it was strange that nobody shouted or cursed at him, even as he forcefully pushed them out of his way. In fact, the more they sensed his distress, the more people tried to clear a path. With more space now, Joe stumbled forward, and then he was there at the fountain in the center of the square. He tilted his head to look up at the man standing on the ledge and, quite suddenly, found himself face to face with Jesus Christ.

Whatever Joe had been expecting, it certainly wasn't this.

In appearance, Jesus was nothing like the long-haired handsome figure depicted in Renaissance paintings. He was of average height and muscular, although more like a day laborer than a bodybuilder, with short black hair and an untrimmed beard. Jesus wore the same white robe as everyone else and could have easily been lost in the crowd if he wanted. His face was familiar and ordinary, forgettable even. Nothing physical about him was remarkable.

Except for his eyes. His olive-colored eyes were layered with complexity and intelligence, and they met Joe's in a disarming gaze that all at once communicated sympathy, patience, amity, and compassion. It was more than that, though. These eyes truly saw Joe. They saw through him, in him, before him, beyond him. They saw the length and width and depth and shape of his every longing. Right now, in the presence of Jesus, Joe felt more naked than the angels he'd seen at the pearly gates. He was totally exposed and judged for every aspect of his character, all of his deeds. He was judged for every vice, every flaw, every fault, every failure. Judged for his very being. Judged—but not condemned. Here was Jesus, and in his eyes the verdict—all was forgiven, all was covered over, all was washed away. Joe was clean. New. Worthy. Wanted. Loved.

You will see others as he does, truly and completely, without a veil over your mind.

Joe Platt knew what it was to be seen.

The idea that Joe had charged across the square to rage at this man now seemed preposterous. This was God incarnate. The recipient of Joe's prayers since childhood. His only lord and savior. Joe felt his emotions turn inward, his anger soften, and his legs weaken as he fell to his knees. The crowd quieted until the only sound was the running water in the fountain. After a long pause, Jesus spoke.

"Truly I tell you, no one can see the Kingdom of God unless he is born again." He stepped down off the fountain and helped Joe to his feet. Again, he gazed deep into Joe's eyes. "Well done, my good and faithful servant."

Then he held Joe in a tight embrace while the crowd erupted into joyful shouts and clapping, much louder than Joe's traveling party when they had been dancing on the road outside the city. Joe blushed as he realized that the same people he'd shoved aside moments before were now applauding for him. The thundering sound of forgiveness.

But, no matter how glorious the moment, Joe couldn't forget why he was there.

"There's something I came to ask you."

The Messiah nodded. "I know. Come, follow me, and we'll talk." He then led Joe away from the square to a narrow pathway sloping up the nearest mountainside. The trail wasn't paved this time but was worn into the dirt from frequent use.

"Are you just leaving them, then?" Joe asked, motioning back to the people who had assembled around Jesus at the fountain. "I didn't mean to interrupt."

"I am with them always in spirit." He gave Joe a knowing look. "Besides, I believe it was your intention to interrupt."

Joe gulped. "Er . . . yes. Sorry. It was just kind of urgent that I got to you."

"Well, then, let us go with urgency."

"We could talk here," Joe said.

Yet Jesus was already off at a run, and Joe found that he had no choice but to follow. Indeed, *urgent* was the perfect word to describe their climb up the trail. Although the grade increased quickly, Jesus leaped forward with the agility of a mountain goat. Joe kept pace without becoming physically winded, but it was somewhat of a mental effort to push himself up the steep pathway. In fact, the ascent had a similar effect as a long workout at the gym. Joe's mind soon had a singular focus, setting aside all other worries and thoughts so that he could concentrate only on the task at hand. *Keep up. Climb higher.*

He followed Jesus up the trail for about twenty minutes and then came to an abrupt halt. They had reached a switchback near an overlook facing out over the gathering square below. The sky was still sunset-orange. Below, Joe could see the golden plaza, the dense orchards and coursing river, the towering stone wall and angels at the gate, thousands of men, women, and children moving freely with discovery and delight. It was absolutely magnificent, unimaginably beautiful.

"There is no hunger or thirst here," Jesus explained, stepping alongside him. "There is no death or suffering. It is my desire to mend every wound and wipe every tear. Your physical pains I can heal, as you found at your arrival. But the burdens you carry inside—your guilt, your shame—those are yours to give to me. And when your grip on them is tight, I will not pry open your fingers."

Joe turned to face him, and again they made eye contact, Jesus still with that penetrating, all-knowing gaze. After a moment, Joe couldn't take it anymore and looked back out over the ledge. It was then that Jesus spoke.

"You wish to ask me about David."

Well, there it was. Joe had wondered how he might broach the subject, but Jesus had thrown it right out in the open. Apparently seeing into somebody's soul was kind of like mind reading. Joe sensed that there was no point in holding back his thoughts, but still it was strange to actually vocalize what he was thinking about. He'd prayed to Jesus countless times before, but face to face was ... different. And how exactly was he supposed to ask for a free pass for his brother when he'd only been here a few hours himself?

"Well," Joe began, "I'm sure you know the situation already. I found out that I'm here, and David isn't, and, well, I just know David was making some changes in his life right at the end. And the car crash wasn't his fault, and I really think if he'd had more time, he would have turned things around and . . . so I guess I'm asking for a second chance for him, that's all."

Jesus had been listening impassively this whole time. He was fully attentive, but his face betrayed no hints of what he was thinking.

"You think David did not have enough chances?"

Well, that was a trick question if Joe had ever heard one. He realized now that he should have spent more time preparing his case before making the request. Joe considered carefully before responding.

"Well, he blew a lot of his chances, for sure, but there were other things affecting him too. I don't think he ever expected this to happen . . . so soon."

"I see." Jesus turned his gaze out over the glorious city below. "And what if I told you he had already received his invitation, that he was welcome here but chose not to come? Would you then stop blaming yourself?"

The question surprised Joe. What did he mean, *blaming yourself*? Was it because he had been driving the car the night they crashed? But Joe didn't blame himself for that. It was an accident. There was nothing else he could have done.

"I'm not sure I understand what you mean."

"You love David, of course, and it's right to want to be with the ones you love. But is it fair to hold yourself responsible for the choices he made?"

Another trick question, and an even more confusing one. Joe knew this came back to that whole *am-I-my-brother's-keeper* thing, and for some reason, he was blanking on the correct answer to that time-honored query. Yes, Joe was the older brother and was responsible

57

for protecting and looking out for David. No, Joe could not control what David did with his life as an adult. And wasn't the original story of Cain and Abel about not killing each other, anyway? Hardly relevant to this. Joe now had a good idea why the first disciples had such a hard time holding a conversation with Jesus.

After a moment, Jesus spoke again.

"Why are you here, Joe?"

Somehow Joe knew that *here* was not a reference to the overlook. A simple question with deep implications, but Joe found an answer at once.

"Where else would I go? I didn't do everything perfectly in my life, for sure, but . . . isn't that why you came? So we could be with you now, in Heaven?"

Jesus gave a strange and curious look, one that Joe wasn't quite sure how to interpret.

"You must understand, Joe, the Father created the world and everything in it. Men and women were the joy of all his creation, his final work. He could not love them more. But his greatest gift was for them to know his love, to feel it, relate to it, and even to choose it. By law, the Earth circles the sun and sound travels through air, but law cannot govern his love. It's too great, too wild. From the beginning, the Father and I have known that love must be free.

"So we ordained freedom for humanity, but it was humanity who ordained its fall. Evil came, and they chose it. You see, I am the good shepherd in search of his sheep. The good shepherd lays down his life for the sheep, but to lock them in the pen would forfeit their choice. It's more difficult than you even presently understand, Joe. But a difficult truth is no less a truth. So it is—free they were formed, and free they must remain."

"So . . ." Joe contemplated these words for a moment. "David's not here because that's what he chose? But when? How? I'm sure if he saw all this now, he'd choose to be here. Isn't there something you can do?"

"Oh, I said the situation was difficult. But I always have a plan."

And without explaining any further, Jesus turned back to the trail and sped up the hillside, again so fast that Joe had to run to keep up. Somehow he knew it was pointless to ask where they were going.

Before long, the dirt path gave way to a gravelly slope. The trees were sparse now, and Joe could see other mountain peaks in the distance. He couldn't tell if the whole range was contained within the great stone walls or if it somehow extended beyond them, but he figured it wasn't the best time to ask for a heavenly geography lesson. Joe felt his bare feet push down on the rocky scree, and he half-wondered what would happen if a loose stone cut him. Jesus said there was no suffering, so would the wound heal automatically? Would it even bleed?

They finally reached what appeared to be a cave. It was a squarish hole in the rock face, partly obscured by some shrubs and a large boulder. There was a sound, too. A crashing like heavy rain. Walking past the cave, Joe discovered the source. They were near a stream of that clear living water, pouring over a ledge opposite them and cascading into a deep pool below. The waterfall was a hundred feet tall, at least. Not impossibly high, but certainly high enough to make Joe dizzy when he stole a glance over the edge.

"Are you ready for a leap of faith?"

Joe gawked. "You're joking, right?"

For the first time since they started this mountain hike, Jesus laughed. "Oh, I'm quite serious, although a swim was not what I had in mind."

"Yeah . . . right." Just to be sure, Joe took a few steps away from the edge of the waterfall. "So what's this plan of yours?"

Jesus found a medium-sized boulder and took a seat, facing back toward the path they had come up. Joe remained standing, waiting for an answer.

"I love you very much, Joe."

Those simple words had a near paralyzing effect. Joe couldn't quite explain why, but something about Jesus' tone, the way a father would speak to his son, was both immensely comforting and immensely foreign. Again Joe noticed the humanity of his lord seated before him. Again he saw those eyes that looked deep into his soul.

Jesus continued, "I also know you, Joe. Before I formed you in the womb, I knew you. I know you better than you know yourself. And I have appointed you for a mission."

"What do you mean?" Joe stammered. "What mission?"

"I know your heart. You can't rest until you see David again, and indeed, part of your work *is* to see David again."

As usual in these conversations, Joe was trying to keep up. They were supposed to be talking about saving his brother, but for some reason, Jesus kept focusing on him. Did Joe have to do something to bring David back? He was reminded of something his mom had told him earlier by the river. *Your work is not yet finished.*

"What do you want me to do?" he asked.

"I am commissioning you to find him."

Joe wasn't exactly sure what he had been expecting Jesus to say, but it certainly wasn't that. *Commissioning you to find him?* Jesus knew and saw everything, didn't he? How could he possibly not know where somebody was? And if he didn't, how was Joe going to help?

"Find him? Is he lost or something?"

"For now, yes. But there will be much rejoicing for finding the one who is lost."

"But, I mean, couldn't you . . . couldn't you just bring him up with that tunnel of light thingy? You know, how I got here."

"Remember, it must be his choice."

Joe considered this statement and its implications.

"So let me get this straight. You can't just pluck David out of Hell because he has to want to come here, like *really* want it. And since he

60

hasn't expressed that desire yet, I have to go down to Hell and find him? Then what do I do?"

"You have known me and seen this place. You have been my disciple. Teach him to obey what I have commanded you."

"I don't mean to be rude," Joe said, "but why don't you do it? You might be more convincing."

If Jesus was offended, it didn't show. If anything, he looked amused.

"Whoever listens to you listens to me. Whoever rejects you rejects me."

"And will David reject you?"

Jesus didn't answer directly. Instead, he gave Joe another strange look just as he had on the trail earlier, clearly knowing something Joe did not. There was a part of Joe that now wished Jesus would have asked him to jump off the waterfall. It would have been terrifying, but in a knowable sort of way. Long fall, sudden splash, and then done. He couldn't get hurt anyway, right? Instead, Jesus was suggesting something Joe hadn't even known was allowed. He would go down to find David. He would bring him back.

"I don't even know where to start," Joe admitted.

"You will not be alone."

"So you're coming with me?"

"I am with you always. But no, I meant a partner. I always send out workers two by two. You might say it's a company policy." Jesus smiled. "I've called someone already. He should be joining us soon."

In fact, at that very moment, Joe heard footsteps lightly crunching on the gravel. He stepped out to get a good look at the newcomer. Approaching them was a man dressed in the heavenly-issued standard white robe. He was a little shorter than Joe and about sixty years old, balding with a thick gray beard and dark tan skin. In the same strange way that people Joe had never met had recognized him in the square earlier, he now recognized this man despite the fact he'd never seen him before. In that instant recognition, Joe's jaw dropped. He could hardly believe it.

Although they'd never met, Joe already knew this man's entire life story. He had lived on Earth as a contemporary with Christ and been one of his closest associates. They had walked together, eaten together, and been together right up until the night before the crucifixion. He continued to teach and serve for the rest of his life, and in the centuries following, this man was venerated as a founding father of the Christian church. Now he was going to help Joe rescue his brother.

So the introduction really wasn't necessary, but Jesus made it anyway.

"Joe, I'd like you to meet Simon Peter."

SEVEN
THE BATTLE PLAN

IRONICALLY, JOE WAS MORE star-struck now than when he'd first seen Jesus. That encounter had left him overwhelmed in an emotional way, amazed and entranced. Yet it was still an expected sort of amazement, like climbing a mountain knowing there'd be a view at the top. Joe had grown up praying to Jesus, talking to Jesus, attributing the blessings in his life to Jesus, and really all-around believing that Jesus was somewhere nearby even when he couldn't see or hear him. In that belief, Joe had always assumed they'd meet in Heaven. So while the power of the experience was surprising, the experience itself was not.

But now Simon Peter—one of the original twelve apostles, author of two New Testament letters, and the man considered to be the first pope in Rome—was standing there in the flesh. Joe certainly hadn't been prepared for that. This was a hero of the faith, now coming to assist Joe on his own quest. What an astonishing honor it was.

"Peace, Joe," he said. "I'm glad to be with you." Peter's voice was deep and gravelly, and his presence exuded courage and confidence. He was straight-faced and tough, like a seasoned army veteran. Joe decided right away that he could trust him.

"Peter is a rock on which I've built my church," Jesus explained. "His experience will aid you. To succeed in finding David, you will have to work together."

All of Joe's attention hung on those last words. *Work together.* With *the* Peter of the Bible. Joe felt more than a little inadequate, but privileged too. If any human being knew the ins and outs of the heavenly realms, surely it would be Peter. Joe had been concerned before, but how could their mission not succeed now?

"It's an honor to meet you," Joe said. He almost added, *I'm a huge fan of your works and used to attend a church with your name on it,* but thankfully stopped himself in time.

"So, um," Joe said, "I take it you've done this before?"

"In a way. I spent the majority of my time on Earth ministering in the enemy's territory. But, until now, I have not gone back across the chasm."

Joe nodded as if that statement made perfect sense, when of course it did not. It was apparently normal in Heaven for people to give answers that were evasive and more than a little foreboding. Joe accepted Peter's reply without pressing, however. There were too many other big unanswered questions, and they could always get to know each other a little later on. They had momentum now, and Jesus' crazy idea suddenly seemed quite doable.

"Okay, so first things first. How do we find David?" Joe looked to Jesus for this, understanding him to be the mastermind of this whole rescue operation.

"We will make our full preparations in the armory."

"The armory? What armory?" So far, they'd spent all of their time together on a nature hike up the side of a mountain. Joe hadn't seen anything that looked like a military base.

"I am sending you out like lambs among wolves. The journey will be dangerous." Jesus got up from his seat on the boulder for this last part. His gaze was even more intense than before, communicating the gravity of the situation. There was no hesitation or fear in his eyes, but Joe did sense his deep concern.

"Well, I mean, how dangerous can it be? I already died once." Joe meant it to lighten the mood, but neither of his companions laughed.

Jesus said, "There are much worse things than physical death."

Right. On that ominous note, the Messiah led them to a trail sloping down toward the base of the waterfall. They had to go single-file—Jesus with Joe following right behind him, and Peter bringing up the rear. The hike was considerably easier than their journey up the mountain, and Joe used the time to reflect on everything he'd learned since arriving at the pearly gate.

So Heaven had an armory. This was the latest in a long list of surprises here. Joe had been in enough Bible studies to know that, in the New Testament, Jesus often spoke harsh words to the hypocrites and teachers of the law. Still, Joe always thought of him mostly as the peace-on-Earth and goodwill-to-men type as opposed to being a warrior. Peter, on the other hand, looked like he could still throw a pretty mean punch for a guy his age—if age meant anything at all here. But Jesus, he thought, was more of an orator than a fighter. Yet as the trio descended the winding path, Joe realized that he hadn't been right about very many things in Heaven so far.

Just like the river he'd seen earlier, the water here was perfectly clear. Joe could see directly through the fall as they came level with it. Beyond the cataract was an impressive cavern extending deep into the heart of the mountain, which they entered at the ground level. The waterfall created a natural curtain to block out sound from outside, leaving them alone in the humid and quiet air. The same pool from out front extended back into the cave, with rocky shores rising up on each side. Moving close to the water's edge, Joe watched ripples from the cascade move gently out across the surface. He gripped the cool stones with his toes, wondering how many secret hideaways must exist in this vast landscape and if anyone could ever explore them all.

Jesus led them back a hundred meters or so. It was far enough that, even with Joe's eyes adjusting and the clear water allowing light into the cave, it became almost impossible to see. To address this problem, Jesus reached up and touched a medieval-looking wall torch, which lit instantly. Right on cue, flames ignited on ten or eleven other torches placed around the cavern, easily illuminating the entire space.

Let there be light, apparently. Just in case anyone was about to forget that Jesus was divine.

Joe took in their surroundings. They had reached a back room of sorts, where the cave widened into a near-circular shape, and the pool shallowed up enough so that one could easily walk all the way across from wall to wall. The ceiling was twenty or thirty feet high, and cut into the walls were various shelves and small recesses, much like a catacomb. Instead of skeletons, however, these walls stored weapons.

There were no guns or grenades, but Joe did see just about every kind of sword, dagger, and spear he could imagine. He recognized an assortment of Roman blades as well as thrusting javelins and composite bows with fine-tipped arrows. He saw armor too—helmets and shields, polished iron plates, and tightly linked chain mail. As a longtime fantasy aficionado, Joe was internally geeking out to see the collection. But, as a pragmatist, he had to voice his skepticism.

"Don't you have anything a little more . . . modern?"

"Bullets are only effective if your enemies are mortal," Jesus replied matter-of-factly. "Our struggle is against spiritual forces of evil."

Joe nodded. "So let me guess . . . there's something special about all this stuff."

Peter was already selecting a shield off the wall, lifting a large, semi-cylindrical, body-length one and wielding it with one arm. He thrust it forward and ducked behind it a few times before nodding in satisfaction. Joe couldn't help but think of *Sir Lanceplot.*

"Try it for yourself," Peter said, handing the shield over to Joe.

It was unexpectedly light and appeared to be made of thick planks of wood covered with canvas. Joe had read enough books to know the round metal piece in the center, called a boss, allowed the shield to be an auxiliary offensive weapon. A quick blow with that would easily take the wind out of anybody. At least, that was how it worked on Earth.

"The Shield of Faith," Jesus proclaimed. "With it, you can extinguish the flaming arrows of the evil one."

"What does that mean?" Joe asked. "Will there be literal flaming arrows?"

"You may see them as such—they take many forms. The danger, however, is not a physical one. The enemy is the father of all lies. Indeed, when he lies, he speaks his native language. You will encounter demons of the most duplicitous nature. They will tempt you to doubt yourself and the Holy Spirit inside you."

Joe swallowed. "Okay . . . so I just use this shield to stop all that?"

"Here," Peter said. "Practice with me." He pulled a handful of stones from the water's edge and took a few steps back. "Get ready to dodge these."

"How is a rock the same as a lie?"

But before Joe had even finished his question, Peter tossed a stone across the cave. Joe blocked it easily, however, and then deflected the one after that. It was like playing goalie in hockey, minus the pads. Peter kept throwing stones as Joe continued positioning his shield, hoisting it over his head, crouching down behind it, accustoming himself to its shape and balance. On Earth, there was no way he could ever wield something so huge, but here, it was effortless. Apparently when his body was remade in Heaven, he'd gained some muscle.

"I think I've got the hang of it," Joe called after several minutes. "It's pretty easy."

Jesus sat leaning against the cavern wall, watching them practice with quiet interest. His body was relaxed and comfortable, but his eyes were alert with anticipation. Joe felt a shiver in his spine. Despite the calm appearance, something was definitely going on here. Joe opened his mouth to ask a question, wondering if . . .

Whack! On instinct, Joe saw the rock hurtling toward him and raised his shield just in time. The impact sent him stumbling backward, but he managed to maintain his footing. Joe looked up to find Peter standing on the opposite side of the water, holding another projectile in his hand and poised to launch it across the cavern.

"Pay attention," he said, cracking a mischievous grin. "Before was just the warm-up."

The apostle hurled the second rock with startling accuracy. Joe twisted his shield to avoid a smack in his face but still found himself off balance. When he looked out again, Peter was pulling some kind of spear down off the wall with a long wooden shaft and an iron shank.

"You gotta be kidding me," Joe muttered. Was Peter seriously about to throw a javelin at him? Joe glanced over at Jesus to make sure. The Messiah made eye contact and merely shrugged.

Unbelievable.

"I need to ensure you have the skills before we go into battle," Peter called, his deep voice booming in the cavern. "The enemy will do more than throw pebbles."

"Yeah, I get it. He throws lies and stuff. But do you think we could . . ."

But before Joe could finish, Peter charged forward with a ferocious battle cry. Dumbfounded, Joe took a step back and planted his feet. There was nowhere to go inside a cave. He had no choice but to fight.

Peter crashed into him with a forward thrust of the spear, which Joe fended off with his shield. Despite his appearance of being an older man, Peter was lightning quick on his feet. He spun and kicked Joe's legs out from under him, sending him crashing to the rocky floor. With the wooden end of the spear, Peter smacked Joe's hands, causing him to drop the shield. The skin stung immediately. Joe had wondered earlier if he could bleed in Heaven. Perhaps he was about to find out.

"When I was alive on Earth, men actually knew how to fight," Peter jeered. "At this rate, you won't stand a chance of saving your brother."

Joe got to his feet, again lifting the shield. "I wasn't ready for you. That's all."

"Then be ready this time. Align your knees. Keep your step, and move into the hits."

Peter swung the spear again and jabbed it forward, but this time Joe stayed up, managing to parry each blow with the shield. Joe had never formally studied martial arts, but for once his video game combat knowledge was actually coming in handy. Once he had the footwork down, he knew where to strike. Peter, however, fought with seasoned instinct. Gaining no headway up top, the apostle feinted down and to the right, leading Joe to lower his guard. A quick flip with the butt end of the spear, and Peter whacked Joe across the face.

"Not strong enough, not fast enough." Peter said. "I hardly have to try."

The exercise repeated for another five or six rounds, each hit more violent than the last, and each time sending Joe to the ground. His infinite stamina appeared to be wearing off. Joe actually felt winded—worse, he felt defeated. Finally, Peter threw his spear to the floor.

"You're unfit," he declared. "I thought I could help with your mission, but it's useless. I'm sorry, Joe. You just don't have what it takes." The apostle straightened his robe and stepped past Joe, making his way to the front of the cavern.

"Wait!" Joe called. "How is that fair? I didn't even know what we were doing."

"Do you think the enemy cares about *fair*?" Peter called without looking back.

"What about David?" Joe shouted. "You can't just leave."

Peter whirled around. "What about him? If you can't save yourself, how will you ever save him? Or are you even more naive than I thought?"

The words stung more than a slap to the face. Joe had allowed himself to be so caught up in the excitement of talking with Jesus and meeting Peter and seeing the armory, but now the truth of the matter was clear to him. The point of this had been to save David, but now they'd never do that at all. Jesus had appointed him—well, that was

69

before he'd seen him fight. What a joke. Who had ever rescued someone from Hell, and what made Joe think that he could do it now? He stared at the cave floor, watching shadows dance from the torches on the walls.

"You failed," said a new voice over his shoulder. Joe turned to see Jesus crouched down beside him.

"Yeah. Thanks for reminding me," Joe replied meekly.

"Indeed, I should. Or are you missing the point of the lesson?"

Joe looked up, thoroughly confused.

"The battle is already won, Joe, but not if you fight it on your own. Let me be your strength and shield." Jesus smiled. "I go before you always. Do not be afraid."

And then Joe understood. *They will attempt to have you doubt yourself and the Holy Spirit inside you.* That was the real exercise. Peter had been throwing more than rocks after all, and Joe had fallen for it. But he wouldn't again. He had the power of God and Heaven inside him and the weapons to use it, but he had to believe in it too.

So that had been round one. Well, the battle wasn't over yet.

With new resolve, Joe pulled himself up and yelled to the edge of the cavern. "Peter! What do you say to one more time? I'm ready now."

Peter turned and appeared to consider the offer, waiting a moment before giving a cautious nod. Although his reluctant expression didn't let on, Joe had the sense that the apostle had been hoping for this all along. Peter returned to the back of the cave and collected his spear.

They began. Peter drove his weapon forward, but this time Joe leaned into it. Unleashing a fierce battle cry of his own, Joe rammed the metal boss into the spearhead, cracking the wooden hilt around it. Peter backed up and swung the spear again, but Joe easily blocked each blow.

"You're better this time," the apostle said, "but still not strong enough."

Out of the corner of his eye, Joe glimpsed Jesus still watching them and felt a surge of encouragement. Why not let out a battle cry?

"I am strong," Joe shouted, "and I have the power of Christ within me."

Raising his shield above him one last time, Joe noticed the center glow with heat like an asteroid entering the atmosphere. He collided with his opponent's weapon, and the spear splintered into a hundred pieces, scattering around the cavern. Peter flew backward and landed on his side at the water's edge. The battle was over. Joe had won.

From where he stood, Jesus applauded. "Well done."

"I agree," said Peter, his demeanor totally the opposite of what it was a second ago. He brushed off his robe, looking no worse for the wear. "I hope you'll forgive me, Joe. I needed to ensure you were prepared."

"Yeah ... no worries," Joe replied, resting his shield on the ground. They certainly liked to do first and explain later around here. Still, it was a good feeling to conquer the challenge. He extended a hand to help the apostle to his feet.

"Now," Peter said, "pay attention. No battle has ever been won on defense. You had to strike to knock me down. Now you need a strong offensive weapon."

And with that, the adventure was underway—Joe could hardly contain his excitement. As he perused his options, he considered a long spear with an iron shank similar to what Peter had just used, but then remembered how easily it had broken. There were a few daggers with ornate hilts, but they looked more ceremonial than practical. The bow was an option, and Joe surprised himself with the accuracy of his first practice shot across the cave. He put an arrow right above the wall torch that Jesus had lit when they first came in. But he couldn't figure out a way to manage with the bow, arrows, and shield using only his two hands, and, after their practice session earlier, he was too attached to the shield to give it up.

Finally, he settled on a medium-length iron blade with keen edges and a finely-honed point. The sword had a thin channel down the center and a tight grip with ridges for his fingers. He deftly parried a few practice swings from Peter to be sure of his decision—swordplay came almost naturally now that Joe had passed the first test. The sword wasn't particularly elaborate or shiny, but it was steady in Joe's hand and, most importantly, battle-ready.

"The Sword of the Spirit," said Jesus. "May it lead you in truth against the devil's schemes."

Peter selected a shorter sword with a sharp triangular tip and a shield nearly identical to Joe's. At Jesus' recommendation, they decided against bringing any additional armor so that they would be able to travel quickly while still carrying other supplies. When they were ready, Jesus dragged two enormous wooden chests from a recess at the far end of the wall.

"You'll need some other clothes," he said. "Outward appearance matters more down there, and at first you'll need to blend in." He tossed an array of pants, shirts, and shoes from the first chest for Joe and Peter to sift through.

"Won't we already stand out with our giant shields?" Joe asked.

"There's a difference," Peter explained, "between being an outsider and being an insider with an outside possession. We're going for the latter."

Joe found a pair of sneakers that fit, as well as some jeans and a gray hooded sweatshirt that reminded him of his earthly wardrobe. Peter dressed similarly, and Joe found the anachronism amusing. A man he could only picture as belonging to the first century was now dressed in a full twenty-first-century getup.

"I imagine that's a new look for you, Peter."

His travel companion smiled. "I suppose I have to keep up with the times."

While they were changing, Jesus laid out some canteens for water, food, blankets, and two canvas packs to carry it all. He informed them that, in descending to Hell, they would experience hunger and cold again just as they had previously on Earth.

"Take this for anything else you might require to complete your journey," Jesus said, adding a hefty pouch of gold coins to their supplies.

"Is that . . . money?" Joe asked incredulously. Even though he'd spent most of the day on gilded walkways, he had never expected Jesus to be handing out sacks of cash.

In response, however, Jesus placed a second purse next to the first one, equally full of coins. "Does a king not have riches? And is his wealth not his to spend as he pleases? But see this as an investment for which the return will be new life in the spirit."

"Yeah, well, thank you," said Joe, embarrassed for mentioning it at all. "So how do we find David?"

Jesus reached into the chest again and pulled out a small sheet of papyrus, an inkhorn, and a pen. He flattened the papyrus against the top of the chest and sketched the crude outline of a map.

"You'll enter the gates here," he said, marking the place with an X. "Much of the land is desolate and abandoned, but true isolation is against human nature. There are places where many souls group together. I can tell you that David will be in such a settlement, one they call Brimtown, located here." He marked another spot on the map. "It won't be hard to locate."

"Does that mean he's with other people?" Joe asked, thinking back to Sahil and the rest of the group he'd traveled with upon first arriving.

"Yes. Brimtown is beside the lake of burning sulfur, and David has accepted a job constructing a bridge across the lake."

"A job? People work down there?" Joe couldn't help but notice the irony. David had struggled to hold a steady job on Earth, but he somehow managed to land one in his first few hours of afterlife. And of all places to find employment.

"The hours must be hellacious," Joe quipped.

"Those apart from me lack true purpose," Jesus explained, "but they do sense that it's missing. They will try any number of labors and pursuits to feel purposeful, all the while missing the true objective for which they were created."

"So the bridge is a useless ambition?" Peter asked.

"It is the Bridge to Nowhere. They toil and build without a true destination in mind. They will never reach across the lake, nor would they find anything there if they did."

Jesus rolled up the map and handed it to Peter. "Take it if you'd like. But finding the bridge will not be your greatest difficulty." Peter accepted the map and carefully placed it into his pack.

"Okay. I think I got it," Joe recapped. "Fend off anything evil, find the bridge, find David, head back here. Anything else we need to know?"

Jesus' eyes twinkled. "As a matter of fact, I've saved the most important thing for last."

He again reached into the wooden chest and removed one more object. He stood for a moment, holding it out in the firelight so both Joe and Peter could get a good look. In his hand was an antique skeleton key, made of brass with a circular handle and two stubby bits protruding from its end, like two little buck teeth. It was an iconic sort of key design, like one might find in jewelry or an insignia. Jesus carefully handed it over to Joe.

Joe studied the object for a moment, trying to determine its significance. To start, the key was unusually large, about the length of his hand. It looked more decorative than practical. Joe noticed a small cross engraved at the base of the handle, but the key was otherwise unmarked.

"What is this?"

"It's a salvation key. You must keep it with you at all times."

"A salvation key," Joe repeated, lifting the object toward the light to inspect it further. "That sounds important. Do we need this to get in?"

"The very opposite. The doors of Hell are fastened with chains of darkness, but truly I tell you, they could be opened at any moment. Confinement there is a self-imprisonment. The locks are turned from the inside. But anywhere you find a lock, this key will open the door. Indeed, press it into the earth itself, and the way back to Heaven shall be opened for you." Jesus reached out and cupped his hands around Joe's. His eyes were intensely resolute.

"You will enter freely. You must unlock the gates to leave."

And with that last solemn statement, Joe felt the gravity of his mission return. He'd been enraged and distraught to learn David was in Hell, but somehow with Peter's arrival and trying out the weapons in the cave, he'd become flippant and carefree, as if this were all just pure entertainment, a fantasy game in a fantasy world. But it wasn't. David—his own brother—was trapped in an eternity of pain and suffering. Jesus Christ had just given Joe the key to release him. Nothing about that was a joke.

"Well, I guess we're ready," Joe said after a moment. "I'll ask the obvious question. How do we get down there?"

"Don't you know?" Jesus replied. "Heaven is the land of eternal life, and Hell is the land of eternal death. To arrive here, you must overcome the grave and live."

The logical conclusion wasn't hard to guess. Peter and Joe stared at each other for a minute, and then back to Jesus. Joe thought he understood, but was afraid to say it out loud.

"So to go there . . ." He waited for Jesus to finish his sentence.

"You must enter the grave and die."

EIGHT
YE WHO ENTER HERE

THEY DIDN'T SAY MUCH as they climbed the path back to the top of the waterfall. Joe and Peter carried their swords and shields, and each had a pack of other supplies slung over his shoulder. The salvation key was tucked in Joe's pocket. For his part, Joe was once again glad to use the hike as time to think. So much had happened since he'd arrived in Heaven, and then he'd been so upset to hear about David that he hadn't really taken time to fully consider what he was asking for. What he was about to do. He was voluntarily leaving this glorious paradise—the trees, the mountains, even his own mother—to descend into Hell. The plan was to come back, of course, but he had no idea how long it would take or what dangers they'd encounter. Obviously Jesus had given them weapons for a reason. *Our struggle is against spiritual forces of evil*, he'd said.

But Joe was hopeful. He had an enormous shield and a powerful sword—not to mention a Bible legend to make the journey with him. More than likely, once they talked to David, they'd be able to return quickly. Joe recalled their last car ride together and how much David had told him about wanting to make changes in his life, so he had little doubt his brother would agree to come with them back to Heaven. They just had to find him first.

The trio backtracked to the main trail, stopping at the cave Joe remembered passing earlier. It was much smaller than the cavern they'd been in below the waterfall, just a hole cut into the rock, not even tall enough for Joe to fully stand up inside. There was a large boulder next to it, about the same height and width as the cave entrance itself. It reminded Joe of a movie he'd seen once about the Easter story, Jesus' crucifixion and resurrection. The movie had depicted Jesus' death and burial, and this little cave looked extremely similar to . . .

Oh. Suddenly Joe understood. The cave was exactly what it looked like. Beads of cold sweat formed on the back of his neck, and a searing dread took shape in his stomach.

The cave was a tomb.

You must enter the grave and die.

Who knew they were supposed to take that literally? If Joe had any misgivings about what was coming next, now would certainly be the time to speak up. Maybe instead of doing all this, he could skip back down the mountainside and find a nice shady spot to lie down, grab a few of those oranges he'd eaten earlier, and just enjoy the evening air. What, exactly, was about to happen anyway? Was Jesus going to sneak up on Peter and him, knock them both out, and toss them into the tomb to be buried whole? Why had he ever agreed to this? Joe nervously looked over his shoulder, half expecting to see Jesus preparing to tackle him from behind.

Then again, he trusted Jesus, didn't he? Wasn't it by invoking his name that Joe had been able to work the shield earlier? This was Jesus' plan to rescue David, and he wouldn't have led them here if he wasn't confident it would work. Besides, they wouldn't have bothered to bring all these supplies with them if they were just going to rot inside a cave. Perhaps this was the leap of faith he'd asked Joe about earlier.

"Heaven and Hell are choices both," Jesus informed them, like a teacher to his pupils. "I can no more force you to enter that darkness than I could force you to climb this mountain."

"Are you sure about this?" Peter asked, looking at Joe.

Of course I'm not, he thought. Who in his right mind would willingly crawl into a tomb? Joe closed his eyes and pictured David as a kid, when they used to play together and race their cars over the basement floor. David, his little brother. That's why he was doing this. If he didn't go now, he'd never be able to see him again. Could he really spend eternity in Heaven knowing he'd been given a chance to rescue David and turned it down? Of course not. Joe thought of the hard times, David's numerous dumb decisions and arrests and court hearings and all the ramifications that followed. Then there was their last phone call, when David had said, *All I need is a ride.* Well, Joe could give him a ride now. Joe could lead his brother to this calm and everlasting refuge. His mind resolved, Joe opened his eyes.

"I'm sure."

With that, Joe and Peter clambered into the tomb. It was a tight squeeze with all of their weapons and gear, and they ended up seated with their backs against the wall and their knees to their chests. Sardines were probably more comfortable. Once they were situated, Jesus poked his head in and addressed them one last time.

"The enemy will do all he can to destroy your faith. You must not let him crush your hope." Looking at Joe specifically, he added, "I must warn you that I am not sending you with peace, but with a sword."

"Yeah, I've got it right here," Joe said, patting the hilt. "Anything evil better think twice before coming near me." Yet despite his strong words, Joe was quite apprehensive. Jesus probably didn't need his godly insight to see that.

"Harder to face will be the enemies in your own household."

Joe didn't know what to say to that. Who was in the household of a bachelor who lived alone? His grandparents were still, to the best of his knowledge, alive and well on Earth. Unless he meant David.

"Will this work?" Joe asked, more anxious than he'd been before. "Rescuing David, I mean. Can't you see the future and tell us whether we'll be alright?"

Jesus reached in and placed his hand on Joe's face, his palm calloused and his touch intimate. "I know the plans I have for you," he whispered. "Plans to prosper you and not to harm you, plans to give you hope and a future." With that, Jesus stepped back to roll the stone over the entrance. It was time.

Peter gripped Joe's leg in reassurance. "Whatever happens, you won't be alone." Joe nodded, comforted to know that Peter's words were true.

Sealing the tomb was a drawn-out process. At first, the anticipation was like sitting in a roller coaster about to launch from its platform, a jittery excitement bursting for release. Joe was anxious to get started, whatever they were about to do. Nothing was worse than sitting still. But as Jesus slowly rolled the stone in front of the entrance, Joe experienced a sudden bout of claustrophobia.

"Peter, what happens next?" he asked, eager just to hear another voice.

"Trust the Lord."

They watched together as the last of the light waned like phases of the moon, down to a tiny sliver. Then came the final thud.

Total darkness. The tomb was sealed.

Being a video game designer, Joe possessed a fairly decent imagination. He wondered now how they would meet death, their guide to the underworld. It was still a little frightening to think about, even though he'd technically already died once. Something quick seemed most likely, as a slow starvation would be out of the question since they didn't need to eat in Heaven anyway. Maybe spiders or flesh-eating scorpions would crawl out from cracks in the walls, or a poisonous gas would fill the chamber, or the rocks would press inward to crush their bones.

As it turned out, the last guess was the closest, although he had the direction of motion wrong. Joe and Peter sat together in anxious silence for only a minute or two before the walls began to move outward. The floor lowered itself too, as if they were in a subterranean elevator. It remained pitch black, but somehow Joe sensed the quality of the blackness was changing from a no-light-black to a nothing-at-all-black, just as he had experienced when he was lifted up from the scene of his car crash to Heaven. The difference, however, was that unlike the first time around, Joe did not have a calming sense of peace. Even the reassurance from Jesus' touch was fading fast.

In fact, every emotion associated with this descent was the very opposite of peace. At first, Joe sensed just some small agitation in his gut, but it soon became a torment. Every disappointment and heartbreak he'd ever known, every strife or tension, every feeling of regret, simultaneously returned to him. Flashbacks of visiting David in jail, failing his first test in college, Max Yearling moving away, his mother's casket carried down the aisle. All of the loneliness, all of the pain, all of the loss he'd ever experienced tore at Joe's heart, ripping it from the inside out. His temperature increased until he felt his organs were literally burning up under his flesh. Although nothing had cut him, Joe felt he was bleeding out from every pore. All of the life and excitement and happiness contained within him was now leaking onto the floor, draining his body of everything meaningful and good and whole.

Then came the voices. Whispers in his mind, accusing him, cursing him, telling him again and again that he was worthless, hated, forgotten, alone. Worst of all was that, despite how boldly Joe might have rejected these charges in the light, here in the dark, he suspected that they may indeed be true. Conflicting were his will to submit, to drown in these accusations, and his will to fight. Joe writhed and kicked at the air, but there were no walls around him, nothing to touch—even Peter was gone from him now. Joe was a prisoner with no shackles, completely alone, trapped in this empty space. The voices became louder, closer, sharper with their words. This whole mission was a fool's errand. Why would David listen to him, a hypocrite, a liar, a selfish idiot? Joe swatted at the air, but to no avail. At last he reached for his sword, thinking if there was nothing to fight then perhaps he might lessen his pain. He might silence his misery. He pulled the weapon from its sheath and slid the blade against the palm of his hand, relishing the cool metal against his skin, longing for sweet oblivion.

Heaven and Hell are choices both.

So they were. Dropping the sword to his side, Joe lay flat on his back and chose.

Peter shook him awake in a desolate land. Joe set his elbows in the dirt and took in the parched and treeless ground. The sky was overcast and dreary, and their surroundings were flat and barren. Not much to see other than a few skeletal bushes and a cluster of dilapidated shacks off to their left. A quick inventory revealed that Joe still had his pack of supplies, the salvation key in his pocket, his sword and shield, and all of his limbs.

"Well, we made it," Joe remarked. "Not exactly paradise, is it?"

"It wouldn't be my first choice," Peter replied wryly.

"Yeah, I guess not."

Joe stood all the way up, brushing the dirt off his jeans and absently wishing he'd brought some warmer clothes. Hell was quite a bit colder than the inferno he'd expected. He had to admit, if anything could be a complete contrast to the Heaven he'd just left, this was it—no color, no life, no energy, no company, no trumpets, no obvious path to take. He'd thought the opposite of good and real would be evil and false, and indeed, he found that the opposite of having something was having nothing at all.

"Alright then," Joe said. His head and every muscle ached, likely from falling through whatever trapdoor had landed them here. "Now we just have to find this Brimtown place and get David. Which way do you suppose we go?"

"I studied the map Jesus gave us while I was waiting for you to wake. It took a moment to orient myself, but I'm certain we must head that way." He pointed to their right.

Joe frowned, skeptical. "How can you tell? There aren't any landmarks." He honestly couldn't remember the last time he'd used an old-fashioned map instead of the GPS in his car, but still, he knew it couldn't be that easy.

"I'm certain," Peter repeated—a little sternly, Joe thought. Well, Peter was the guide wasn't he? Why else had Jesus sent him?

"Alright then. Lead on."

They walked for close to an hour without saying much. Joe's back muscles whined with every step. Maybe his sparring match earlier was catching up to him now. It was also considerably more challenging than it had been to carry his shield and the heavy supply pack, as if he were an astronaut finally coming back to the full gravity of Earth. No, that wasn't it. It was more as if his muscles had atrophied since leaving the mountaintop. He was the champion athlete who'd gotten out of shape. Heaven was the fullness of Joe's strength; this was a shadow of what he knew to be real.

To make matters more dismal, the vibrant hues he'd known in Heaven had stayed there too. The gray sky was so gloomy here, and it only seemed to be getting darker as they went. Twice they stopped to sip water from their canteens and discuss which way they should go next, Peter's confidence in his navigating never once wavering. They did appear to be going in the direction of more settlements, which was a good sign. Most of what they saw, however, had a barren, post-apocalyptic air to it—a few rotting trees, cabins in disrepair, and a lean-to so rickety that Joe thought he might collapse it just by exhaling. No people, no animals, not even bugs. Everything was empty and crumbling, as if the world itself were in decay.

"I'd imagined more licking flames and devil horns," Joe remarked.

"Instead, you found that death is cold and bleak."

"I'll admit, it's kind of a letdown." Their laughter pierced the air like a sprout shooting up through the dirt.

"I don't think I've said this yet, Peter, but thank you for being here. I mean, you don't even know me or David, but you're helping out. I really appreciate it."

The apostle turned his head and regarded him for a moment, his deep brown eyes thoughtful and knowing.

"Jesus is the Messiah for all people, not just for those within the heavenly gates. Some call him Lord, but many do not."

"So," Joe continued, "I don't mean to sound conceited or anything, but why has nobody else ever thought of this? I mean, I can't be the only one with somebody I care about stuck down here." A chilling wind picked up, as if to make his point. Surely if people could avoid this desolation, they would.

Peter wrinkled his brow. "If you know anything about my story, Joe, then you know I was persecuted—as were all the believers in my time. Many who came here were enemies of the gospel."

"I thought the Bible said to love your enemies," Joe replied, puzzled.

"True, we are called to love our enemies and can rightly lament over their choices and their rejection of the truth. Yet we have always known that anyone who does not listen to God will be cut off from his people. Narrow is the road that leads to life, and few find it."

Joe paused a moment to adjust his grip on his shield. It was actually quite cumbersome, now that he had his Earth strength again. He had no idea how Peter was managing it so easily. At least the conversation was a welcome and interesting distraction. He was genuinely curious, too. *Many who came were enemies of the gospel.* Somehow David had ended up down here, and, despite the numerous dumb choices he'd made throughout his life, Joe wouldn't really consider him to be anyone's enemy. He ventured another question.

"It seems like a lot of people, though, aren't really *evil*. You know, not mass murderers or rapists or anything like that. Like David. You know what I mean?"

An abandoned outbuilding creaked in the wind.

"All have sinned and fall short of the glory of God."

"Right—I mean, I know nobody's perfect and we all make mistakes. But isn't that why Jesus came?" Joe pressed. "To save the whole world from sin?"

"From the moment of the first sin of the first rebellious angels," Peter explained, "I believe God has always had redemption as his plan. He loves too much for anything otherwise. But with love is freedom, and with freedom, there are really only two possible courses of action."

"And what are those?"

"To accept or refuse. To relent or resist. To dive in or climb out. It is human to speak of achievement and legacy and diversion and comfort, as if those alone could sustain. People everywhere seek to build lives for themselves although they lack the required tools. For what we saw on Earth was only a reflection, images and shadows of the glory that is to come. And so we have faith in the one who saves us and hope that he already has, but at the end of all days, when we see him face to face, even those become unnecessary. When all else passes away, we are left with only love. That is, love, and what we choose to do with it."

"But what if people don't know about Jesus or don't know they have to make some kind of choice? It just doesn't really seem fair, you know."

"Quite right. Everything about love is unfair."

That doesn't exactly answer my question, Joe thought.

Joe studied his companion, his powerful frame, his bristly beard, his impressive endurance. He considered the fact that this grandpa-aged man was the one he had to keep up with, and not the other way around. Peter was more of a warrior than a mystic, and if it weren't for his reputation, Joe might question his wisdom. Yet for all his talk about love, Peter's views on the matter didn't exactly seem loving. *Enemies of the gospel*—well, Jesus wouldn't have sent them if David fit that category. Joe placed his hand around the salvation key in his pocket, just to be sure.

As they walked on, the buildings they passed became more frequent and of sturdier construction. A few of them actually looked habitable, although they still were empty. Eventually they reached a group of houses on both sides of an unpaved street. The houses were all two-story and modernly suburban, in excellent condition compared to the shacks they'd passed earlier. Joe was reminded of pictures he'd seen of abandoned real estate developments in the middle of the desert, unfinished subdivisions with perfectly livable houses but no actual residents.

"Should we go inside?" Joe asked.

"No. We can rest before continuing, but outside the homes."

Joe was taken aback. "Are you sure? I kind of want to check it out."

"For what reason? We are neither vagrants nor looters. It would be unwise." Peter dropped the subject by moving a few steps down the road to stretch out. His exercises were swift and precise, with an athlete's discipline.

Joe huffed in annoyance. He'd been following Peter this whole time. Couldn't he lead the way for once? Joe felt like a child being told no. What would be the harm in just looking? They might gain valuable information that could lead them to David. Peter had no reason to be obstinate about this. Joe hadn't questioned his decisions all day, but now . . .

Joe stopped himself. If they were going to succeed, he had to trust Peter. They had to work together. This would be a stupid thing to fight over.

Stay focused on David, Joe thought. *He's the real reason we're here.*

He looked up at the house nearest to him while he snacked on an orange. It looked pretty innocuous—two stories, faded blue paint, steps leading up to a covered porch with two rocking chairs by the front door. The blinds were drawn on all the windows. Ironically, it was the normality of the house that made Joe so immensely curious to see the inside. Everything they'd seen so far had been falling apart, but these houses were in fine condition. They could be on a street in the neighborhood where he'd grown up if it weren't for the dusty desert landscape.

In fact, come to think of it, it did kind of remind him of the Nelsons' old house on the corner. Joe and David used to play kickball there with the neighbors after school. Once, David drilled a line drive straight into a flowerpot and shattered it across the porch. They were all ready to make a run for it, but Mr. Nelson, the football coach, just laughed and said David would make a fine placekicker someday. Then he swept up the shards without another word. Still, David had asked Joe not to tell Grandma about it, and Joe had kept his word.

The good old days, Joe thought, *when the worst David did was smash a flowerpot.*

Joe smiled at the memory and was about to stand up again when suddenly he saw something. There—a slight movement in the blinds on the front window. It had been quick, but Joe was sure of it. Someone had peeked out from the blinds. Someone was watching them.

"Hey, Peter," he said, as loud as he dared. Joe gripped his sword at the hilt. "Somebody's in there."

Peter snapped to attention, eyes wide and alert. "A person? You're sure?"

"I just saw whoever it was spying on us. What should we do?"

Peter thought it over for a moment. "I doubt a demon would stay so long in hiding and not seek a foothold. Let us speak with him— but keep your guard."

In a strong, authoritative voice, Peter called out, "Come out and show yourself. We mean you no harm."

No response but the wind.

"We're just looking for Brimtown," Joe added. "Do you know how to get there?" Thinking of the coin pouch in his bag, he added, "We could pay you."

A moment of eerie silence, and then Joe heard a deadbolt move. He watched as the front door inched open. An older man with stark white hair and wild eyes stepped onto the porch, holding a shotgun. In a swift motion, he leveled the double-barrel right at them.

"You fresh meat, ain't ya?" he spat.

Joe hesitated, not knowing what to make of the question.

"Well, y'all better move along," the man continued. "This here's private property. You ain't bringing no demons on me."

Joe was flabbergasted. He hadn't seen a single sentient being the whole time they'd been wandering around, and now the first guy they ran into had a shotgun leveled at their heads and a whole *git off my lawn* routine to go with it. Joe wasn't sure would happen if he got shot in Hell, but instinct told him he didn't want to find out.

Peter recovered his wits first. "I assure you, we don't intend to stay long. Perhaps you could direct us. Do you know—"

A loud pop sounded from the gun as Joe ducked his head and recoiled behind his shield. Joe heard a spray of little pellets above him, meaning somehow the man had missed. A quick glance told him Peter was okay too.

"That there was a warning shot," said the man. "That's all the direction I got for ya. Now move along." The gun clicked as he pumped the slide to reload.

"Okay, okay!" Joe called frantically. "We're leaving." He tugged at Peter's arm, and the two of them hurried down the street away from the man's porch, Joe awkwardly holding his shield over his head as he moved, just in case. But no shots followed. Joe and Peter reached the end of the row of houses gratefully unscathed.

"Holy crap," Joe panted. "I mean, that was crazy, right?" He glanced over his shoulder to make sure they weren't being pursued. There was the white-haired man, still on his porch, hoisting his gun into the air like a baton.

Peter slowed to a walk. "We should not have run so quickly. Perhaps he could have informed us about this place. He mentioned the demons."

"Are you nuts? Talk to that guy? He was shooting at us."

"Only to chase us away. I suspect it was fear, not malice, that ruled him." Peter rubbed his fingers along the top of his shield and licked them. "It's salt."

Joe blinked. "Wait, what? What are you talking about? He shot *salt* at us?"

Peter nodded. "Not everyone wishes to leave Hell, Joe. Although nothing threatens their ability to do so, some will defend their right to stay."

"I gathered that," Joe mumbled.

But before either of them could say more, they heard a rumbling in the distance and turned around to see something coming. *Now what?* Joe thought. Hours and hours of walking through an absolute wasteland with no action to speak of, and now it was one quick thing after another. Joe squinted at the fast-approaching cloud of dust to see what it was. He immediately did a double take.

It was a truck.

A real, Earth-built, gas-engine truck.

Well, strange as it was, Joe supposed that if there were houses in Hell, why not vehicles too? There was no real road to speak of, but the truck sped diagonally across the desert floor, obviously headed right for them. With nowhere to hide, Joe and Peter had two options—turn back toward a half-crazed man with a shotgun, or wait to see this new arrival.

"Be ready," Peter said, drawing his sword and taking a defensive stance.

"Oh, so now you want to fight someone?" Joe quipped, still on edge and doing nothing to hide it.

"I only said be ready. Our mission will find enemies here."

Joe closed his eyes and took a deep breath. What happened to all of the bravado he'd had in Heaven? He'd been strong and confident in the armory. Hadn't Jesus himself appointed him for this mission to rescue David? Yet at the first sign of real danger, Joe had run away fast. And it hadn't even been real danger—just some old guy dousing them with salt. Joe gripped the hilt of his sword and stared out at the horizon. *Lord*, he prayed, *give me strength.*

The red Chevy Silverado drifted to a stop right in front of them, spraying sand and gravel. Seconds after killing the engine, a woman, maybe early fifties, hopped down from the driver's seat, her light hair pulled back into a bun and a no-nonsense attitude on her face. She was dressed in a khaki-colored uniform with a badge on her chest and a gun at her hip, giving Joe the sense that they were about to be arrested.

"You know most people just sit there all dazed and confused after they come down the pipe, but no, you two decided to take a little tour. I've been trying to track you idiots all day. And what in the . . ." She raised her brow in disbelief to see their swords and shields. "What are you, some kind of gladiator reenactors or something?"

Intrigued, Peter cautiously lowered his sword. "Who has sent you?"

In response, she pulled a paper from her shirt pocket and unfolded it. "I'm guessing from the syntax that you're Simon son of Jonah, called Peter." She regarded him with a quizzical expression. "And that would make your friend here Joseph Platt. We got your death alerts this morning."

"I'm sorry, who are you?" Joe blurted.

She tapped her badge impatiently. "Agent Nora Barnes, North Abaddon Customs and Immigration. Now c'mon. You can save your questions for the drive over."

"Immigration? Like, for a country?"

"I told you, questions on the drive over. Now hurry up. It'll be nightfall soon."

Joe looked to Peter and hesitated. With David's soul on the line, there was no time for a detour. But, then again, access to a vehicle certainly wouldn't hurt. It was his turn to be brave.

"Actually," Joe offered, "maybe you can help us. We're looking for a place called Brimtown. If you could give us a ride or something, maybe we could work out a deal."

For a second, Agent Barnes broke her composure. "How do you . . . who told you about Brimtown?"

Joe swallowed, hoping he hadn't overplayed his hand. "We've . . . um . . . heard of it, that's all. You know, while we were wandering around, like you said. Anyway, it seems like a good place to go. Can you take us?"

"No," she said immediately, although her face still showed the confusion from a few seconds back. "No, absolutely not."

"We could pay you," Joe offered, trying the money angle once again. He could count on a little greed from the people down here, right?

Agent Barnes gave an indignant snort. "You should be paying me anyway just for the work of tracking you down." She shook her head, then returned to her assertive composure.

"Look, I don't know how you've been here one day and already have your whole afterlife mapped out, but clearly you don't know why that can't happen tonight. You'll learn quickly that the sky here has two colors, gray and black. And when it turns black, the demons come out. Not even a fool is still outside when the demons come out."

"We do not fear the demons," Peter replied emphatically.

"Well, you should," she snapped. Despite her tone, however, Nora's scowl was speckled with curiosity. Joe had the sense they weren't anything like her usual customers.

"Look," she said after a minute. "I get paid for bringing you in. That's how it works. If tomorrow you have somewhere you want to go, be my guests. You have all of eternity to see the sights down here. But whatever it is you think you have to do, believe me, it starts by coming with me. You have no idea what happens at night around here and no idea how dangerous it is. So you're right, I can help you. But first, we play by my rules."

Joe glanced at Peter in hopes of reaching some silent agreement, but the apostle had his eyes closed and was muttering a few words that Joe couldn't quite make out. A prayer, maybe?

At last, Peter acquiesced. "Very well. We'll follow your lead."

Nora Barnes rolled her eyes. "Sure made that harder than it needed to be. Throw your packs in the bed. We need to get going." With that, she climbed back into the truck.

"So you have a good feeling?" Joe whispered. "You think this is the right move?"

"I think," Peter replied, "we should test every spirit. The land is full of false prophets. She claims to be an agent of this place, yet she speaks as if the demons are her foes. I sense we may have found an ally."

"The whole enemy-of-my-enemy thing?"

"For now, we are merely sojourners. The time has not yet come to reveal our true purpose. Besides, it seems unwise to camp here."

"You can say that again," Joe replied, thinking of the man with the shotgun. "Okay then. We go with her tonight, then find Brimtown first thing tomorrow. Remember, we're here for David."

"I haven't forgotten," said the apostle.

Joe and Peter loaded their belongings into the truck bed as instructed, Joe feeling some nerves as he parted with his shield, even if it was just for a car ride. He left the front seat for Peter and climbed into the back of the cab.

"I have to ask," Joe said as buckled into his seat, "what exactly did you mean when you said you're with customs and immigration? Do we have to go through some sort of inspection or something?"

Nora Barnes smirked as she started the engine.

"Welcome to Hell, my friend. Welcome to Hell."

NINE
THE PARDONER AND
HIS SCHEME

JOE FOUND THE DRIVE across the desert to be quite nerve-racking, and strangely enough, it had nothing to do with Nora Barnes's daredevil maneuvering. His thoughts held him captive as the truck hurtled toward its destination, desperate to arrive before nightfall. For better or worse, they were involved in the place of Hell now and were no longer just outsiders looking in. It also didn't help Joe to think about how the last time he'd been inside a vehicle he'd ended up pulverized by a semi-truck. Just remembering it made his palms sweat and his head feel dizzy. Up in the front seat, meanwhile, Peter was watchful and calm. Somehow a man who'd lived and died centuries before guns or cars even entered the human imagination had been fazed by neither. All that time in the glorious city of Heaven must've really changed his perspective on what qualified as extraordinary.

One huge bump followed another as they tore through a dried-up creek bed. Joe felt sick to his stomach. He closed his eyes and tried to relax, but to no avail. When was the last time he'd actually slept? He hadn't been physically tired in Heaven, but now all of his exertions since leaving the crash scene on the highway were catching up to him at once. The sooner he could get out of this place, he thought, the better off he'd be.

As soon as we *get out*, he corrected himself. *Me, Peter, and David.*

After a few more minutes of watching the desert landscape blur by his window, Joe's attention drifted up to the front of the truck where Peter and Nora Barnes were talking.

"I'm curious," Peter was saying. "How did you know to expect us?"

"We call it a death alert," she said. "It prints out like a fax each morning giving us the names and locations of any new arrivals in the sector."

"The sector?"

"North Abaddon—that's where we are. Supposedly Hell started off as a single unified state, you know, way back thousands of years ago or whatever. But, not surprisingly, the first people to show up brought their conflicts with them. Ever since the beginning, political disputes and personal quarrels have led to Lord knows how many different districts and zones and territories and municipalities, each wanting nothing to do with the next."

"Do you mean that people are at war with each other?"

She gave a snorting laugh. "War requires that you actually care enough to do something about it. Maybe they would on Earth, but something about eternity dulls the fighting spirit. No, most people who decide they're unhappy in one place just pack up and move somewhere else. There's plenty of land to go around, as you can see."

"Indeed." Peter looked straight ahead to study the undeveloped wasteland. "So North Abaddon, then. Do all people come here first when they die?"

Nora shook her head. "It's all just random, I think. You've got as much choice in the matter as you did about where you were born on Earth. I've heard enough to know other sectors run it more or less the same way, though. Each morning we get the alerts for whoever's gonna pop up inside our borders and then we go get 'em. A pretty good system, actually. It orients the arrivals and supports the local tax base, especially with a multiple." She glanced in the rearview mirror and added, "Arrivals usually show up alone."

Joe swallowed hard and tried to act like he hadn't heard her. She already seemed a little suspicious of their swords and shields. How much did they really stand out?

94

Peter, however, played it off nonchalantly. "I see. Was it strange to find us together?"

"Not especially. I see pairs from time to time, even small groups, typically if they all died right together. Not finding you terrified out of your minds, though, that was strange."

He grinned. "Should we take that to be a compliment?"

"Take it how you want. Either I'm calling you brave, or I'm calling you stupid. You'll realize soon enough, a healthy fear is what keeps people sane around here."

Peter asked a few more questions, keeping it light and casual in what Joe assumed was an effort to build a rapport. Did it ever rain here? Not for as long as anyone could remember. Was the truck new? Since last month. Could they take it out for a spin later?

"We're not that friendly," she teased. "But maybe I'll help you find your own ride."

In fact, while Nora Barnes had been impatient and a little pushy earlier, she was quite amiable now that they were in motion. A nice person in Hell—imagine that! Back in Heaven, Jesus had made it sound like everyone and everything would be against them here. The old man with the shotgun certainly came to mind. But perhaps there were some good people mixed in with the loonies and the criminals. Maybe Nora Barnes just made a lot of mistakes in her life and through one unfortunate circumstance or another had ended up here. Like David.

It was nearly dark when they arrived at the town, a sudden reminder of civilization after miles and miles of barren wild. The little downtown area had a down-on-its-luck sort of feel, an urban center well past its economic prime. On either side of the road was a hodgepodge of cafes and liquor stores, walk-up apartments and shady boutiques, dark office buildings and private dispensaries advertising various remedies and concoctions in the windows. It was hard to tell what was closed for the night and what was closed for good. The streets themselves were potholed and crooked, appearing to overlap with one another rather than intersect, as if each avenue were jostling for prominence. Wrappers and plastic cups littered the walkways, and less than half of the streetlights were functioning. Joe mentally compared the dirty and chaotic layout to the elegance and careful planning of the city in Heaven. It was like a child's finger painting held up to the blueprint of a master architect.

"Where are all the people?" Joe asked.

"Inside by now. Like I said, you don't want to be out at night. We're pushing it."

They made a tight turn, and Joe thought he glimpsed a church steeple a few blocks over. He almost asked about it but then caught himself. Of course there wouldn't be a church down here. He'd almost forgotten where they were.

Finally, they reached a dead end on one of the streets and pulled into a large parking lot. Theirs was one of several dozen vehicles, all of which looked fresh off the assembly line. In contrast, Joe saw that the building before them could do with more than a few renovations. It looked like a mid-century elementary school, similar to the one he'd attended as a child, a squat, red-brick affair with wide rectangular windows and a covered sidewalk leading up to the entrance. The black lettering over the doorway read "North Abaddon Municipal Service Center." Joe and Peter gathered their belongings and quickly followed Nora to the door.

Stale air and fluorescent lighting greeted them inside the cramped lobby. Joe took in the disorderly mess of winding queues and service counters, cartons of paper forms and overstuffed rows of filing cabinets, checkpoints and security desks set up like roadblocks. He'd wondered where the people were. Well, now he knew. There were about fifty men and women standing in line for one thing or another, most of them old and all of them grumpy, and about the same number of employees—although few of them were engaged in anything remotely useful. Joe's programmer heart cringed at the obvious inefficiencies. If he hadn't died already, surely waiting around in this bureaucratic nightmare would have done him in.

Nora Barnes led them over to a small counter with a stack of forms and letter trays. Manning the station was a similarly uniformed guard reclining in a swivel desk chair, a giant bear of a man who looked like he'd just come out of hibernation.

"You're late," he grunted.

"Believe me, I know. I'm getting overtime for this one." Nora reached into her pocket for the same paper she'd shown Joe and Peter when she picked them up. "Two for ingress processing. Simultaneous entry, department four, verbal identity confirmation. A little more talkative than usual, I might add." She signed the bottom of the form and handed it over to the guard. After a brief examination, he stamped the paper and placed it in a tray.

"Entry tax and declarations on top, housing and work permits on the bottom," he muttered, handing a clipboard to each Peter and Joe. "Fill these out and take your belongings over there." He half-heartedly motioned to another counter about ten feet away where currently a cadaverous old man was attempting to apply for some sort of license. The poor guy lacked the required documents, however, and, at least from what Joe could overhear, wasn't winning any sympathy.

"There's a holding period while they process your paperwork, usually no more than twenty-four hours," Nora was saying as they shuffled over to stand in line at the next station. "After that, you're officially residents."

"We're not planning to stay," Joe reminded her, still a little distracted watching the old man haggle at the counter.

"Most folks aren't when they first arrive, till they realize this is the final stop. Might as well make something of it if you're gonna be here forever anyway."

"No, uh, that's not what I meant. We're going to Brimtown tomorrow, remember?"

She smiled coyly. "That's right. You mentioned it."

"Yeah, well, if you're able to help at all with that, I know we'd certainly appreciate it." Joe looked to Peter for support, but, strangely, the apostle was seated at a table and carefully filling out the forms they'd just received. Earlier, Peter had been all about focusing on their mission, and now he was in a rush to complete some meaningless paperwork that had nothing to do with rescuing David. The more Joe learned about Peter, the less he understood the man.

"You'll find your way, I'm sure," Nora said, somewhat indifferently. "Well, I'll leave you boys to it. Goodnight."

"Oh, one other thing," Peter said, jumping from his seat, "before you leave us for the evening." He whispered in Nora's ear.

"I did promise you that, didn't I?" she said with a laugh. Nora reached for a pad of paper and scribbled an address on it. "Tell 'em I sent you, and best of luck." With that, she left them and exited to another room inside the building, looking back just before she shut the door. Peter folded the paper and pocketed it. Joe waited for the apostle to explain, but he didn't.

With a heavy sigh, Joe heaved his pack up onto the table. He dug out his canteen and took a drink, then grabbed an apple for a snack. Peter continued to scribble away.

"So what's up with you, anyway?" Joe said after a moment. "You've hardly said a word since we walked in. And why do you suddenly care so much about some useless paperwork?"

Peter set down his pen and scratched his thick gray beard. When he turned to face Joe, his deep brown eyes flickered with intrigue.

"I was arrested once, very early on after Christ had risen from the grave. It was during the Festival of Unleavened Bread, not long after King Herod had put to death James, John's brother and my friend. The only reason he didn't do the same to me was because a public execution during the festival would displease the people, and the fool valued his reputation above all else. I thought there was no reason he'd spare my life, although my only crime had been to preach the resurrection. So there I was, suffering in prison, alone, afraid, but also at peace. It was a strange and remarkable thing for me to wonder if that night would be my last on Earth, but still sleep soundly knowing that my life was in God's hands."

Joe chomped on his apple. Still delicious, even this far from Heaven. "I take it there's a reason you're telling me this."

Peter smiled. "The Lord did indeed spare my life. The very night I was imprisoned, an angel came to me in what I thought was surely a dream. We walked right past the guards to the wall surrounding Jerusalem, and the city gate opened by itself. As soon as I was inside, the angel vanished. It was truly a miracle. Even when I arrived at the house where my friends were praying, they insisted it couldn't be me outside knocking at the door."

"I'm not sure I understand what you're getting at."

Peter held up the form he'd just completed. "Our bodies will need to rest before we continue on to Brimtown. By staying indoors, we can both lie down without needing a sentry, and as we are effectively detained while they process our documents, I suggest we take advantage of the opportunity. We'll need our energy come morning." He stood up and then leaned in to whisper in Joe's ear. "Sleep now, for help is on the way."

"What help?" Joe asked.

But now the man at the counter had gone, and Peter rose to register them with the clerk. Joe slouched in his chair, left to answer his own question. He felt for the salvation key in his pocket, wrapping his fingers around the cool metal.

You will enter freely. You must unlock the gates to leave.

Joe almost laughed. What holding period? Who could possibly detain them? They could leave at any moment if they wanted to. How absurd they were appeasing the system at all! Peter's reason made no sense. They could rest anywhere. But as the minutes ticked on, Joe sat back in his chair and waited for Peter to finish, griping, then yawning, then finally resting his head on his pack and drifting off to sleep.

Joe awoke to find a stranger in the room. The man was so unobtrusive that at first Joe thought he was only imagining him. He was tall with round glasses and ebony skin, smartly dressed, and calmly reclining in a wicker chair against the wall.

"Good morning," the man said, aware of Joe as soon as he opened his eyes. "Excuse me for the intrusion, but I wanted to make sure I spoke with you in person."

Joe sat up on his cot, still groggy and trying to make sense of his surroundings. Windowless room. Bare walls painted a hospital beige. His sword resting on the small nightstand between the two beds, an easy reach if he needed it. He rubbed the sleep from his eyes and squinted in the bright, incandescent light.

"I'm sorry, but who are you?"

"Apology not necessary. My name is Isaac Washington. They tell me you're Joe Platt."

"They? What do you mean, *they*?"

"Take your time. It's normal to feel disoriented waking up for the first time."

Joe did feel unusually out of it. Had he been drugged? He tried to remember if he'd drunk anything strange the night before. Someone had led them here, a chubby guy with a huge key ring, after they'd cleared customs and given up more than half their food and coins as some bullcrap entry tax. The man with the keys had taken them to this little room with military cots and a naked lightbulb and told them he'd send someone to release them in the morning, and then he'd locked the door, and Joe had crashed immediately.

The stranger leaned in to whisper. "I'm a friend, Joe. I'm here to help you."

A friend. They weren't supposed to have friends in Hell, were they? Joe had a vague memory of Peter's story about the angel saving him from prison and a promise that help was on the way. Was this what he meant? Joe still wasn't quite conscious enough to piece it all together. He couldn't remember the last time he'd slept so deeply. He reached for his canteen on the floor beside his bed, hoping the hydration would wake him up a bit. There wasn't much left. His supply was dwindling, and he wasn't sure yet where they'd find more.

"What time is it?"

"Almost midday," Isaac Washington replied. "Only a few hours until darkness."

Joe swung his legs over the bed and stretched. Midday? They were wasting time. His mind urged motion, but his body was slow to follow.

Peter was still out cold on the bed next to Joe, wearing the same clothes as the day before, his chest rising and falling in the steady rhythm of sleep. He looked older now than when Joe had first seen him in Heaven. More vulnerable, too, no longer exuding the same confidence and strength. Maybe yesterday had exhausted him more than he'd let on.

"There are a few urgent matters I came to discuss," Isaac continued. "They're processing your release as we speak. As soon as I'm finished here, you're free to go wherever you wish."

Joe nodded, relieved. Although he'd agreed to come with Agent Barnes in her truck yesterday, he wondered now if it'd been the right decision. They'd wasted a lot of time without gaining any real information. He was eager to get back to their mission.

"What do you need from us?" Joe asked.

"I assume the agent who picked you up yesterday warned you about the demons."

Joe shrugged. Stealing Peter's line from the day before, he said, "We're not afraid."

"A valiant thing to say, although courage alone won't save you. You see, they find you no matter what. It's impossible to avoid them."

"I thought they only came out at night," Joe said, remembering what he'd heard already.

"Most of the time that's true. But those who pridefully think that they can hide forever in the safety of their own homes without some kind of supernatural protection, well, they're like children playing in a pit of snakes. They try all kinds of buffoonery to ward off the spirits, what with amulets and dreamcatchers and who knows what else. But none of it works, you see. The demons force their way through every gap and crevice until you're surrounded without even realizing it. Your soul is damaged forever."

"I'm sorry. Who are you again?"

"All you need to know is that I'm here to offer my services to new arrivals. Your agent told me that you were especially lively. I want to protect that life."

"I thought you said I'm doomed no matter what?" Joe couldn't hide the sarcasm. Whoever this guy was, he'd probably never seen a Shield of Faith straight from Heaven.

"Ah, but there is hope," Isaac continued. "You see, unenlightened, most people don't understand the true nature of the beasts. All demons are parasitic. They feed on iniquity like insects boring through trees. Tell me, Joe, have you ever committed a sin?"

Of all questions—Joe had been going to church his whole life. Of course he knew the answer to that.

"Everyone has. We all sin, myself included."

"That's exactly right. And I'll tell you now, these demons will feed off your wrongdoing and wickedness, all of the sins you ever committed on Earth and all the new sins you will commit here." Isaac Washington spoke fervently but quietly. Only later did Joe realize how strange it was that he didn't want to wake Peter before issuing this warning.

"The big ones, sure—murder, adultery, betrayal. But it's the little ones people forget to count. Every little indecency, each indiscretion in thought or word. Every time you ever lusted after a woman or stored up hatred of your fellow man, those demons know about it. They'll come upon you and remind you of everything you've ever done wrong, big things and little things, making you feel the hurt and relive the pain you caused in ways you've never imagined, amplifying your own suffering to a thousand times what you've ever felt before. No, there's nothing like the guilt you'll feel then, knowing that they're the ones right in naming you the one wrong. You'll weep and gnash your teeth together, regretting your very existence until at last you try to end your life again, only to realize that you can't. Such is the rub—there's nowhere else to go from here."

Joe was captivated, but cautiously so. The observations rang familiar, but surely there was some part missing from the story, like wise words taken out of context.

"Thankfully," Isaac continued, "we are not without means of protection. You see, there is no sin to feed off of as long as it's forgiven. Only by receiving a pardon for your sins can you be certain that you'll be safe."

"What do you mean, a *pardon*?"

"An official action of removing your offense. I happen to represent the North Abaddon Holy Sanctuary, right here in town. You probably saw it on your way in. We minister to North Abaddon and nine of the surrounding—"

"Wait," Joe blurted, cutting him off. "Are you talking about a church? In Hell?"

Isaac flashed a knowing smile. "Indeed I am. You'll find my rates commensurate with the gravity of the crime. A courteous young man such as yourself can have invaluable protection at little expense, as long as you continue to abide by what's right."

"Well, I appreciate the offer, but I think my conscience is clean."

"Oh, my good friend. If that were true, we both know I wouldn't be here."

David. From nowhere, the thought entered his mind. Joe took another drink, remembering the trumpets and gold-paved streets, so far away now.

"We should get going," Joe said, "but thanks for stopping by." He reached over and shook Peter by the shoulder to wake him.

Isaac suddenly stood and spoke in a hurried voice. "I can take away the burdens you're carrying, Joe. For just a small sacrifice on your end, I can pardon your sins. Let your soul's rest here be a blessing and not a curse." He reached into his pocket and pulled out a business card. "Here's my address. You come when you're ready, and not a minute later."

At that moment, Peter awoke and, upon seeing the stranger in the room, jolted upright.

"Who has asked you into our room?" he snapped.

Ignoring him, Isaac stood and made to leave. "Well, it's been a pleasure meeting you. As I said earlier, you're free to go." Facing Joe, he added, "For your sake, I hope we meet again soon. You know where to find me." Then he swung open the door and was gone.

"Who was that?" Peter growled suspiciously.

Joe glanced at the business card thrown on his cot. *I'm here to help you*. That was becoming a popular refrain down here: Nora Barnes yesterday and this Isaac Washington character just now. Both of them had seemed sincere enough. So why was it so hard to believe?

"I'm not really sure. I think he was trying to sell us something."

Peter frowned. "Of what nature?"

"I don't know. It was nothing, really."

"You should have woken me sooner."

"I can handle myself," Joe insisted. He picked up the card and slipped it into his pocket, hoping Peter hadn't seen it yet. Joe didn't have time for a lecture. They were already late.

"I think we slept in later than we meant to," Joe said, intentionally changing the subject. "We need to get going and figure out how to get to Brimtown."

Peter studied him for a long moment. His gaze wasn't nearly as intense as Jesus' in Heaven, but it had a similar penetrating quality to it. He probably realized that Joe wasn't being entirely honest with him, but thankfully he decided to let it go.

"Indeed," he said, fighting back a yawn. "I've already made some arrangements for our transportation."

"Oh yeah?" Joe hadn't heard any mention of this last night.

"At my request, our Agent Barnes referred me to a dealership here in town."

"Like a car dealership?" Joe replied in disbelief.

"I hope you don't mind driving. I never had the chance to earn a license myself."

Joe cleared his throat, something between a cough and a laugh.

"I still can't tell if you're being serious."

But Peter was already up and collecting his belongings, taking a long drink from his canteen and fastening his sword around his waist, readying to set out again.

TEN
THE LOOKOUT

AS IT HAPPENED, Peter turned out to be quite the haggler. Maybe it was from his days working as a fisherman—Joe could just imagine him bartering in an open-air fish market alongside the Sea of Galilee, trading buckets of fresh tilapia for a pair of sandals or a new tunic or whatever it was people wanted back then. Simpler times, that was sure. For a moment as he looked out over the dealership with its flashy signs and well-polished vehicles, Joe felt like an old man sick with nostalgia, pondering how it was that consumerism had touched even a desert on the outskirts of Hell.

Come to think of it, the very existence of the car dealership was ironic. *Where does anyone go*, he wondered, *when there's nowhere worth visiting and all of eternity to get there?* It was a surprisingly cynical thought considering how eager he was to reach his own destination and find David. But it was like Peter said, they were merely sojourners, passing through on their way back up to paradise. A totally different situation than those stuck here forever.

"We possess a treasure to be desired," Peter had said on the walk over, carefully counting their remaining gold coins in the little canvas pouch, "but foolish is the man who spends it all at once." Joe had taken this to mean that they were on a budget. For all the riches he'd seen in Heaven, it was hard to imagine a need to be frugal. Perhaps Peter only wanted to maintain an ordinary appearance. Either way, Joe was glad not to have to make the transaction.

So while the great fisherman-turned-apostle was still seated inside the sales office, stroking his thick beard and brokering a deal for a rusted-out jeep—already marked as the cheapest vehicle on the lot and for reasons not hard to imagine—Joe had stepped outside for a breath of air. He welcomed the chill after the dry heat blasting inside the building. Ever since waking up on that flat cot earlier, he hadn't been able to get comfortable. His muscles ached even more than the day before, and his shield weighed heavier with every step. The bread they'd bought from a street vendor was stale and lifeless, and the water they'd found to refill their canteens was grossly insipid compared to that heavenly elixir he'd had before.

Joe unfolded the map he'd obtained inside the dealership and located Brimtown. Quite unhelpfully, there was no scale to show distances, only routes and major landmarks. He glanced up at the ashen gray sky, wondering how many hours they had until dark. Agent Barnes's words from the day before rang sounds of caution.

Not even a fool is still outside when the demons come.

Peter was still convinced they wouldn't have any problems, but how could he really know? He'd never actually fought one of them, had he? And Joe's strange conversation this morning with Isaac Washington had reminded him that they needed to be prepared. Well, he had a few minutes right now . . .

Joe looked around to make sure he was alone. A few customers silently browsed on the opposite side of the lot, and his companion was still occupied with paperwork inside the office. Joe carefully loosened his sword and pulled it from its sheath. Setting his other belongings on the ground, he stepped away from the building for some space to move. He tried to remember a few of the maneuvers Peter had shown him back in the cave under the waterfall. Pivot forward, swing, step, block, jab. Joe lifted the weapon above his head and lashed at the air, twisted his hands, thrust forward, stumbled— but kept his balance. His sword dropped, and the tip clinked against the asphalt.

C'mon, Joe. Focus.

He remembered bounding up the mountainside with Jesus, full of limitless energy. Joe recalled the anger he'd felt just before that, pushing through the crowd to get to the fountain, and he thought of David's face, bored and cautiously optimistic, pressed against the gas station window the last night they'd been alive.

He'd come here to fight, not to run away.

Joe went at it again, moving more forcefully this time, spinning, slashing, stabbing, and then suddenly surrounded. Those black-hooded wraiths, their flame-red eyes and bony fingers, their fetid breath choking him like smog. Frightful beings, but it was they who should be afraid! Joe Platt lifted the Sword of the Spirit, sharper than the finest scalpel and more blinding than Excalibur. And he roared as he tore through the air with perfect choreography, cutting down his foes in quick succession, slaying one, two, three at a time, all with a single cut. They turned to flee but had nowhere to go. Joe was faster, stronger, reaching them in every direction. With another slash, he choked their screams of terror. With another turn, he silenced their evil threats. He was unstoppable now. By the power of God, nothing could hinder his quest!

A small cough shattered the fantasy.

"My friend, what has evoked your fury?"

Startled, Joe turned to see the apostle standing behind him and looking rather amused.

"Sorry, I was just ... practicing," said Joe, hoping his embarrassment didn't show.

But Peter simply nodded. "I suspect an hour will soon be upon us when our preparations will be put to use." He tossed a key ring to Joe. "Do you still want to drive?"

And as their new jeep exited the small town of North Abaddon, Joe found himself thinking of family and Christmas lights and fresh snow on highways. Some twenty minutes into the drive, he could have sworn his ears detected a horn blaring behind them, but he must have imagined it. They were totally alone on the road. The good news was that they had no more uncertainty about which direction to go or how to conduct themselves. With any luck, they'd find David and be back in Heaven by this time tomorrow. It felt as if their mission had only now officially begun—Peter, navigating in the seat next to him while snacking on a half loaf of that stale and awful bread, and Joe, back straight and arms fully extended, ever aware of the salvation key inside his pants pocket, eyes locked on the bare and lifeless desert stretched out before them.

Despite all their warnings, the first attack came wholly unexpected.

By this time, it was well after dark—dark being the operative word. No stars, no moon, and the headlights their only illumination as they sped over the flat and rocky ground.

"You need to sleep," Peter remarked.

"I'm not tired," Joe lied.

"The spirit is willing, but the flesh is weak," the apostle recited. "Better that we rest and keep watch than press on in such a vulnerable state."

Not arguing, Joe glanced down at the dashboard. "We almost need gas anyway. When's the next town?" So far, they'd driven through four or five little hamlets, whistle-stops along the unpaved highway, each more despondent than the last. By comparison, the jumbled streets of North Abaddon seemed like a booming center of commerce. Not wanting to waste time, Joe and Peter had stopped only once, at a dingy convenience store with bars over the windows and shotguns in a glass case behind the counter.

"For the demons," the clerk had explained, his arms covered in tattoos and a pentagram charm dangling from his neck. "Box of salt shells free with every purchase. Buy two and save thirty percent, today only."

"Do you ever suspect," Peter had asked on their way out, "that a demon might cower only to perpetuate the myth? A pretense of power over them is in reality their power over you."

In response, Joe had offered to share his bag of trail mix.

The jeep hit a small bump in the road, and Peter turned on the interior light to see. He crinkled the map against the dashboard.

"We should be approaching Brimtown proper, assuming we can find a station willing to sell fuel at this hour."

"You think they'd be closed?"

"If our stay in North Abaddon was any indication. Fear rules the land."

Joe remembered how empty the streets had been at dusk, let alone late at night. And just about everyone they'd met so far had warned them against going out.

The demons force their way through every gap and crevice . . .

Joe shook the thought from his mind. *Jesus sent us here*, he reminded himself. *I should trust him.* But, then again, Jesus wasn't with them now, and what if . . .

No. There was too much at stake to give in to fear.

"Tell me another story," Joe said. "I need a distraction."

A silent beat passed before the reply. Perhaps Peter was thinking.

"I can. But first, there's still a story you haven't told me."

"Oh yeah? What's that?"

"This morning. What did that man in our room really want?"

Joe groaned. He thought they'd moved on from this. "I told you it was nothing."

"I know what you told me."

"Are you saying I lied?"

"If omission was meant as deception, then yes."

A piercing bluntness. Joe sincerely felt offended. *Deception* was a strong word, wasn't it?

"I mean, he just warned me about demons and said something about needing forgiveness. Something about a holy sanctuary in town, too. Like I said, I think he was selling something."

Peter's concern showed with an audible growl. "You cannot buy what's already been given. The price for your sins has been paid in full."

"Yeah, right. Anyway, it's not important. Nothing that would help us find David."

"You must beware, Joe. It's by the grace of God I awoke in time."

"I woke you," Joe pointed out. "Besides," he added defensively, "I wasn't in danger."

"Perhaps it was danger of a different sort. The advice of the wicked is deceitful. They will introduce all kinds of destructive heresies in broad daylight, and yet their own condemnation is hanging over them like heavy chains. We must look out for each other so that we are not ensnared in the trap. You must take care that you are not led astray."

And with that, Joe remembered why he hadn't talked about this earlier.

"I'm not an idiot," Joe said. "I won't be roped into anything."

"You're young," Peter replied. "Why do you suppose I'm here?"

"Wow, okay. So I'm not some two-thousand-year-old saint, but I mean . . ."

Joe's sentence trailed off—he saw a child.

Up ahead was a small boy caught in the headlights, walking toward them along the side of the road and looking down at his feet. He hadn't seemed to notice them at all.

"What the heck?" Joe swerved out wide to give the kid space and slowed to a stop. "What is he doing out here alone?" Joe had seen kids in Heaven, but not here, not until right now. This boy couldn't have been older than ten. His skin was ghostly pale, and his dirty shirt had a noticeable rip along the bottom. He might have been a runaway if he'd had some sort of pack over his shoulder, but the boy carried nothing at all.

Being the closest one to him, Joe rolled down his window and addressed the child.

"Hey, buddy. What's going on? Are you lost?"

No answer. The boy continued walking toward them, now almost even with the jeep.

"Be careful, Joe. Things in darkness are not always as they seem."

Another gem from Peter the Wise. Joe swallowed his smart reply.

"Hey, buddy," he called again to the boy. "Where are you going?"

The child stopped a few feet from the car.

"You almost hit me, mister." The murmur drifted across the night air like an echo.

"It's okay. I saw you in plenty of time. You're perfectly safe."

"You almost hit me, mister," the soft voice repeated. "You almost killed me."

Peter gripped Joe's arm like a vice. "Drive now. Go."

But Joe's eyes were locked on the boy. Maybe he was new here too. Maybe they could help him. He looked so terribly alone.

"I don't know if you know this," Joe explained as gently and tentatively as possible, "but you're already dead for some other reason. I know it's hard to understand, but this is the place where you go after you die. Do you remember what you were doing just before—"

"You almost killed me, mister," the boy repeated.

"Hey, buddy. Look at me. You're fine. I promise."

"You almost killed me like David."

David. At the sound of his name, Joe went numb to his deepest marrow. His rational mind knew it must be a trick, but his heart forgot to beat.

"What . . . what did you say?" Joe stammered. "How do you—how do you know . . ."

"He told me."

"Who? David? You talked to David?"

111

"He told me everything about you."

"Where . . . when?" Joe sputtered. "Is he here?"

"David told me how you killed him."

In a sudden flurry of motion, a silver blade darted up from the dark and plunged its tip into the boy's throat. Peter had climbed out and stealthily circled the jeep, and he now unleashed a wild battle cry as he pushed the weapon in deeper. The boy choked as the dagger surged with blinding light.

"In the name of Jesus Christ," Peter roared, "be gone from here!" He ripped the weapon free, and, utterly defenseless, the boy crumpled to the ground. In the shadow of the car, Joe could just make out the child's body contorting in agony, dark blood gushing out from his wound and soaking the thirsty ground.

Joe swore loudly and tumbled out of the vehicle. He shoved Peter aside and knelt beside the boy, trying to soothe him as he gagged and rasped, wanting to stop it but having no idea how. But it was too late. With a final shudder, the child fell still and perished on the side of the road.

So indeed, there was life in the land of the dead, and with it still death, and now they had seen it. Was tragedy so inescapable as to follow them beyond the grave?

As Joe stepped back, he became aware of the warm blood on his own hands, and the grisly look of it, and he doubled over and retched. He purged any food he'd eaten since waking, then heaved dry and painful breaths until he barely had the energy to stand.

Peter calmly cleaned his blade by plunging it into the ground. "We should go," he said after several minutes, his voice even and steady, his strong figure backlit by the jeep's headlights.

"Why did you do that?" Joe panted.

"Come. There will likely be other attacks to follow."

"But he was just a boy."

"I suspect that he was not."

"Did you even hear him? He knew David. He was starting to say—"

"He spoke only lies."

"You killed him!" Joe screamed, suddenly furious. "You killed him, Peter! You killed a kid! And for what? What did he do to you?"

"I acted for your protection as well as my own."

"Yeah, and since when did I need your protection? Huh?" Joe fumed, every ounce of shock turning to anger. "Or is this all just some game to you like it was in the cave?"

"Still your rage, Joe."

"Ever since we got here, not once have you listened to me. You read the maps, you decide where to stay, you decide when to go."

"Listen to me, Joe. You will bring them upon us."

"Oh good, something else that's my fault."

"They will distort the truth and prey on your every weakness."

"Oh, *my* weakness, huh? Because I guess you don't have any, right? It's all fine and perfect for you, huh? You don't even care if we find David, do you?"

Peter, although his reply came sharply, still did not raise his voice. "Were you not told the journey would be dangerous? Were you not given these spiritual weapons for the purpose of fighting? Yet when the first temptation came, you were unwilling to see it as such."

Joe slammed his fist hard into the side of the jeep, the stinging impact a painful reminder of his physical body, his genuine life with beating heart and breathing lungs. He studied his companion and saw his face dark with shadow and his posture even and collected. This was Simon Peter, the great disciple of Jesus, the legendary leader of the early church, the man who'd trained him in the armory and led him on this mission. The man who'd just slain a helpless child without a moment's hesitation. And now, not for the first time, he spoke as if he'd known something all along that Joe was only now realizing.

And it pained Joe to admit it, but he was right, wasn't he? The boy had been a demon.

David told me how you killed him.

The blood on Joe's own hands had dried and caked on, like mud after splashing through a puddle. He knew there was water in the jeep to wash it off, but he made no move to get it.

"David," he whispered, "what did I do?"

Joe could picture every detail of his little brother's face—his scruffy brown hair, the little black gauges in both of his ears. Except his eyes—no matter how he tried, Joe could only imagine David with eyes closed or looking away, but never looking right at him. Joe had lent him money plenty of times and even bailed him out of jail, but when in recent years had he spent time just for the sake of knowing his brother? When had he ever called just to talk with David, just to hear about his day? Oh, it was all too obvious now. What sympathy had Joe given when David lost his job? What praise had Joe offered when David finally finished rehab? While Joe followed his dream career and volunteered at church at Sunday mornings, all in the name of serving others, had he ever harbored more than blame and skepticism for his own brother? Had he ever helped him from a place of joy and not one of compulsion?

"We should go," Peter said, "before the demons surround us. More will surely come."

When Joe didn't move, the apostle said it again.

"Alright," Joe replied, his voice barely audible in the desert night. For he couldn't help but notice it too—a growing urgency, a pervading malaise settling in the air. They might be alone for now, but it wouldn't stay that way for long.

"Quite the sssstrike . . ."

"What was that?" Joe looked up, trying to locate the voice. But it was no use. The starless night gave nothing away.

" . . . a mighty ssssword . . ."

More than he actually heard that terrible hissing, Joe felt it like goosebumps on his skin. They'd waited too long, and now there was nowhere to run.

"Ready your shield, Joe," Peter commanded. "We will not outrun these foes."

"*. . . hoping you'd want to fight . . .*"

Adrenaline took over, and Joe ran around to the back of the jeep to pull out their armor. He handed off Peter's shield before taking a defensive stance with his own.

"What do we do now?" Joe asked frantically.

"Remember your training," Peter said. "You have the Spirit of God inside you. By faith, you shall overcome."

"I can't see anything," Joe replied, crouching in the shadows.

"The Spirit is your light."

"*. . . those who draw the sssword . . .*"

The sounds were everywhere but nowhere at once. Joe tensed his body and backed up against the jeep.

"*. . . will die by it . . .*"

On his right, two cracks and shattered glass. Both headlights were now out. The darkness was complete.

Overhead, flapping wings and frightful sibilance. The demons had arrived.

"In the name of Jesus Christ," Peter bellowed, "I command you to leave!"

An explosion of red sparks flashed against the apostle's shield, like hot iron against an anvil. Short bursts of fire rained down like small meteors, causing both men to duck. Joe heard a scampering along the ground to his left and jabbed his sword downward. He hit only dirt.

And what about you? asked the same hissing voice from before, although this time the sound came personally, invasively, an echo inside his head. *He's the fighter, not you.*

Joe looked right to see Peter's blade burn red as he slashed upward at some terrifying creature with a vulture's body and two heads in the form of vipers. The demon spat fire, but Peter deflected the shot with his shield. Joe watched in horrified awe as the apostle opened a gash in the monster's side and invoked the name of their heavenly God. The creature retreated back into the night, fleeing on injured wings.

"That was a demon?" Joe gasped.

"Yes. And more will follow. Joe, you must listen to me. They'll try to separate us. Believe nothing you hear. They speak only lies. You bear the Sword of the Spirit."

"Peter, stay close."

Soon the residual embers faded, leaving them again in total darkness. Their reprieve was not for long. Joe heard another wingbeat up above. Then a scraping against the jeep—Joe imagined the talons on the beast he'd just seen. They were closer with every breath. A prickle on his arms. A sudden, stabbing pain in the back of his neck.

Joe cried out and stumbled forward away from the jeep. He swung his sword but was completely blind, and his attackers were adaptive and dangerous. Surely he was surrounded now. He felt a cut on his ankle, a sharp prod in his shoulder, what felt like insect bites on his left hand holding the shield. How many were there?

"Peter!" Joe shouted. "Help me!"

Yes, come quickly! mocked the voice. *Come save your helpless friend!*

A shower of light as Peter slayed another demon, its innards bursting like fireworks into the night. With the light, every shadow was an enemy, every small rock a creature waiting to strike. Joe swung his sword frantically, feeling the burn in his shoulder and panic racing through his veins. More colors flashed like lightning as Peter continued to find his mark. Joe thought he heard his companion shout something, but he seemed impossibly far off. Which direction? They had to stay together. Joe was hardly aware if he was running or stationary, if the jeep was to his left or to his right.

He tried to call out, but his throat was dry and hoarse. His arms ached, and his constant slashing with the sword was clumsy and futile.

"Peter . . ." Joe rasped. "Where are you?"

No reply.

Who is your lookout now?

Joe closed his eyes, for the first time shutting out the darkness, and tried to control his breathing. He couldn't go down now, not when David still needed him. He thought back to his training session in the cave in Heaven. Joe pictured the running water, the cool rocks under his feet, sparring with Peter while Jesus looked on. The Holy Spirit inside of him. He'd won before. He could do it again now, couldn't he?

"The Lord is my strength and my shield," he intoned. Joe waited until he felt another jab against his skin, and then he spun with a wild slash of his sword. He missed, but he sensed his attacker retreat. A small victory to surge his confidence.

"The Lord is my strength," he repeated as loudly and confidently as he could manage. He heard a wing flap to his left and jabbed with his sword. This time, he made contact.

A flash of red light irradiated another of those grotesque two-headed vultures. Joe was close enough to see its tar-colored feathers and serpentine eyes. His blade had clipped the creature's wing, and now it struggled to fly away. The burst of light showed him exactly where to aim. Now or never. This was his chance. *God help me,* he prayed.

"In Jesus' name, be gone from here!"

Instinct seized Joe as he drove his sword deep into the foul bird's belly, twisting the handle for maximum effect. A nauseating pus seeped out onto his hand—if Joe hadn't vomited already, he certainly would have now. The creature's two heads shrieked and tried to strike at Joe's arm, but he batted them away with his shield. Joe felt its body rumble on the verge of eruption, and as he yanked his sword free, the demon exploded with a shower of burning luminescence.

He'd done it. He'd defeated the demon.

The second bird was an easy target, and after spearing the third, there were none who dared to enter his reach. Each swing of Joe's sword brought another ray of light into the darkness, another burst of hope, and whatever demon corpses there were caught fire until the whole surrounding area was a brilliant conflagration that soared and brushed the sky.

As the remaining demons flew away from the blaze, Joe collapsed to his knees, dizzy and panting, staring at his hands as if he did not know to whom they belonged. Those sinister voices were gone, and now his mind swirled with true words of gratitude. *You gave me strength. Thank you, Lord Jesus. Thank you.*

Finally spent, Joe put his face to the ground and wept.

And in the last of the lingering glow from the demon fires, Joe saw a silhouette cross in front of the battle scene. Peter? No. It was a woman he'd never seen.

She gently approached, her body backlit and some sort of pack slung over her shoulder. She knelt close and spoke to him, a young and soothing voice, a gentle touch on his shoulder. And then a piece of his strength returned, and Joe sat up to greet this strange and welcome comforter. But her face was covered in shadow, and the last of the embers were quickly fading, like the details of a bizarre and frightening dream just upon waking.

ELEVEN
ALLIANCE

JOE ADJUSTED THE BINOCULARS and scanned the desert one more time, again with no luck. The expanse was empty and voiceless, the morning sky and rocky ground two shades of the same dismal color.

"Where are you, Peter?"

The desert shrugged in response.

Joe had been in and out of consciousness last night as they'd driven him to the house. He'd asked about Peter several times, but they repeatedly claimed to have found Joe alone, with no jeep in sight. He'd slept on a couch and awakened to a gray light peeking in through the window shades, still with his sword and salvation key, and now with more questions than answers.

This would be the perfect time for a cell phone, had they thought to bring any. Joe had noticed a landline inside the house, but what number would he call? No email, no texting, no signal flares. Being separated was the one scenario they hadn't prepared for.

He'll go to Brimtown, Joe guessed. *It's the most logical place to meet.*

Peter had shown he was perfectly capable of handling himself. Not to mention the fact that he still had all their supplies. No, the real worry was that they were wasting time to find David. Joe's aching body and the sword at his belt were reminders enough of the terror of an actual demon attack. Peter could slash them as they came, but

119

David didn't have that luxury. After what Joe had seen last night, the need to reach David was more pressing than ever.

Abandoning his search efforts for the moment, Joe rested on the porch step and gazed out pensively at his immediate surroundings. They were in sight of the highway leading into Brimtown, a fact Joe gathered only from the occasional passing cars, intermittent as they were. The house itself was clearly neglected but still functional, the only residence on its dust-covered lane, like a farmhouse without the farm. Parked to the right of the house was the white van that had brought him here, and leaning against it was the bald and broad-shouldered militiaman involved in the previous night's rescue/abduction—Joe wasn't quite sure yet how to label it.

Whoever they were, these people lacked the official air of the North Abaddon customs squad. Joe had met four of them, each appearing normal enough, at least as far as he could tell. Perhaps the one exception was the aforementioned guard—named Brody, apparently—who had an assortment of weaponry strapped to his belt, a salt gun slung over his shoulder, and a permanent scowl etched onto his face. It was still unclear if he was there to keep intruders out or to keep Joe in, although his best guess was a little of both. To the man's credit, however, he'd been kind enough to let Joe borrow his binoculars.

I wonder if he'd let me borrow the van too. It'd certainly be nice to drive into Brimtown, but another look at the guard's countenance answered that question easily enough. There were only so many requests Joe would get away with. On the other hand, there were others who might be more sympathetic. It wasn't just the watchman who lived here. Joe's thoughts wandered back to the shadowy figure crouching by his side the night before.

The front door behind him creaked on its hinges. He glanced back.

Well, speak of the devil. Or however people said that in Hell.

"I brought you some coffee."

The woman handed him a mug before joining him on the porch step.

"Were you able to get some sleep?" she asked.

"More or less. I'm still a little sore this morning."

She smiled, like sunlight breaking through the clouds. "I bet. Do you remember much of anything from last night?"

Joe sipped the warm beverage, slightly embarrassed at how readily he did recall certain events, although perhaps not for the reasons she was asking. She must have been close to his own age, late twenties, with curly black hair and a flannel shirt to complement her forest green eyes. Joe fondly recalled those eyes sparkling with curiosity as she inspected his wounds in the back of the van, asking him questions with cool medical detachment, softly touching his skin to apply a salve to the cut on his neck.

"I remember you're Maya."

Her lighthearted laughter was infectious. Joe the computer programmer shrank back against the unfamiliar attention.

"Well, you got the important part, I suppose." She nodded toward the binoculars around his neck. "Looking for your friend?"

"Er ... yeah. Peter. I told you about him last night. We got separated in the attack."

"I remember. You said he had your vehicle."

"Yeah, that's right."

"With all your money and belongings."

Her tone was innocent, but Joe caught the implication. He quickly clarified. "We arrived here together and had a ... job to do. He never would have left me on purpose."

"I see." Maya's tone was flat and nonjudgmental, and that somehow made it worse. Joe broke eye contact, folded the binoculars and set them aside. Well, he didn't need to defend himself. Whatever she really thought, it certainly wasn't worth the argument.

He changed the subject. "How'd you find me, anyway? You never really said what you were doing out there last night."

Maya twirled a strand of loose hair. "You certainly caused a commotion. I woke up and could see the fireworks from the house. I figured it had to be demons."

"And so you just came out to join the party? I thought most people here were afraid."

"Well, with my bodyguard and from a distance, yes. We only moved in after we determined it was safe. I can honestly say I've never seen anything like that before."

"What, that many at once?"

"Fear in their eyes instead of yours."

Joe's face grew hot, and he pretended his coffee was the reason.

"May I see it?" Maya asked, motioning toward his sword with genuine fascination. How could he deny such a request?

"It's called the Sword of the Spirit," he explained, holding it out in both hands for her to examine. "It fights against evil and lies with good and truth."

Wow, that sounds ridiculous, he thought. But Maya appeared unfazed. She studied the object with a kind of scientific appreciation.

"I wonder if it's the iron. I've heard demons don't like it, but I've never really seen evidence to prove it. Most of the arms dealers use salt. Toss a pinch over the shoulder as my mom used to say, or be like most people and just buy a shotgun. But this really is impressive." She moved her fingers gently along the blade's edge. "Are you the original owner?"

Joe wrinkled his brow in confusion. "Someone gave it to me, if that's what you're asking."

Maya nodded. "Right. I almost forgot you're new around here."

She handed it back, and Joe carefully returned the blade to its sheath. "I take it then that you're not."

Maya stretched out her arms and gazed at the horizon for a moment, as if deciding how best to respond.

"I suppose I should give you the rundown, huh?"

"Please do."

"When I was still on Earth," she began, "my mother used to tell me that there was no value in material things because you can't take them with you when you die. Well, as we all come to find out, that's not exactly true. The afterlife is itself a hollow wasteland. There's nothing native except the dust under your feet. Its inhabitants, however, are also its suppliers. Each new soul brings with it that person's most prized possessions from life, some of personal meaning and some of practical worth, like clothing and food. Their most coveted desires come too, although they aren't already in hand. Everything from real estate to stock portfolios to name recognition—even one's darker gratifications—can be sought and obtained. Some of the wealthier ones have prepared for their whole lives to fare well in death—they arrive with deeds already in their pockets for the homes they've been building for years."

Joe recalled the subdivision in the middle of nowhere and the crazed old man who'd shot at them. "I think I met a guy like that when we first arrived."

"I've been here long enough to meet a thousand. But you have to remember, everything comes with a price. With always more to have and an eternity in which to want it, people readily trade away what they value most for what they desire in the moment. When someone is willing to make that kind of compromise, the exchange is always unequal. Examples of it are everywhere. The so-called governments impose all kinds of tariffs to buy luxuries for themselves while infrastructure chips away. Businesses are built on corruption. Religious leaders delude their followers for their own selfish gain. Some even go so far as to deal with the demons themselves, trading their own dignity for a quick fix and a false sense of security. Ironically, it's often the ones who deceive many others who then fall for the lie themselves."

Joe thought of the crumbling shacks he'd seen along the road and the new cars decorating the lot in North Abaddon.

"Each new generation comes looking for wealth and industry," Maya continued, "only to find their very existence rotting away. You go into these towns and cities, and everyone you meet will have been here no more than a few decades, a century at most. After that, they've got no reason to even go outside, let alone get up from bed. More time passes, and soon their souls are all but forgotten—mere shadows and shapes, a patch of cool air drifting in the night."

"That sounds awful."

"And yet it is what it is. Hopeless oblivion is as certain as the death that precedes it."

A lone yellow sports car zoomed down the dirt highway in front of them, creating a cloud of dust in its wake. Maya finished her coffee and set the mug on the porch.

Even after Joe's experiences so far, this was a lot of gloom and doom to take in at once. How many billions of people had come down here since the start of humanity? And was this the reason he'd hardly seen any of them since arriving? Joe felt the weight of despair pressing down on his shoulders. He studied Maya, so vibrant and intelligent, and yet someone who had just described her fate as inevitably grim. It hardly seemed fair. For the first time since coming to Hell, Joe wondered if his mission was woefully beyond him.

A new thought presented itself. *Maybe David isn't the only one who needs saving.*

"So," Joe said after a few minutes, "if you know all that, how do you avoid it? Or are you just doomed no matter what?"

"Most people would say doomed no matter what. It's kind of the law of the land."

He took the bait. "Most people. But what about you?"

Maya flashed a mischievous grin. "Well, to tell you the truth, I was never one to play by the rules." She tossed back her hair and got to her feet. "Our numbers go up and down, but there're four of us now. Based on what I saw last night, I take it you're like-minded. With you, we'd be five."

"I'm sorry"—Joe stood to keep from losing her—"but I'm not sure I follow."

"The world takes from us. We take back." With a wink, she added, "It's a job offer, Joe."

The information took longer than usual to compute.

"People trade away everything that has meaning before they even realize it," Maya continued. "We return what makes them who they are by targeting those responsible—anyone who's sold his soul to the demons to profit at others' expense."

"So you're like the Robin Hoods of Hell then? A group of thieves?"

"I prefer rebels, fighting for justice."

"Right. And what do you need me for?"

"As you could imagine, fighting the system gives us some enemies, and I always hate to be defenseless. We have a job coming up that could use a man of your . . . talents."

Joe's skin prickled with possibility. "What kind of job?"

"For that," she said, "we'll have to go inside."

The team plus Joe sat around the kitchen table in mismatched chairs, snacking on dry bagels and potato chips, watching Maya sketch out the plan on a loose sheet of paper. She was obviously the leader, and Joe the newbie. Brody, the guard from outside, and another man and woman completed the group of five. A box fan hummed and rattled in the corner of the room, circulating the stale air and cigarette smoke.

"So, to review for Joe's sake, our target calls himself the Rook. Simply put, he's as vile as they come. He operates a series of warehouses and storefronts in Brimtown, extorting goods from locals and shipping the merchandise to buyers all across the region.

He uses intimidation and threats to keep his empire running and supposedly makes deals directly with the demons. Trust me when I say he deserves a whole lot worse than what we have planned for him."

"His reputation precedes him," said Charlie, a tanned and charming-looking fellow who appeared to be in his late thirties. "Even back when I lived there, he had half of City Hall on his payroll. To hear he's still in business now, well, you've got to admire that kind of tenacity."

"This is why I moved to the country," griped Ethel, a bespectacled senior citizen who would make Grandma look young. "Never had to worry about a thing. People mind their own business and don't butt into yours." She took another drag on her cigarette and lazily exhaled.

"We're not the only ones who want a piece of this guy," Maya went on. "For his own protection, he keeps his cash assets divided among his properties so he's never at risk of losing everything all at once. By design, however, this presents some challenges in maintaining consistent security. As we know, even the best technologies aren't fail-safe, and loyalty is hard to come by with hired help."

"That's why you get my devotion for free, my dear," Charlie quipped.

Ignoring him, Maya went on. "One of my old contacts in the city has provided information identifying a weak link in the chain at this warehouse by the lake," she said, indicating the spot on her paper. "The Rook is planning to close it in a few weeks, so activity is limited, but it's still holding his profits from a recent sale. Now, discretion is key here. We want to get in and out unnoticed to leave the possibility of hitting other targets before drawing too much attention. If we play our cards right, we've got several opportunities to strike before leaving Brimtown."

"How reliable is this intel?" asked Brody. "This sounds like Dumah all over again."

Maya shook her head. "Not this time. I can vouch for this one. We used to work together at my first job. The guy's named Sheqer. Same one who provided the house you're in right now."

"That's what concerns me," Brody replied with a growl. "The whole thing could be a trap."

"Lighten up," piped Charlie. "If we're going after the Rook, trust me, everybody and their mother's brother's got a reason to help us. He's got the most hated name in Brimtown, and believe me, that's saying something. People'll take the first chance they get to throw us some ammo, so long as they don't have to pull the trigger."

Maya nodded her agreement. "Like I said, the intel is from an old contact. We don't see eye to eye on everything, but he's a businessman if nothing else. He'll honor my deal."

Joe risked his first question. "Is it near the bridge? The warehouse, I mean."

"Ah," Charlie sighed. "The bridge. What a nightmare. Must have heard about that gargantuan monstrosity already, huh? Biggest waste of money I've ever seen in my life. I'll tell you something, when I lived there, all it ever did was create more traffic. I used to have to drive by it every morning on my way to—"

"Save us the history lesson," Ethel groaned, tapping her cigarette into the dish.

"What? My first visit back in nearly two years—can't a man get sentimental?"

Maya, however, was still staring at Joe. Her eyes burned with a question that, for whatever reason, her lips decided not to ask. He wondered if he'd somehow spoken out of turn. After a pause, she continued.

"Yes, it's near the bridge. The building schematic Sheqer gave me shows the best access point to be this side entrance away from the main street"—she marked it on the sketch—"and closest to the facility's main vault. I estimate the Rook has about a hundred thousand in cash and coin, all of which we plan to steal."

Charlie jabbed Joe's shoulder. "Before you get any grand ideas, she makes you give most of it to charity. I learned that one the hard way."

"Okay," said Brody. "Say we do this. How's the security?"

"Minimal," Maya answered, "and even better, you'll have some backup this time to clear the exit." They all looked at Joe.

Oh. A lightbulb sparked to life inside his head. This was the reason Maya had asked him to join their team. They'd seen him fight the demons, and now they thought he was some kind of superhero. In a horrible, ironic, flattering sort of way, it all made sense. At least to some of them.

"No," Brody said firmly. "With all due respect, we're relying on outside intel—I don't care what you think of this contact of yours. We haven't done our own stakeouts. We need experienced support, not an untrained newbie we picked up on the side of the road last night. He hasn't been here long enough to vest an interest. How do we know he won't get cold feet?"

Maya, however, held her ground. "After a demon attack like last night? We all saw what Joe can do. I'm not risking leaving that skill set behind only to realize too late that we need it."

"That's what concerns me," Brody pressed. "When have you ever seen that many demons at once? For all we know, he attracted them in the first place."

Charlie smirked. "C'mon, Brody. Don't be jealous because the man's got a big sword."

The bodyguard flipped a finger in response.

"Well, I'm for the newbie," chimed Ethel. "He seems nice enough to me."

"Excuse me," Joe interjected. "I don't mean to be rude, but I haven't exactly agreed to anything yet. I think I need a little time to think about it before—"

"Honey," Ethel said, exhaling a puff of smoke, "when I was in your shoes, I didn't trust a soul, either. But I promise we're the good guys, even if you don't believe me yet."

"I said we fight for justice," Maya added. "We give people hope. All you have to do is look around out here to see why that matters."

"The thing is," Joe began, "I kind of was in the middle of something before I met all of you. Don't get me wrong, I'm very grateful for all you've done, but I really can't stay."

"What's the rush?" Charlie asked. "You've got all of eternity, don't you?"

Only Brody said nothing, although he held his silence with a scowl.

Joe considered his options. Pros: A free ride to Brimtown, the chance to learn more about Hell, and the possibility of taking down a notorious criminal in the process. Cons: He knew almost nothing about this group, and it was hard to imagine Peter would approve of this little excursion to go rob a bank. Well, Joe didn't need the apostle's permission, did he? And he didn't exactly have another way to get to the bridge and find David. That was still Joe's main and only purpose in being here. He wrapped his fingers around the salvation key in his pocket. Find Peter, find David, use the key, all go back to Heaven. Simple as that.

Perhaps a rebel, he thought, *is the best ally I'll have.*

"I'm in," he announced. "If you'll have me."

"Alright then," Maya said with a smile. "We make our strike tomorrow afternoon."

"In the middle of the day?" Joe asked. "Won't they see us coming?"

"Ah, but no demons at noon," Charlie replied. "Some might chance it at dawn or dusk, but you learn to play it safe when you can. Not everyone's as nutty as you."

"Roles are same as usual," Maya said. "Charlie and I will run the heist. Brody and Joe, you'll cover for us while we're in the vault. Ethel, you're driving."

"I'm telling you now," Charlie whispered, "she's got lead blocks for feet. Never let looks deceive you."

TWELVE
BRIMTOWN DOCKS

"SO HOW'D YOU GET involved with this little group?" Joe asked Charlie as they carried supplies out to the van.

"You want to know my story?" He gave a low whistle. "A humble man like myself, I'm afraid it might bore you to tears."

"I doubt it," Joe replied. "Need a hand with one of those bags?"

"What a gentleman to offer. Here, take 'em both."

They stepped down off the porch at the start of another cool, gray morning. After sharing potato soup with the group last night and losing to Charlie in several rounds of backgammon, Joe had nodded off easily. He'd slept solidly but lightly, awaking without the dense grogginess he'd felt on his first morning in Hell. Actually, he felt quite refreshed after a cold shower and warm breakfast. He'd been able to shave and borrow a clean shirt from Charlie too—luxuries after two long days of traveling in the desert. All in all, Maya and her crew had been quite generous, and Joe was almost getting used to this place, strange as it was to admit.

"Well, since you're asking, I'll give you the short version. I was living in Brimtown a few years back and had a little business enterprise of my own go south. I lost absolutely everything, up to and including the shirt off my back, if you can imagine it. Seeing as homelessness was never really my style, I thought about ripping off an electronics dealer just to get back on my feet. One of those real big

131

corporate types—stick it to 'em, I said. Well, I went early for a little scoping out of the security system, and right while I was conducting my surveillance, I got a tap on the shoulder from this foxy little lady cop. So there I was, thinking my cover was blown and she's about to tase my lights out."

Ethel flung open the front door, a cigarette in hand and sporting a black leather jacket. "We're rolling in five, boys. Be ready."

"Count on me, darling," Charlie called. As they returned to the house, he continued, "Anyway, turned out the whole security getup was just Maya's own clever disguise. Joke was on me the whole time. She was there to rob the place, same as I was. She'd been watching me scope it out all along, waiting to see if I might be of any assistance. The electronic door locks had her stumped, if you want to know the truth. Anyway, to my great astonishment, she said we'd have better luck working together and asked if I'd mind forming a partnership. Well, what do you know? We made our first clean getaway the very next day. I've been under her thieving tutelage ever since."

They moved into the kitchen to pack sandwiches and drinks into a cooler, a surprisingly ordinary thing to do considering they were about to commit a robbery. *Can't crack a safe on an empty stomach,* Joe supposed.

"So you've just been doing this kind of . . . work the whole time, then?"

"At first I was thinking we'd be regular Bonnie-and-Clyde types, you know, conducting our bandit spree throughout all the boroughs of Hell. But Maya's got this special disease called morality, you see, and she only ever picks targets who truly deserve it. And what do you know? It's contagious, as much as I hate to say it. But honestly, corruption's so deep, we vigilantes do more good just by looking at someone than every courtroom in Hell combined. And it's not just us giving back. We've trained plenty of others along the way. We picked up Brody while he was down on his luck outside a bar in East Nergal and sweet old Ethel trying to pilfer from a grocer in Beherit with a ski mask and pepper spray, misguided soul that she was at the time. There've been a few others who've come and gone for one reason or another, most leaving the group after they've settled whatever score they had with the universe. That's Maya's real talent—finding those who've lost purpose and then giving it back."

Joe grabbed an armful of pop cans from the back of the refrigerator and packed them away. "I see. So how'd Maya get started in all this then?"

"Funny thing, in all the time we've known each other, she never wants to talk about that. I asked once, and she gave me this whole speech about seeking justice and dismantling the system and a bunch of other idealistic claptrap like that. She keeps to herself mostly, if I'm being honest. But hey, we all have our traumas, and it's never my place to pry. You'll get used to her, just like the rest of us did. As I said, I'm just happy to do something productive with my afterlife. My guess is that she's running from her own troubles, but she never told me what they were. I suppose it's her business, not mine."

Charlie took the cooler, and Joe collected his shield. They reached the entryway just as Maya was coming down the stairs. She looked every part the robber with her hair tied back and a tight-fitting black shirt and pants. Stunning, actually. With flushed cheeks, Joe took a sudden interest in the floorboards.

"You ready for this, newbie?" she asked. He looked up and nodded.

"I've been prepping him all morning," Charlie said. "He's my little protégé by now."

"That's what I want to hear." Maya clapped Joe's shoulder and waited to meet his eyes. "I need you to have my back out there today." Her touch was invigorating, and her freshly-rinsed hair smelled of citrus and lavender.

Be careful, warned the voice inside his head.

Don't worry, he answered back, although the tone was hardly convincing.

Maya left ahead of them, and Charlie turned back to whisper, "The first time's always a rush, isn't it?"

Outside, Ethel blared the horn.

Compared to all the derelict towns Joe had seen so far in Hell, the city of Brimtown was a downright metropolis. Its skyline was crowded and blurred by factory smog, and its structures grew up from the ground like black weeds in a rocky garden. There were markers of industry but none of beauty, towers built for function but devoid of elegance, let alone basic upkeep. In the high windows, Joe counted wood boards and glass panes to be almost equal in number. As with North Abaddon, the city showed a complete lack of urban planning, only now on a much larger scale. Intersections were random and chaotic, vehicles bullied their way onto sidewalks, and rotting trash bags sat heaped on every street corner. And of course, there were the pedestrians—more people existed on a single street than Joe had seen total since arriving in Hell. Currents of forlorn humanity rushed past the graffitied newsstand, the silent beggars, the man and woman loudly arguing beneath a ripped and faded awning. If smiles were currency, the land would be bankrupt. If misery were a place, it would be Brimtown.

David, Joe thought, *is somewhere in this city.*

"Always feels like home, doesn't it, Maya?" Charlie scratched behind his ear as he looked out with ironic nostalgia. "Sometimes I really do miss this craphole."

Ethel honked at a jaywalker as the van veered left into an open lane, he shouting a long string of obscenities, and she returning the favor in kind. Joe absently wondered if Ethel had any grandchildren. She must have been a riot at family Christmases.

They passed several apartment buildings abandoned mid-construction and turned right at an outdoor clothing bazaar. Everywhere were groups of people, but nowhere were people in groups. Gray-clad individuals moved about, tending to their own matters and speaking only to conduct a transaction or shout some angry oath. As they drove on, they entered a warehouse district, and the crowds thinned out. Joe noticed a gradual change in elevation as the streets sloped downward. They were getting closer now. The van drove over a sidewalk and turned at the next intersection. At last, Joe saw it.

The lake of burning sulfur.

This was the Hell he'd always imagined. The liquid churned blood-red and lustrous yellow. Tongues of fire leaped up like geysers from the pool. The lake extended outward for miles and stretched back to the horizon, really more like an ocean in its magnitude and power. Even from their distance and inside the car, the rotten-egg stench of sulfide gas permeated the air. Joe instinctively covered his mouth and nose with the top of his shirt.

Most peculiar, however, was the human activity out on the lake. While one might think the sea was completely inhospitable, several steel docks jutted out into the magma, and a dozen or so boats ferried back and forth between them. As the van drew closer, Joe could see dockworkers loading goods to be shipped down the shoreline. Both men and women labored away with sweat-drenched faces and wearing coveralls to repel the flames lapping at their feet.

Finally, Joe glimpsed what he came for. Maybe a mile or two down the coast was an enormous suspension bridge, reaching out over the lake only to abruptly halt partway, an aptly named Bridge to Nowhere. There were giant cranes and long beams of steel and, somewhere among the workers, David Platt. Joe's heart raced in anticipation. Soon—maybe today—he would reunite with his brother. What would David say when he saw Joe's armor, when he heard stories of true paradise and their mother in Heaven, or when he learned that the little key in Joe's pocket could take them there right now?

Press it into the earth itself, and the way back to Heaven shall be opened for you.

They'd have to find Peter first, of course, but for all Joe knew, the apostle was already there waiting for him. He imagined him with David, leaning against the rusty old jeep, joking together about what was taking Joe so long to get there. And he'd certainly have a story to tell.

"Joe!" Maya snapped him from his reverie. "I need you to focus. We're here."

The van parked near an alleyway two blocks up from their target. The Rook's warehouse was bigger than most in the area, but otherwise nothing special—a large rectangular hangar with high windows and a loading dock near the lakefront.

"Remember the plan. We drive up to the side door, Brody takes out the guard and stands watch, Charlie and I unload the vault while Joe covers us inside. If something goes wrong, we regroup here in one hour. If you don't meet us then, you're on your own for a way back."

"Don't worry, Ethel darling, I'll be sure to make the bus."

"Don't think I won't leave you, Charlie dear."

"Listen to you. Always such a tease."

Five minutes later, they were at the warehouse, and Brody landed an uppercut on the lone guard's jaw just before checking him into the wall. The unfortunate sentry slumped motionless to the ground before he even had time to shout. So much for security—and discretion.

Maya snatched the man's keyring and made for the door.

A rare eddy of wind brought a fresh scent of sulfur, and Joe's breakfast threatened to resurface. He refocused on the man lying prostrate before him and was relieved to see him still breathing.

Joe ventured a question. "Hey, Brody, I was wondering, when you, you know, kill a person in Hell, does he actually die? Again, I mean. Since we've already died once."

"What, our mighty warrior has suddenly gone pacifist?"

"I'm just curious."

Brody's shrug spoke of callous indifference. "Nothing kills you here, strictly speaking, but eventually people reach a point when that doesn't matter. For some, it's a head injury. For others, it's just a little old-fashioned despair and the bottle. What you call it isn't important when life and death both feel the same way."

Joe shuffled uncomfortably with the idea. He knew what the Sword of the Spirit did to demons—and was glad for it—but he shuddered to think he might need to battle a human soul.

Maya swore and banged her fist on the door. "None of the keys fit. The Rook must have set up the perimeter and not actually given them access." She eyed Brody. "Do you think you can force it open?"

"We're on the clock, my dear," Charlie reminded them.

"Well, do you have any other ideas?" she asked.

An eighteen-wheeler passed on the road beside the lake and parked within view of the warehouse. Joe decided to play his trump card.

"Let me see it." He removed the salvation key from his pocket and fit it against the lock. The teeth molded like clay—a square peg into a square hole. Just as advertised.

Anywhere you find a lock, this key will open the door. Score one for the good guys.

"Amazing," said Maya. "What can't you do?" Joe blushed, but she quickly moved on to give orders.

"Alright, Brody, you stay. We need a clear exit when we come out. Joe, you're with us."

Maya switched on a flashlight and silently led the way forward. Charlie followed carrying a backpack full of supplies, and Joe brought up the rear. They were in.

They moved noiselessly, passing a stairwell and a storage closet, before turning down a longer hallway to their destination. The smell was noticeably improved inside the building. They reached a small office in the middle of the hall, which Joe again opened with the salvation key. A quick scan with the flashlight—two metal filing cabinets, a desktop computer in sleep mode, a swivel chair with no occupant. In the far corner was the safe, about four feet on all sides.

This is the part when we trip the alarm, Joe thought.

Maya absently studied the few papers on the computer desk while Charlie knelt by the safe and laid out his supplies. Joe reluctantly took up his position by the door.

"Why is no one here?" he whispered after a moment. "It's the middle of the day. Shouldn't they be at work?"

Charlie snickered. "Who cares? They're at the wharf, out for lunch, taking a dump—be thankful luck's on our side for once."

"He's closing it in a few weeks, remember?" Maya said. "They've probably cut all major operations. Stay alert, though. You can never be sure."

Joe, the sword-wielding guardian, kept one eye on the hallway, his sight having adjusted by now to discern shadows in the darkness. Joe, the computer nerd, however, kept his other eye on the safe's electronic lock and Charlie's setup to crack it. To his fascination, they weren't drilling a hole in the side but were actually trying to hack the passcode.

"I used to be a programmer, you know. If you need any help—"

Charlie held up a hand. "My friend, when I told you my first job was ripping off an electronics store, understand that was not by accident. Pay attention. You finally get to witness what I contribute to the team." With a screwdriver and pocketknife, he removed the outer cover to expose the keypad's contact array. Joe watched as Charlie methodically connected a few wires to a relay board then pulled out a laptop to begin running a script of some sort. It was the most technology Joe had seen since arriving in Hell.

"Are you just trying a brute-force attack? There's no way we have time."

"Pish posh. Watch the master work his magic."

"Depending on the protocol, you could speed things up by trying a—"

A gratifying click. Joe stared in disbelief as the safe door popped free.

"And *voilà*. Under three minutes is a new personal best." Charlie looked up in smug satisfaction. "You're not the only computer nerd in the house. Like I told you, Joe, never let looks deceive you. Maya, my dear, would you care to do us the honors?"

She unfolded a duffel bag meant to transport the money and crouched down beside Charlie. Maya gingerly lifted her gloved hand to pull the door all the way open. Her body obscured Joe's view into the safe, but he observed as she brought the flashlight around for a good look at their plunder. Stacks of cash, he imagined.

He was wrong.

"Where's the money?" Charlie asked.

"It was supposed to be . . ." Maya stopped and leaned in closer.

"It seems like your source was a bit misinformed, hmm?" Charlie pressed.

But Maya had pulled a small object from the floor of the safe and was carefully examining it with her flashlight. It appeared to be a bracelet or necklace of some sort—Joe was too far away to tell for sure.

"Is this . . . he told me . . ." She suddenly snapped to attention as if she'd just broken a trance. "The whole thing's a setup. He knows we're here. We have to go now." Maya quickly grabbed their supplies and shoved them carelessly into Charlie's bag.

"Are you mad? What's going on?"

"No time. Get your stuff."

An audible whoosh in the hallway outside caught their attention. All three of them froze. Joe had been so caught up in the safe-opening drama that he'd neglected his watchman duty. Now he anxiously peered out into the darkness beyond the small office, fearing it was already too late to make their escape.

"*Dirty thieves . . .*" said a voice from everywhere and nowhere at once, an all-too-familiar hissing sound that chilled Joe to the core. Maya dropped the bag she'd been stuffing. Charlie carefully rose to his feet, clenching the computer desk for support.

" . . . sssslinking around in ssssecret . . ."

"It's too early for . . ." Charlie stammered. He didn't need to finish. They already knew.

Demons. Surrounding them. In the middle of the day.

" . . . how does it feel to be betrayed . . ."

Lord help us. Joe rapidly scanned the room with his sword at the ready. The malevolent voice seeped out from every corner, but he couldn't locate a source to strike. He'd seen the innocent-looking boy, the two-headed vulture—had the demons now taken another form?

"Don't move," Joe said. "I'm going to try something."

Charlie laughed in nervous panic. "Don't move? Hate to burst your bubble, but I think now is actually the perfect time to—"

Fire like lightning burst across the room and struck Charlie square in the chest. He leaped back in terror, frantically patting his shirt as the hungry flames spread across his torso. Joe lifted his shield just in time to block another burning arrow, this time flying from the opposite direction, and then the attack came from all sides at once. The demon voices amplified, and more fire rained down from the ceiling. Their stealthy heist quickly turned into a scene of absolute pandemonium, with Maya screaming and Charlie rolling on the floor to smother the flames.

Joe instinctively ran to Maya and pulled her under his shield. "In the name of Jesus Christ," he shouted, "be gone from here!" An unseen wave rippled across the room like a sonic boom, cracking the glass pane in the door and sending papers flying off the desk.

The fire stopped.

"Go," Maya shouted. "Get outside."

Joe helped a still-smoldering Charlie to his feet and then led the trio back into the hallway. The made it about halfway before the ceiling tiles above them ignited, raining balls of fire like hailstones. Joe raised his shield again, but the umbrella wasn't large enough for all three. Charlie took another hit to the shoulder before moving his body against the wall, trying to avoid the bulk of the impact. From around the bend in the hallway, Joe thought he heard Brody calling to them. They couldn't be far from the entrance.

But the burning ceiling had begun to crack. Small pieces were already crumbling down, and if they didn't get out soon, they'd be buried in a fiery collapse. Seeing the danger, Charlie steadied his injured figure and prepared to sprint to freedom.

"No," Maya said, tugging at Joe's arm. "We won't make it."

"Charlie!" Joe called. "Wait!"

Charlie briefly looked over, his fear-stricken eyes glowing with the same heat that had already scorched his body. His mind had committed. He stepped forward into the blazing hall just as a mighty tear ripped across the ceiling directly above. The whole section caved in, crashing down with searing and reckless violence. Joe took cover just before a tile slammed into his shield, throwing both him and Maya to the ground. Adrenaline surging, they scrambled to their feet and backtracked past the office. Their way out was now a wall of impenetrable flame.

Charlie was gone.

"Go," Maya urged. "We can't wait."

They bolted down the hallway away from the firestorm. Soon they were lost in blackness again, weaving through the darkened halls in a series of turns, Maya leading with fearless instinct, and Joe still lifting his shield for protection. At last they reached a wide loading bay, empty save for a few crates and pallets, and containing a double-door exit faintly illuminated with emergency lights. They made a beeline for it, their hurried footfalls resounding in the cavernous space. With no hesitation, Maya frantically tried the handle. Locked.

"Move," Joe commanded. The salvation key worked its magic one more time, and Joe rammed the door open as they raced to safety.

They collapsed on the ground about forty yards from the building, thankful for the light of day. Joe's arm was exhausted from holding up the shield, and his breaths were shallow and quick. His arms were singed in several places, but nothing too horrible. He'd been lucky.

But not Charlie. Joe's mind could barely comprehend the horror. Brody had said a person couldn't actually die in Hell, but what about literally burning alive? No—it was too terrible to even think about. He had to have made it. Or if he hadn't, Brody would get to him. Or if he couldn't, they'd wait until the flames died down and then they'd all search together until . . .

Joe dared to look back, and the quiet building mocked him. So far, the outer structural integrity was holding, but who knew for how long. Joe thought he could see smoke trailing up from the roof, a nearly invisible cloud on the monotonous gray afternoon.

What now? he wondered. Did the warehouse have a sprinkler system? Did Hell have a fire department? Did any of it matter once demons were involved?

"He promised," Maya said, still panting from the run. "He promised me."

"Who?" Joe asked, still thinking of Charlie.

"How could I be so stupid?"

She flopped back on the dirt lawn and groaned her lament in long, painful wails. Joe averted his gaze, feeling much like an intruder upon her private grief.

"He'll be okay," Joe offered. "We'll find him."

She moaned in reply.

Although he barely knew these people, Joe felt a rush of sympathy. Nothing had gone right today. There wasn't even the consolation of some money from the safe, some way to know they'd harmed the Rook. Well, nothing except for—Joe looked back to be sure. Even as Maya lay sprawled out on the ground, she kept her right hand balled into a fist. Whatever Maya had pulled from the safe, she still had it.

"Maya," he began.

At length, she propped herself up. Joe decided it was best to be direct.

"What is it?" he asked, pointing.

She opened her hand uncertainly. "I, um . . . I don't know. It's just a little chain, I think. Pretty worthless, probably." Joe saw what appeared to be a necklace without the pendant—and how tightly her fingers kept their hold. "I'm not even sure why I grabbed it."

Joe smirked. "You're a terrible liar."

She looked away. "You don't know the half of it."

A section of roof collapsed as the fire finally took its toll.

In his work as a programmer, Joe had often worked at his computer correcting code. Every once in a while, the source of a particular bug would elude him until, after hours and hours of testing, he'd finally discover the error in the middle of the screen, holding its tongue out and squatting in plain sight. His present revelation was that kind of moment.

"The Rook wasn't a random target at all, was he?"

No answer. Maya's green eyes dared him to continue.

"I mean, you're from Brimtown, so of course you'd heard of him, but this was personal. That's how you had a source who knew every detail of his operation and how you didn't get lost in the warehouse and how"—he motioned to it—"you know exactly what that necklace is. You've been here before, haven't you?"

"You're smarter than most, Joe. I'll give you credit for that."

"And what about the demons? Were you expecting them to show up too?"

"Not like that."

"Oh"—he threw up his hands—"well, like what, then? Because that was a pretty important detail to leave out. If I didn't have my shield, we all would have been burned to a crisp in there, just like . . ."

He couldn't say it. Maya stared.

"Yeah, and what's your point?"

"My point is that if you'd been honest . . ."

"Hey!" she snapped. "You've been in Hell, what, three days? I've been here seven years. You can't even begin to understand what it's like. You have no idea what decisions I've had to make or what it costs me to do what I do. You think you can just show up here with some flashy gadgets and figure me out—well, you can't. And don't forget who pulled your sorry carcass off the desert floor and gave you a place to stay. So you know what, Joe? You're the last person who gets to judge me."

A fresh wave of that putrid smell carried up on a breeze from the dockyards. Joe's cracked lips longed for a drink.

"Sorry," was the most he could manage. "I'm sorry for everything."

Beyond the still-burning warehouse, they could see the great lake of fire. Its red-orange currents swirled between ships and piers, and its smoldering waves crackled against the metal docks, dangerous and enchanting.

"You know," Maya said, her tone softer now, "I hadn't been back until today. Not for almost two years. Brimtown is exactly the same, though. I remember my first few lonely weeks in Hell tucked away by the wharfs and watching the flames dance out on the lake. I kept thinking I'd wake up, only I never did. Outside of customs, the Rook was the first person who ever spoke to me here. He found me one morning pulling scraps from a dumpster by the dock. All he said was, 'What's your name, child?' It was like my whole life I'd just been waiting for someone to ask."

Joe listened without comment, picturing her words as she spoke them.

"At first, it was just a normal job. He had me doing accounting for city imports and exports, menial office kind of work, you know, but enough to keep me occupied. I honestly thought he was a good guy, just giving me a chance. Well, the more I learned, the more I saw he was a good guy to a lot of people. The Rook gave out loans and pay advances like peppermints off his desk, letting people just run up a tab without a second thought. It's a working-class city, so most people were grateful for a little extra. That is, until he called to collect. The Rook waited until a person owed an impossible amount, then he'd demand immediate repayment plus interest, lest they be thrown to the demons.

"He asked for my help one evening. I didn't know what was happening when we went with two of his goons down by the jetty to meet one of the dockworkers, this older guy with a buck tooth, not the kind of man you'd ever see as a threat. The Rook handed me a legal pad and made me read off everything the man owed—millions and millions, I mean, just an absurd sum. Then he demanded cash right there on the spot, and when the guy didn't have it, the Rook pulled out an iron brand and dipped it into the lake. He just held it there for the longest time, letting it heat up while the guy moaned and pleaded. You think your skin burns from the fire just now? The Rook made me watch. His guys held the man's arms while the Rook ripped open his shirt and seared his bare chest. Trust me, the only stench that overcomes sulfur is burning flesh. That sick monster just stared at the man and said, 'You're a slave now, forever indebted to me.' You know what the worst part was? There must have been two dozen other people working that dock, and every single one of them just looked the other way. Every. Single. One.

"So you can imagine that the very next morning, when I went in to tell him I quit, the Rook had a running tab laid out for me too—a detailed record of all his supposed charities toward me. He said I couldn't leave with a balance still on my account unless I gave some kind of payment. I wasn't going down without a fight, though. I was ready to rip his eyes out of their sockets if he tried to force himself on me. But instead, he just calmly pointed at my necklace and said, 'That's the price.' My diamond necklace that my mom gave me when I turned eighteen, the one thing of mine I truly cared about in Hell. She was a single mom, you know? We didn't have a lot growing up, but she worked hard and saved her money, and when I finally moved out, she bought it just for me. She said I was worth it and to never forget it. And every time I touched that diamond, I thought of . . . anyway, I don't know how he knew. And like we were haggling in the market, he said I could give him the necklace for my debts or keep it and go back to my desk. I told you, didn't I, that people here trade away what they value most for what they desire in the moment? Ironically, since my release, the only thing I haven't felt is free."

Joe allowed the narrative to settle in the air. He couldn't help his response. Compassion touched him from the outside in, like dewdrops condensing from her story.

"So," he began, "that necklace in the safe . . ."

"Yes," she answered. "It's missing the diamond pendant, but it's the one. I'm sure of it. He knew I was coming, and this was his taunt."

Cruelty, Joe thought, *keeps an armory of tricks.*

She wanted to be free. Well, she could be—but not here. He'd been so distracted by their mission to the warehouse that he had almost forgotten why he'd come in the first place.

He chose his next words carefully. "Maya, did you ever believe in Heaven?"

She shrugged. "I'm not the religious type. Honestly, I didn't believe in the afterlife at all until I came here." With a chuckle, she added, "Turns out, joke was on me."

"Well, what if I told you that there's not just a Hell, but a Heaven too?"

"I suppose I'd be skeptical."

"Well," —Joe found his courage—"that's where I came from. I mean, you said yourself that you'd never seen anything like my sword and shield to fight the demons, and that's why. And this key you saw me use, well, it doesn't just open doors. It can get us out of here, Maya, I promise. All of the pain, all of this, it can all be gone."

Maya regarded him carefully, staring at the large key in his outstretched hand, and for a moment, quite incredulous. But the moment soon passed.

"I've been here a lot longer than you, Joe. You're not the first one to think you can escape to a magical land of milk and honey."

"But you've seen it!" Joe exclaimed. "You've seen the proof! You know it's true."

She laughed. "I woke up one day in an alternate universe where demons exist, lakes are made of fire, and souls live on forever. What is truth?"

Joe smacked his palm against the ground. "This, Maya. The things I can touch and taste and see. Your feeling that the Rook is evil and that part of your heart that wants to be free. That's real, Maya. And Heaven is realer than all that. It's where we were created to be. Everything else is just a shadow."

"So now you're a philosopher?"

Joe groaned. "I'm just not good at explaining it, that's all. If only Peter were here, he'd tell you . . ."

"No, Joe, I understand you just fine. I'm just a here-and-now kind of person, that's all. I'm just fine with what I have."

Now it was Joe's turn to laugh. "Right. And that's why you just told me that whole story about how you'll go to all these lengths to get back what the Rook stole from you."

"Hey," she snapped. "Watch it."

Joe sighed. Their conversation was going nowhere. This whole time, he'd thought he should keep his mission a secret, but maybe now was finally the right moment. He tried again.

"Pretend for a minute that I really am from Heaven. Well, the reason I came here was to rescue my brother. His name's David. We both had kind of a rough time growing up, but he was the one who could never quite fit the mold he was supposed to. It didn't matter if it was school or family or church or whatever. He made a lot of mistakes, but he's not a bad person. And it's not too late. So I came here, and once I find him, we're going back to Heaven together, and"—he hesitated—"I want you to come with us."

Maya gave a half-hearted smile. "How sweet of you to offer."

"I mean it."

"So let me get this straight. You're the good guy, here to save your brother's lost soul?"

"Well . . . yeah, I guess."

"And what about me, Joe? Is my soul lost as well?"

Her green eyes contained a dangerous spark. Joe fumbled for words.

"Look," he started, "I don't mean to say that—"

"I'm not like the Rook," she said, more sternly than before. "You have no contract with me. You owe me nothing, and I will never ask anything of you that you don't want to give. You said you're looking for your brother. So if you want to go, then go. I wish you the best. But I already have a purpose here, Joe. And maybe it's not easy, but it's what I chose to do. And you can accept it or not, but either way, it's who I am." With that, she brushed the dirt off her backside and rose to her feet.

And with new clarity and pain, Joe's heart comprehended what his mind had long suspected. "So that's it, then? This is where we leave?"

"Hey, if you change your mind, you're still welcome to join us," she said, readying to go. "We'll be at the house a few days to recover before moving on. We'll need it, especially if Charlie was able to . . . Anyway, you can find us there until then."

"And what about after that?"

Maya met his gaze one last time, her green eyes noticeably duller than before.

"I hope you find your brother, Joe. Really, I do."

He sat a few minutes longer, replaying their conversation as he watched her disappear, idly tracing circles in the dirt with the salvation key. Tight, concentric spirals on the ground, like currents swirling beneath the lake of fire.

THIRTEEN
THE BRIDGE TO NOWHERE

JOE RECALLED A SERMON he'd heard at St. Peter's that discussed a story in the Bible about a rich man in Hell. To his torment, the man died and suddenly found himself surrounded by agonizing fire. He could see Abraham and a beggar named Lazarus across a great chasm, and the rich man called out to them, asking for just a drop of water to cool his tongue. The distance, however, was too great. No one could cross it, and no one could help him. Now the man, who'd had everything in life, was condemned to suffer, and Lazarus, who was afflicted and starved in life, had eternal comfort and peace. One of the more alarming parables, to be sure.

Am I now the rich man, Joe pondered, *or am I Lazarus, waiting for the torment to end?*

What Joe had thought was two miles was now feeling closer to six. The water and sandwich he'd brought were still in Ethel's van, and his pack from Heaven was with Peter—wherever he was at the moment. Joe's wandering toward the bridge had so far lasted over an hour without a single reprieve.

But all of his aches, soreness, and pain were temporary. He endured it for David. Soon they could go together back to paradise. Shouldn't that fact alone be motivation? Joe was closer than he'd ever been. The end of the journey was literally in sight.

Yet to the desperate wanderer, mirage became truth and reality a shimmering illusion. Joe felt his empty stomach, and of Heaven, he could only dream.

Joe stopped to rest for the fourth time, sitting alongside the road and using his shield as an awkward chair to prop up his back. He felt dizzy and sick. Worse was knowing that people could help him but didn't—the cars and trucks that passed by every so often never once slowed or gave a second thought. After a half-dozen attempts early on to hitch a ride, Joe had resigned himself to the long and plodding hike alone. He'd never seen such rudeness. It wasn't hard to believe why Maya had been so taken by the first person who'd simply acknowledged her existence.

Maya. There was that, too. She came in and out of his thoughts like a bird at the window, landing for a moment and then darting away. Most everyone he'd met in Hell had been distrustful or aloof, or, in a best-case scenario, simply professional, like the customs agent from North Abaddon. But not Maya. She'd cared for him, risked for him, and even believed in him—or so at least he thought. It was confusing to piece together. She'd tended to his wounds after the first demon attack and trusted him enough to share about their mission. But she'd also been dishonest, withholding details about her history with the Rook. Perhaps there were different kinds of dishonesty. If stealing from a criminal could be justified, might deceiving a friend also have its grounds? Perhaps more to the point, after their brief encounter and his willing departure, would Maya consider him a friend?

You have no contract with me, she'd said. *You owe me nothing.*

So why does it cost me to leave you? he wondered in reply.

On the bright side, he did have an excellent view of the lake, if any view of that acrid and molten sea could be described as such. To think, the lake had been enchanting at first, like the backdrop for an epic fantasy saga of which he was a part. But now Joe resented its fiery expanse as much as he'd come to hate the empty desert they'd traveled through to get here. Thankfully, he was now close enough to the bridge to make out the details of its construction, which meant his travel was almost done. Level with his eyes were several boats parked underneath the enormous structure as workers reached out to make repairs. As the lava swirled relentlessly against the bridge, Joe imagined it was a never-ending task to check the integrity of the supports. Literally never-ending.

With the thought came a fresh pang in his heart. David would be out on this lake of fire for eternity—unless Joe found him now. He had to remember that. No matter how tired or thirsty he got, he couldn't quit. Rescuing David was why he was doing this. Slowly, Joe forced himself to his feet and trudged on.

The asphalt stretched out along the coast with sand and rocks filling in its cracks.

The gloomy warehouses cast no shadows under the sunless sky.

He struggled to say if his shield felt heavier in his right hand or left.

At long and painful last, Joe arrived at the bridge.

It was almost dusk now—the darker sky created an even sharper contrast with the currents of burning sulfur. Joe guessed he had less than an hour before workers would go inside for the night. The base of the construction site where the bridge met the shore was still a center of steady activity, however. Six or seven trucks towed concrete mixers, and several dozen workers moved from one task to another, carrying various tools or welding masks or even rolls of blueprints, all of them wearing yellow hard hats and orange vests that matched the fiery sea below.

Surrounding the site was a chain link fence, and at the roadblock guarding the entrance were a man and a woman seated in folding chairs and eating deli sandwiches. A checkpoint for deliveries, Joe presumed. Well, the search had to start somewhere.

"Excuse me," Joe said, coughing a little, his voice hoarse from the walk. "I'm looking for someone. Would you mind helping me for a minute?"

151

"The foreman's done for the day," replied the man, an irritable-looking fellow with sunken eyes. "If you're looking to interview, you'll have to come back tomorrow."

"Oh, no, I'm not here for that. I'm looking for a worker. David Platt. He should be pretty new here. Do you know him?"

"Sounds familiar," said the woman, using her finger to wipe a smear of yellow mustard from her upper lip. "But hard to say for sure."

"Is there a way you can check? It's very important."

"Oh, that depends." She held out her hand, palm up. "What's it worth to you?"

Joe cursed his luck that the bags of coins were still in the jeep with Peter and not in his own pocket. Where was a bribe when he finally needed it?

"Please. I've come a really long way to get here."

She took another noisy bite of the sandwich, utterly indifferent.

Unbelievable. He'd walked all the way from the warehouse only to be stonewalled by a pair of bad-tempered hard hats on their dinner break. Joe did not have time for this.

"Excuse me, then. I'll just look for him myself." He moved to sidestep the roadblock, but the man leaped up and held out his arm. He was at least six inches shorter than Joe and was armed with only a half-eaten sandwich.

"Hey," the man snapped. "What's this about? There's no unauthorized entry. I don't care if you think you're King Arthur with all that getup. You're not barging in here."

Joe guessed he could knock the man over with one hit from his shield, about as quickly as Brody had dispatched the sentry at the warehouse. But then again, Joe was not Brody, and it made little sense to cause a scene before he found David. Who knew what kind of security or backup might be nearby? Joe racked his tired brain for a better idea.

152

"My apologies," Joe began. "Perhaps we got off to the wrong start. Like I said, it's been a long journey. I've come all the way from North Abaddon. I'm David's brother, and it's kind of a family emergency."

"What kind of emergency?" The man blocking his path glared with distrust.

Joe floundered for a moment—death, sickness, tragic accident—none of the usual excuses made sense in Hell. He had to switch tactics.

"Well, um, he's wanted, actually. David Platt is, I mean. I've been chasing him."

"I thought you were his brother," the woman replied skeptically.

"Well, sort of. Not so much in the biological sense. Actually,"—Joe was improvising now—"I meant in the spiritual sense. He was part of my congregation."

"What congregation?"

Joe reached into his pants pocket and produced a slightly wrinkled business card. No way would they believe it, but what options did he have?

"I represent the North Abaddon Holy Sanctuary."

The woman took the card and carefully examined it.

"Isaac Washington?" she asked tentatively.

"Um,"—Joe swallowed his panic—"yes. That's me."

Her eyes returned to the card. Joe positioned his feet to run. The man took the last bite of his sandwich and licked each finger clean.

"You know," the woman said, her expression softening, "I think I've heard of you. Aren't you the one who does those revivals downtown? I've seen the posters."

Either a lucky break or a battle of wits—although she appeared quite sincere.

"Uh, yes," Joe responded. "I'm the one."

She set down her sandwich. "To think, here I am, asking for my due, rude as can be. Forgive me, Reverend, as you can tell it's been a long time since I've been to a service of any sort. Why didn't you just say who you were at the beginning?"

"Well, I, um, try to keep a humble profile."

"By carrying around medieval weapons?" the man inquired suspiciously.

"Um, yes. These are to fight off the demons, you know," —Joe appealed to the woman— "at revivals and such. And there's another specific...relic that I require for this good work."

"And what's that?"

"It's … um … a diamond. A diamond with very special properties. And, unfortunately, this David Platt whom I mentioned, he stole the diamond, and now I'm here to collect it."

"Why don't I just call security?" asked the woman.

"Oh, thank you, um, but I'd prefer to handle the situation privately."

"We can have you file a report."

Joe shifted nervously. "I don't think that's necessary."

"We have certain procedures here," said the man.

"Of course, but with all of the sudden attention, I'm afraid he may hand off or hide the diamond before I can confront him, and then we might never recover it. It's very important, you see, and due to its nature must be handled quite delicately. And I'm sure anyone who helps" —Joe knew to tread carefully here— "will receive their own reward for doing good. Can I trust that you two are such good people?"

It appeared the woman was buying it more than the man, but they both studied him intently, being either quite fascinated or just plain baffled. Joe willed the uneasiness in his gut to stay put and did his best to fake a confident stance while he awaited their verdict.

"Well," the woman began, "I've lived in Brimtown long enough to know there's a need for such things. Society's not what it used be. The demons get worse with every generation of arrivals. So I suppose it can't hurt to let a reverend do his work, especially if it'll bring some favor to me too. You'll grant me some protection, then, against the demons' attack?"

"Of course. What's your name, for the, um…pardon?"

"Rhonda Hastings."

"Wonderful, Ms. Hastings. Your kindness has been noted."

She took out a pad of official visitor's passes and filled one out in the name of Isaac Washington, then tore it off and gave it to Joe. The man scowled but didn't protest, and Joe fought to contain his excitement.

"Platt's working receiving today. Turn right. Loading bay at the base of the platform."

Joe shared his gratitude and blessing, then entered through the gate.

He saw David before David saw him. Six or seven workers were unloading a shipment from a large truck that Joe vaguely recognized as having driven past him on his long walk over. But sure enough, there he was. Joe's only brother—the family troublemaker, for whom he'd crossed the desert and fought off demons—stacking three wooden crates onto a dolly with his back to Joe. His orange vest looked a size too small and his hair as mangy as ever.

Should I surprise him? Joe wondered. Encouraged by his successful acting at the gate, he imagined now sneaking up from behind to startle his brother with a booming voice and a draw of his sword—"Turn around slowly with your hands in the air." And then after a jolt of fright and dropping a crate, David and he would come together in a tight embrace, sharing a laugh like the best of friends. They'd find a quiet corner to sit, and Joe, tired from the walk, would prop up his feet as they resumed their conversation from that fateful car ride home from the gas station, recalling the joy and not the sorrow, picking up at the exact point where they'd left off on their last night alive.

"Hey, you looking for something?" called a fat man from across the loading bay.

And then everyone snapped to attention, and David spoke next.

"Joe? Holy crap. Dude, you're here!"

"Hey, David." So much for the grand entrance.

David set down the crate he'd been holding and strode across the concrete with eagerness but perhaps not urgency, his eyes wide with astonishment.

"Dude, where did you come from?"

"I, um ... It's a really long story. I've been looking for you, though. Ever since I got here."

"I figured you must've survived the crash," David said, "you know, since I didn't see you here at all. Like, have you just been wandering around this whole time? And what the heck is all this stuff? You've got this like, a Protector of the Realm thing going on."

"Yeah, I'll tell you about it. Hey, David, is there somewhere we can—"

"Here," David interrupted. "Let me get you a drink. Is water okay?"

"Um, yeah. Thanks."

By now, the other workers had lost interest and returned to their tasks. David fetched a bottle of water from a cooler, and Joe downed it in exactly three gulps.

David said, "Man, I've got something to tell you you're not going to believe."

Joe crushed the empty plastic bottle and tossed it into a nearby trash can.

"Me too, actually."

But David didn't seem to hear this. Instead, he went on excitedly, "We have to wait until the work shift's over. I'd tell you right now, but I don't want to ruin it. In the meantime, I can give you a tour. This place is sweet."

Joe hardly had time to respond before his brother took off, leading the way around the compound. Between Joe's tired state and his brother's enthusiasm, it took all of Joe's energy just to keep up. They saw the various bays for parts receiving and assembly, and David spoke animatedly about the types of steel connections and joints, even showing off the special paints used to protect from heat and corrosion. He named the items with pride, as if each piece of equipment were state-of-the-art and each step in the process were revolutionizing the industry. Most of the other employees ignored them or gave only a cursory nod as they walked past, but David gave out waves and salutes and greeted everyone by name. Joe could barely handle it—stranger than a lake of burning sulfur was David's newfound confidence.

To be honest, Joe had expected to find his brother miserable and alone. Wasn't that what Hell was supposed to do to people? Yet David appeared happier now than Joe had seen him in years. In fact, David wouldn't shut up about how much he loved the place. The more he showed off, the more Joe's heart sank.

There's more to this, Joe reminded himself. *Remember why you came.*

"And this is the final product," David said, gesturing to the bridge. The tour ended on a dirt-covered peninsula, a small protrusion of land with a set of picnic tables and a side-angle view of the construction in action. Work had just finished for the day, but Joe could still see the enormous crane used to lift the steel trusses into place. Joe had to admit, the bridge was impressive. He studied with interest the geometric support of the diagonals and chords, and the suspension cables stretching from the land to a fixed point on a high vertical beam some ways out onto the lake. It was hard to estimate, but Joe guessed the bridge was more than a mile long—an incredible undertaking over a sea of raging fire.

"What do you think?" David asked.

He thought, *It's a colossal waste of time and resources, a spectacular and effective distraction from the cold reality of Hell.*

He said, "It's quite the project."

"I bet I can get you a job here if you want. The pay is good, and we get benefits too."

Well, how about that? David helping him get a job—now the irony had come full circle. But Joe knew better than to even feign interest. That's not why he was here. Joe took a few steps toward the edge of the lake and kicked a pebble into the burning sulfur. It dissolved with a quick sizzle, like a drop of water falling into a hot pan.

"So, David," Joe said after a moment, "what would you say is the point of all this?"

David laughed. "What are you talking about? It's a bridge. Isn't that obvious?"

"Yes, but"—Joe turned to face his brother—"you have to realize that it will never actually reach the other side. I mean it's literally melting as you build it. So what's the point?"

"I don't know." David shrugged. "I guess there's a part of me that's just drawn to the challenge, you know, wondering if we can do it. You get that, don't you?"

"Maybe. There's a difference between challenging and impossible."

"You know a few days ago, I might have said life after death was impossible, but here we both are."

"Well, life's more than just having a heartbeat."

David threw up his hands. "C'mon, Joe. Are we seriously having this conversation? We're dead, right? Dead as it gets. But it turns out we're here and talking instead of rotting six feet under. So what are we supposed to do for eternity if it's not at least trying to make some kind of difference?"

And at last—such was the question Joe had come to answer.

He told David everything. Joe spoke of Heaven, the mighty trumpets, the streets of gold, the endless fields, the marvelous city with angels at the gates. He described the sweet water and delicious fruit, always in season, and told of mountain passes and unlimited strength.

"And Mom is there—I talked to her, David. And Jesus—he's real. He has flesh and voice and eyes like you've never seen. He knows everyone and everything, David, and he loves them for it. And most importantly, he sent me here to find you. He sent me to bring you up to that glorious place, and to do that he gave me this." Joe held out the salvation key.

"What is that?"

"Here, look at it." He pressed the key into David's hands, allowing his brother to feel the smooth brass that would unlock their way home. "It's from Jesus himself. It's our ticket out of here, David. So what do you think? Will you? Will you come with me?"

There was nothing to say for a long moment while David collected his thoughts. He looked away, and soon Joe followed his gaze, watching the crowd walk away from the bridge. The workers, done with their shifts, were now filing out away from the main construction site. Many had cars or motorcycles parked in a gated lot near the checkpoint where Joe had first walked in, but many left on foot too, their limbs tired and their hair slightly matted from removing the hard hats they'd worn all day. There were dozens if not hundreds, ensnared by the daily routine, ceaselessly laboring each day until the gray sky turned to black. Indeed, it was the fact of their diligence that made Joe pity them more, desperately wishing that their energies might be spent on a project with a true destination in mind.

A Bridge to Somewhere, he thought, *must be preferable to this.* And for all he'd been taught and come to know, wasn't Heaven that Somewhere?

"I don't know, Joe," David replied at last. "I mean, I believe you went somewhere and all that—I've heard Hell is a big place—but Brimtown really isn't as bad as you'd think. There's a lot happening here, and I've got a place to stay, and—"

"And all the cold shoulders, the corruption, the demons . . ." Joe interrupted.

"You know," David said. "It's funny you mention it about Mom."

Joe blinked. "What do you mean?"

"Well, I told you I had something to show you too."

David waved as a bridge worker stepped out from the crowd to join them on the peninsula. The man was about fifty, wearing dark jeans and the same orange vest as everyone else, with a round face like David's and a brow line like Joe saw in the mirror each morning. Joe couldn't have described this person only a moment before, but in that same way that people in Heaven knew one another, so Joe already knew this man even before he walked up. Or rather, he recognized him, for how could he truly know a man who'd been absent for most of his life?

Facing them now with his hard hat gripped in one hand stood Bill Platt.

His father.

"I wanted to surprise you," said David. "Joe, this is Dad."

Those three simple and gut-wrenching words.

Joe failed to raise his shield before some invisible hand punched him in the stomach—punched him very hard. He tried to speak but found his jaws tightly locked together. Hadn't it been twenty years since they'd last shared a roof? And back then, hadn't Joe's innocent ears been too young to comprehend the late-night shouting and his mother's sobs? Although he remembered it well enough, or least as well as he dared, for what had been his memories were now repressed or ignored or simply forgotten. Or, perhaps more accurately, they were replaced, superseded with vivid images of Grandpa's smile and Uncle Russ's jokes and the encouraging words of every teacher or coach or pastor that had for a season, a day, or even a moment stopped to know him. And the pain that had long gnawed at his heart, like a mouse hidden inside the wall, now crept forward and unveiled a new emptiness, a wrong that was never righted, a wound that was never treated and had long since festered and spread its infection unchecked. Of all places and of all times to finally meet! Oh, the absurdity of this whole situation! Which was worse, the fact that this stranger-not-stranger required an introduction to his own son, or that David had the audacity to call this man *Dad*?

"Well, look at you. David told me you might be down here, but we weren't sure. Glad to see you again, son." No hug, no handshake, not even a wave from across the short distance that existed between them. Joe had seen too many wonders to still be shocked, too many demons to still be afraid, and had spent all of his joy and sadness on the complicated reunion with his brother. All that remained now was anger. Joe was angry for reasons he could hardly articulate, the conflict swirling inside him like a tropical storm, with increasing intensity even before it was named.

"Is that it?" he asked, the words slipping from his lips laced with both incredulity and accusation. "Is that all you're going to say to me?"

"Well, maybe while we're standing here," said Bill—Joe couldn't yet think of him as father. "I mean, look, it's almost dark. Why don't you come back with us? I have a place nearby where David's staying too. We can grab a beer or whatever and talk all you want."

"No," Joe replied. "That's not happening."

"Hey, nobody's making you do anything. I'm just saying it'll be dark soon, and if you're looking for somewhere—"

"No," Joe repeated, his blood rising to the boiling point. "That's not why I'm here."

"Look," Bill started, opening his hands in a conciliatory gesture. "I know it's been a while. And if you're not happy to see me right now, I get it. I really screwed things up. For what it's worth, I had every good intention, but things never worked out the way I wanted them to. I always regretted not being there for you, Joe. But if you give me another chance . . ."

"Is that it?" Joe asked, shouting this time. "Is that your whole apology? Am I supposed to just say everything is fine after not hearing from you for years, after you abandoned us?"

"Hey," David interrupted. "I get what you're feeling, Joe. I mean, I was in the exact same boat. But trust me, it's not like that anymore.

I mean it's *Dad*, Joe. Give him a chance, and I promise you'll see what I've seen the last few days and—"

"No!" Joe cried. "You're not listening." How he wished he weren't trapped on this small peninsula with fire on three sides and his so-called father blocking the other. If he had space to run, Joe would be miles from here by now. He would go in a straight line, kicking open the doors to every warehouse and slashing through every wall with his sword until he was beyond Brimtown, beyond this desert, beyond this truly godforsaken place. For how could Jesus have sent him only to be starved and lost and confronted by so much confusion and torment? And even Peter had gone from him now, his only companion on this agonizing journey.

But there was still hope. There had to be. Why else would Jesus have sent him at all?

Joe closed his eyes and fought to compose himself. He couldn't ruin this, not here, not now. He counted his breaths in and out, not caring how long he stood like that, or who saw him. Neither David nor his father spoke, but neither did he hear them leave.

The silence broke at the sound of a police siren, and Joe opened his eyes to see a patrol car come to a stop and a pair of bulky officers step out onto the dirt.

"Which one of you is David Platt?" said the first.

"Who's asking?" Bill replied.

"We're following up on a call, sir. We just have a few questions."

Joe nearly fainted with dread. This was his doing, wasn't it? Had those two at the gate actually filed a report? They must have, despite his request.

"Wait," Joe said. "I'm, uh, I'm Isaac Washington. I made the complaint. There's no problem here. Sorry for the false alarm."

"You're who?" asked David.

"I'm sorry, Reverend," said the officer, "but we have different orders."

"Reverend? What's he talking about?"

"I had to say something to get in here," Joe frantically explained. "I made up a story."

"A story that involves the police asking for me? What the heck, man? What'd you say?"

"My son's done nothing wrong," Bill Platt assured the officers. "Why don't the two of you just move along?"

"We leave when I say so," said the second officer, the bigger of the two. He stepped forward to move past Bill on the peninsula, making a point to brush his shoulder in a gruff show of authority. Feeling the challenge, Bill made the mistake of grabbing the man's arm—a little too abruptly, a little too forcefully—and then everything came undone.

The ensuing scene went off like a flash. The officer next to Bill shoulder-checked him, and they both fell to the ground, wrestling to gain an advantage. The first officer drew his nightstick and attempted to aid his partner, although it was hard to find a clean shot in the skirmish. David leaped into the melee to even the numbers, and Joe shouted for all of them to stop. But they ignored him, and it was hardly a fair match anyway. The stronger and better-trained officers quickly subdued Platt and Son, cuffing the both of them.

Joe reached for his sword but then lowered his hand.

Don't hesitate, he thought. *Peter didn't.*

But he wasn't the apostle, and these men weren't demons. Despite their brutality, the officers had a true aura of humanity, one which Joe could hardly describe but could readily see. Was he supposed to attack these people? Would stabbing someone really be a solution?

"David," Joe begged. "Listen to me. As soon as we figure this out, we can go. Did you understand what I told you? It doesn't have to be like this. I came here to rescue you."

"You know, that's a funny thing to say while I'm being arrested."

"Just let me explain," Joe pleaded to David, to his father, to the officers, to the wind.

"You know what, Joe?" David met his eyes. "I've had a lot of problems in the past. But not here. Not until today. For once in my life, I didn't need you to rescue me."

The officers yanked the two men to their feet and led them to the patrol car. On the way, David spotted the salvation key lying on the ground, dangerously close to the edge of the lake, where it had fallen out of his hand during the fight. And in one final, thoughtless moment of frustration and defiance, David kicked it as hard as he could. Time stretched and warped as the key sailed through the air, a dark line against the churning inferno.

Not a splash as it entered the flames.

"We'll be in touch, Reverend," said the first officer.

Then the siren and engine both started up again, and the car drove away toward the construction site gate. For the first time since arriving in Hell, Joe truly was alone.

FOURTEEN
FOR WE ARE MANY

DARKNESS CAME LIKE a heavy rain. Joe felt exposed, caught in the storm with no shelter or cover, watching helplessly as all promise and optimism washed away in a mighty torrent. Of course, in reality, the air was as dry as ever, and increasingly cold as he moved away from the lake of fire.

David is gone, he mourned, *because I failed to save him*.

Even if Joe went straight to the police station to arrange for their release—even if he could do so, now that both David and his father had assaulted two officers—he doubted that David would listen to what he had to say. He wondered if he'd even believed him in the first place. From what Joe had seen, David loved working on the bridge and was in no rush to give it up for the dream of a promised land.

Not that they could go back anyway. The salvation key had sunk to the bottom of the lake, where surely it had melted like wax on a candle. It was of little importance that David had been the one who kicked it. It was Joe who'd been responsible for its safekeeping, and somehow he'd managed to botch that too.

There were other concerns of the moment—namely, where he might find a place to take shelter from the cold and sleep for the night, although he had no money to his name, and how he might find

165

a meal, since he'd last fueled his stomach at breakfast. But none weighed upon Joe as heavily as David's last words.

I didn't need you to rescue me.

Even if Joe could find another way back to Heaven—Peter would know what to do if only Joe could find the apostle again—could he bear a return to paradise without David? Could he live with knowing he'd been unsuccessful in his mission? Could he face his own mother with the shame? Although she'd been right all along. *It's not the kind of decision we can change*, she'd said.

But was there no hope for the relationship at all? If there wasn't a way back to Heaven, and indeed Joe was trapped in Hell, would there forever be enmity between the brothers? Was eternity a wellspring of second chances, or was it a festering wound that never healed? Maybe it was like Brody had said, that eventually life and death became together blank and vain, like two sides of a penny, not worth its own weight and discarded as easily as it was spent.

Such were the dismal thoughts that followed Joe into the night.

The Brimtown streets curved and twisted as if Joe were a rat to be observed in a circular maze. Not that he had a particular destination in mind, but forward motion was preferable, if only for offering a sense of progress that constant backtracking did not. Still, it was difficult to find his way. Here was a dead end, there was an alleyway identical to the one through which he'd just come. Streetlamps were intermittent and patchily functional, as if their purpose was more for the shadows and less for the light. Disquieting whispers rode up on the sulfuric breeze, and plastic bags on every corner trash heap resembled those two-headed vultures from the night they'd first been attacked. Joe walked with both eyes wide and one hand on the hilt of his sword.

But no danger came. He passed a dormant gas station and a darkened clothing shop, shuttered apartment windows and vacant taxi stands, crooked street signs meant to govern the empty intersections. Still not a soul. All of Brimtown stayed in fearful slumber with Joe as its lone, restless wanderer.

At last his fatigue won out, and Joe stopped in front of an upscale café. The lights were off, and the door was locked—he rattled it to be sure—but a sidewalk partition that enclosed the outdoor seating area offered some cover and privacy. He lay down with his shield as a pillow, hugging the wall and tucking his arms inside his hoodie to stay warm. As much as he could, he tried to get comfortable. A real soldier would be used to sleeping out in the open, so naturally Joe struggled to rest. Strange shapes moved behind his eyelids, and the silence was unnerving.

Maybe I should pray, he thought. That's what he used to do when he was anxious, right?

"Jesus," he whispered, "if you can hear me, I need some help right now. You sent me to find David, but I screwed up. I don't even know how. But if you can help somehow, I just—"

A creaking noise, like a gate swung open.

Jesus? Joe sat upright and looked around. Maybe he was sending a sign.

Joe counted to thirty but saw nothing other than the dark outlines of the café tables and stacks of chairs. No Jesus. It must have been his mind playing tricks.

"Be a little more obvious next time," Joe said to the air.

If only he had just kept his mouth shut, he could have gone with David and his father to share a drink and sleep in a warm, lighted apartment. They could have figured this all out in the morning, after some food and a good night's rest. Joe would have gladly taken Maya and her gang for company, or even a lecture from old St. Peter— anything not to be alone in the darkness.

He lay down again and was nearing sleep when he heard another sound, this time an audible voice. A person—now he was sure. Joe reached for his sword and carefully stood.

"Who's there?" he asked the night, as loudly as he dared.

"I am," replied the voice, and then Joe saw the body to go with it. Seated at the farthest table in front of the café was a man dressed in a long black coat, his face obscured in shadow. How had Joe not seen him before?

"This place belongs to me. What's your name, child?"

"Joe Platt. I'm sorry if I'm intruding. I have nowhere to stay tonight." He immediately wished he'd given a better story than that, or least stuck with his fake name from before, but there was something about intense fear that gave rise to honesty.

The man stood. He was at least a head taller than Joe and had his back to the nearest light, so that Joe could discern no more than an outline of his face.

"Then you are welcome to stay here, Joe Platt. But do so as my guest, and not as some kind of vagrant. You tense as if I were a dog to chase you off."

The man appeared sane enough. Joe did relax a little and let his hand off the sword hilt. The stranger's voice was confident and rhythmic—thankfully, Joe noted, without a trace of that horrible demonic hissing.

"Thank you. I appreciate it, sir."

"I assure you, the pleasure is mine."

Joe waited for this stranger in the dark to explain himself further, but he merely stood there like an apparition. Had he not heard the man speak, Joe might indeed have thought he were a ghost.

"So, um, I told you my name. May I ask yours?"

"I have countless names, given to me by people in every age."

"Uh . . . right. What's the one you want me to call you?"

"Some call us Legion, for we are many. My spirit is entwined with presences and entities not only in this city, but across this whole land and every continent and sea on Earth." The man circled closer and leaned in, as if to whisper. "But tonight, you'll know me well as your friend Maya knows me, as the one they call the Rook."

And just like that, any comforting moment from before was over. Terror again gripped Joe in its claws. The Rook! Maya's story had been warning enough of his evil ploys, but the fact that he mentioned her specifically showed that he'd already known who Joe was, even before their introduction in the shadows just now. Whatever trap this was, it'd already been sprung.

Joe drew his sword and hoped the darkness hid his shaking arm.

"Stand back."

"Come, now. First you accept my hospitality, and now you threaten to fight?"

"The Rook I've heard about is no friend to me."

"Oh, surely you don't believe everything you hear."

"I know who to trust and who not to."

"Ah, but I know you."

This ominous reply was enough to surmise the answer, but Joe asked anyway. "Tell me, are you a man, or a demon?"

"Tonight, I am your savior."

A gust of wind swirled up and reached its crescendo, rattling the café awning and chilling Joe to his core. With a voice that was hardly his own, he boldly declared, "Jesus Christ is my savior." He lifted his sword point to touch the Rook's chest, thinking this was the moment that the power of God would crash down from above, that like the demons before him, the Rook would shrink back. He couldn't withstand this power. He wouldn't dare try.

But no—the air was quiet again.

Then the Rook laughed. It was a sad, pitying sort of laugh, like how one might respond to a child who'd said something that was both innocent and ridiculous.

"And where is your Jesus now? Around the corner, perhaps? Still on his way?"

The mocking question found its mark. Already, Joe's quick surge of confidence had come and gone. The sword sat heavy in his hands.

"He's with me in spirit," Joe replied. Jesus himself had said so, hadn't he? Yet Joe's tone was unconvincing—and, possibly, unconvinced.

He thought, *Was this how I sounded talking to David about Heaven?*

"Yes, the hope in things not seen," the Rook mocked. "I've heard this song before. But I put stock in what I do see, and looking at you, Joe, I have to wonder. Your only friends are lost, and now your brother is taken from you also? If I fed on hope itself, I'm afraid I'd go hungry in your presence."

"How do you know about David?"

That laugh again. The Rook continued, "There's a reason you haven't impaled me, Joe, although you've positioned yourself well to do so. But come now, let's be civilized. Have a seat, and I shall tell you what you have every right to know."

The Rook brushed aside Joe's sword as if it were a tree branch on a hike. If this was meant as a show of dominance, he didn't gloat in the moment. He simply moved on while Joe lowered his weapon and considered his options. Given the Rook's self-assurance, a fight seemed ill-advised, and a flight supposed he had somewhere to flee to. There was, however, an invisible pull to this danger, like magnetism, and Joe wondered what harm a conversation could do.

Not waiting for a response, the Rook pulled two chairs around the nearest café table and then both of them sat, he with comfortable ease and Joe with cautious trepidation. The Rook's face was still away from the lights, wearing the shadows as a mask. By now Joe realized he'd positioned himself this way on purpose.

"Okay," Joe said. "Go ahead. What is this you want to tell me?"

The Rook made a dramatic show of stroking his chin.

"Hard to know where to begin."

"What you're doing here is a good place to start," Joe demanded.

"And here I thought you were the traveler and I the gracious host. I should ask, how have you been enjoying Brimtown so far?"

"It stinks."

"Quick on your feet! How wonderful. I appreciate a sense of humor, and I think so might your father, if you gave him the chance. How was it, by the way, finally meeting your real dad?"

Joe scowled. "Are you here just to taunt me?"

"Such hostility! My friend, it's only a question."

Joe shifted in his seat. It was hardly just a question, he knew, but to be honest, the situation had been on his mind ever since he'd left the bridge.

"I don't know. Surprising?"

"I see. Do you mean for you or for him?"

"Both, I guess. He was certainly the last person I thought I'd see today." *Or ever again,* Joe thought.

"Indeed. How . . . fortuitous that it came about."

Sarcasm was harder to detect in the dark, but Joe picked it up anyway.

"What are you saying?"

"You tell me, Joe Platt."

"My father at the bridge—you set that up just to screw with me, didn't you?"

"Oh, I'm quite flattered. But it's not I who orchestrate such elaborate plans."

"What's that supposed to mean?"

"And here I thought you were smart."

"Enough with the games already," Joe snapped. "If you have something to say, say it."

"Oh, dear Joe," the Rook replied, "can you not recognize what's been done to you? Don't you see the plot holes by now? The sudden appearance of your long-lost father, just as timely and inexplicable as the appearance of the police who took him away? Or what about the lovely Maya—yes, even her—who happened to be squatting in the one house with a view of your battle, awake at night when all of Hell sleeps, let alone willing to come to your aid? Then she just happened to require your assistance on a sham of a mission, a mission that took you exactly where you wanted to go? And let's not forget Peter, the venerable saint and master swordsman, who was chummy with the customs agent despite his own warnings, who could slay a hundred demons with a turn of his wrist but somehow disappeared when you needed him most?"

"I can see how it looks that way, but some of that was coincidence . . ."

"Is there such thing? Was it really chance that brought you here?"

Joe considered this for a moment. "Well, originally, it was a mission from Jesus."

"Ah, yes! And what about Jesus, the so-called Christ? He who claims to have humbled himself but sits exalted over all. It's curious, isn't it? Why would he choose an unassuming young man such as yourself for a mission he's never allowed before and then not come alongside you? What king sends men out to battle while he hides in his palace—except for the spoiled, cowardly, or corrupt? If he had a tenth of the power he claimed, wouldn't he have given it in your aid to ensure your success? I wonder, was it always his plan to leave you, or was it only at the moment of your request to save your brother that his heart became so hard?"

"What are you saying?"

"Oh, come now, Joe. You profess faith, but tell me, how does your résumé compare? Never served as a missionary or elder in the church, kept your beliefs private while you pursued wealth and career, made God and family secondary to your personal wants. You even tried to dissuade others from eating the fruits of Heaven. Tell me, what shines bright in your testimony? Where is your sacrifice? Where is the cross you've borne? Are you not ruled by fear and selfishness? Are you not far more sinner than saint?

"No, Joe, you may think it chance that you find yourself wandering these streets tonight. But truly I tell you, everything up until this very encounter of ours was ordained and purposeful, although never to your advantage. How cruel that he couldn't just send you here first and forgo the drama. But perhaps it was his way of proving a point. You were never good enough, I'm afraid, or at least not in his eyes—for I would never make so bold a judgment about anyone. But, alas, the judgment isn't mine to make. So allow me to bear the bad news, but to do so in truth. You were banished, Joseph Platt. All this has been a ruse. You were never meant to stay in Heaven, and now everyone has played you for a fool."

Joe's brain was a swarm of hornets trying to escape its nest.

"But . . . how?"

"Oh, who can fathom the mind of God? In one breath, he claims to be a merciful lord, but then he sends Jesus, who calls himself Christ, that fastidious and disparaging hypocrite, who says not one iota will fall from the law, and small is the gate and narrow is the road that leads to life. How prejudiced and disgraceful to accept only a few! How pretentious, how overly conceited to demand perfection from those entering his kingdom!

"No, unlike this claim to exclusivity, here we value all humanity. Hell is the ultimate inclusion, where everyone has a chance no matter what he's done or failed to do. We reject the divine inheritance. Men are able to make their own fortunes, to decide their own destinies. I give you autonomy, for isn't it better to be free and independent than the vassal of an unjust king?"

"But," Joe stammered, "Heaven's not like that at all."

"Oh, I don't suppose a single conversation will convince you, but perhaps in time you'll come around. But for now, the night is long, and you need a place to sleep. I haven't forgotten that you're my guest. Here, take this as a token of our new relationship." The Rook pulled a pouch of coins from his inner coat pocket and slid it across the table to Joe.

"I don't need your charity."

"It's not so much a gift. If roles were reversed, I'm sure you'd do the same for me, and perhaps someday you will. Are not good friends constantly indebted to each other?"

"Like I said, we're not friends."

"Pity the man who falls and has no one to help him up."

The Rook rose from his seat.

"There's a loft on the second floor of the café," he said. "There's a stairway to it around back. I've left the door unlocked. A soft bed and thick blanket beat the bare pavement, I should think. But then again, you are free to do as you will. Goodnight, Joe Platt. It was a pleasure conversing with you."

After the Rook had gone, Joe again tucked his arms inside his hoodie. The night was at its coldest, and it was tempting to consider the room upstairs. But would it really mean he owed a debt? Maya's warnings were still fresh in his mind, especially the image of the man branded at the lake. Yet how could a single night of lodging be so wrong to accept? Was he really so proud that he'd sleep out on the street just to avoid owing a few coins? Besides, Joe could pay it back once he found Peter and the money they'd brought—that is, if Peter was still here.

He couldn't overthink it all now. The Rook had cast all kinds of doubts that surely would shrink back after a good night's sleep and some food in his stomach. The sensible thing was to do just that and then make a plan in the morning. Joe picked up the bag of coins on the table and felt its weight. A modest amount, far less than they'd brought with them from Heaven. Certainly it wouldn't be any trouble, with the understanding that it was only a loan. Yet for reasons he couldn't quite name, even touching the bag felt like a violation of principles, as if the coins themselves were unclean. His mind and nature battled against themselves.

The wind picked up again, stealing what little heat remained in his body. Surely he'd freeze to a second death if he stayed outside all night.

The other option, he thought, *is to keep walking.* But he'd tried that already, and he wasn't sure his body could do more. His fingers again touched the coins on the table.

A streetlight flickered and died. A haunting whisper carried in the wind.

Pride, Joe decided, *is the deadliest of sins.*

FIFTEEN
THE PROPOSAL

THANKFULLY, THE CAFÉ served breakfast. A dour-faced seating hostess guided Joe to a small table against the front window and wordlessly placed a menu before him. Joe needed only a minute to decide on a large platter of pancakes, bacon, and eggs. As he waited impatiently, listening to the sizzle of fresh coffee dripping into an empty pot and the low grumble of his equally empty stomach, he couldn't help but think of his last meal twenty-four hours ago at a wobbly kitchen table in a house on the outskirts of Brimtown.

You're welcome to come back, she'd said. He considered the offer as his food arrived, mouthing her words between forkfuls drenched in syrup. He had to admit, his circumstances looked no better in daylight than they had the night before—brother in jail, Peter gone AWOL, salvation key melting in the lake. Perhaps it was finally Joe's turn to run away.

Outside the window, cars, trucks, and pedestrians moved in a steady current, another gray morning of industrial monotony. Joe had no idea what day of the week it was, but he supposed it hardly mattered. Even if weekends did exist in Hell, what would anyone do? Catch a matinee in the Brimtown theater district? Take a scenic stroll along the boardwalk or a nice boat ride on the lake of fire? He imagined fishing from the dock, casting his line with gusto, only to

175

reel it in and discover the lure had burned to a crisp. Much like his hope of ever leaving this place.

Joe sighed, finding his plate clean and his thoughts poor company. Really nothing had changed since he'd left the bridge, although the Rook's accommodations had provided temporary relief. The bed had been comfortable, as promised, and it'd been a mercifully short night of deep and dreamless sleep. He'd awakened, however, with tired eyes, a growling stomach, and a mind racked with guilt. Coffee and food had done their best to alleviate the first two, but it was the last one that now wholly consumed him.

The problem, Joe supposed, *is that I still don't have a plan.*

There were few possible courses of action, and none that jumped out. Should he bail David out of jail? He had the money now, but not the words to see his brother again so soon. Plus, any visit to the jail would lead to an encounter with his father, which, to be sure, was its own dilemma. Bill Platt might have done nothing wrong in last night's mix-up, but innocence of one crime did not absolve him from the rest. On top of that, what would Joe do with them anyway once they were released? With the salvation key gone, they had no quick escape. Joe would have to find Peter first—surely he'd know another way out. The apostle might be waiting at the Bridge to Nowhere (where else would he think to meet Joe?), but then again, he might not be, and to search for him there and not find him would bring about all kinds of implications that Joe wasn't quite ready to entertain. Then there was the final option, which Joe had already considered…

The café, Joe realized, was the wrong place to think. The walls were painted a cheery sort of yellow and sparsely decorated, doing little to contain the color. The decor clashed like bright neon against the otherwise dismal hues of Hell, ironically making one long for the gray outdoors. Except for hot griddle sounds from the kitchen, the place was fairly quiet—although not for a lack of customers. The restaurant held at least two dozen businessmen and women, all professionally dressed and true regulars, displaying a familiar rapport with the waitstaff. Even so, beyond the necessities, Joe witnessed very little interpersonal communication. Indeed, from his vantage point Joe could see that the café booths were at the same time both full and empty—every table had an occupant, and every occupant dined alone.

At the register, Joe paid for his meal with a single gold coin. He caught his reflection in the mirror beside the counter. Jeans stained with soot, eyes red, hair tousled and dirty, shield awkwardly draped over his arm, appearing more comical than threatening. He'd pay another coin just for a shower right now. All things considered, Joe looked like he'd come from a roadside ditch, not a heavenly paradise. No wonder David hadn't believed him.

Joe left his change as a tip and was on his way out when the newspaper rack by the door caught his attention. Balancing his shield against the wall, Joe picked up a copy of the morning's *Brimtown Express* and read the headline twice to be sure.

PREACHER, CITY OFFICIALS CLASH OVER REVIVAL EVENT

A stock photo showed a drab government building, and the full story was printed below. Joe skimmed the whole thing, noting the relevant details with increasing panic.

North Abaddon preacher . . . rising popularity and sellout crowds . . . controversial sale of indulgences . . . denied permit extension . . . final event scheduled tomorrow afternoon at City Hall.

By name, the story mentioned the Reverend Isaac Washington— the real one, not Joe's impersonation. If he were in Brimtown, it wouldn't be hard for the police to figure out Joe had lied about his identity at the bridge. The officers had referred to Joe as *Reverend* yesterday, but with the real guy making headlines, they'd catch on pretty quickly. Thankfully, the news story was without a picture of the real Isaac, but for how long would that save him? If yesterday David had been so quickly investigated for a mere accusation, what would they do to Joe when they discovered evidence of his actual crimes? Identity theft, false testimony—not to mention breaking and entering at the Rook's warehouse, a fact he'd more or less confessed to last night while speaking with the Rook himself. No, Joe couldn't risk going to the station for his father and David today, not without exposing himself to the possibility of also being arrested. What good would it do any of them to have all three Platt men in jail? And of course, looking for Peter would involve going back to the bridge, where Joe might be recognized by any number of construction workers . . .

His only safe option was to flee Brimtown.

Joe tucked the newspaper under his arm and collected his shield, suddenly feeling enormously conspicuous. Was the waiter in on it, or maybe the hostess? That man in the corner booth sipping orange juice and staring across the room, was he an undercover cop assigned to tail Joe? If the Rook had found him so easily last night, couldn't anyone?

Joe stepped outside, but the street was no better. The creeping shadows of the night were nothing compared to the flesh-and-blood people crowding the walkways. Despite their indifference toward each other, everyone turned to look at him. How could they not? His giant shield alone was enough to draw attention. Joe was sure of it. Every man or woman was his newfound enemy, as if there were a bounty on his head. Every cough or motion in his direction was the stealthy glance of a predator about to strike.

Joe walked as fast as he dared, always moving away, but still people brushed and bumped against him like leaves whirling in the wind. Indeed, the very air itself was malevolent. The sulfur smell ebbed and flowed with the breeze, and carried in the gusts were whispered curses and muted threats. Joe ducked across the road amid car horns and obscenities, nearly tripping on a bag of rank trash left to rot against the gutter. A man turned and bumped into him. He swore a woman called his name.

You were never good enough.

He had to get out of here. He had to get out of Brimtown. He had to find his way back, somehow, if not to the jail then to...

You were never meant to stay in Heaven.

A car swerved onto the sidewalk in front of him, and Joe darted down an alleyway. Police sirens sounded in the distance, coming his way.

You were banished, Joseph Platt.

There was no time left.

Now everyone has played you for a fool.

No—there was all the time left. An eternity of it! Well then, he'd worry about David and his father later. Or maybe not at all. If they didn't want to listen to him, Joe wouldn't make them.

He'd go back to Maya, save up some money, then maybe buy his own place, as far away as possible. Maybe he couldn't leave Hell, but he could at least leave Brimtown and that awful lake of fire, he could at least go . . .

Brakes squealed as Joe stumbled out in front of a vehicle, inches away from being splattered across the road. The shock jolted him to his senses, and he looked up at the rusty black jeep.

It was missing both of its headlights.

"There you are," said Peter. "Get in."

Joe blinked several times before registering the familiar face leaning out the driver's side window.

No. This didn't make sense at all.

Joe stood frozen in his tracks, stupefied. He stammered, his brain searching for a coherent response. "You . . . what . . . but . . . how . . . I thought you said you couldn't drive."

The apostle raised an eyebrow. "You haven't seen me in three days, and that's the first thing that comes to your mind?"

Joe's senses, however, were catching up to the moment. Whatever small part remained of his rational mind voiced its objections. What were the chances of this random encounter? No—nothing was random anymore. After all he'd been through, Joe knew by now not to trust his eyes. Shaking off the shock, Joe drew his sword and took a defensive stance.

"How do I know you're not a demon?"

Peter sighed. "Regrettably, Joe, I can't explain everything while holding up traffic."

True, the car horns blared as they came up behind the stopped jeep, all before swerving around it on the sidewalk. Patience was not a strong suit in Brimtown. Still, Joe was not about to be intimidated.

"Prove it," he insisted. "Prove you're really him."

"We arrived here together in search of your brother."

"Obviously."

"His name is David. We came for his rescue."

"Duh." This Peter-look-alike would have to do better than that. But now time was of the essence: Joe swore as he heard a siren nearby. Whoever was coming for him would be here soon.

Peter continued. "Jesus sent us on this mission, but it was you who made the request. You care for your brother deeply, Joe, and for this reason I am with you."

"So what?" Joe snapped. "Even the demons know that, don't they?" He was frantic now, his head turning in every direction while his feet remained planted with indecision.

Peter, though, calm as ever, leaned further out the window and locked eyes with his companion.

"I taught you to use that sword in the armory under the waterfall. I have seen you lift it in battle to slay the very demons of which you speak. I know well both your courage and faith. Doubt me if you must for leaving your side, but do not doubt the Holy Spirit inside you, whom you have received from God. Test your heart and see. Not all is lost, Joe. Indeed, there is still much to be found."

A police car whipped around the corner, lights flashing and siren still blaring. Joe quit his hesitation and climbed into the jeep's passenger seat, shutting the door just as the patrol car swerved around them on the sidewalk. He slouched low to be sure, but the cops didn't even slow down. But they must have seen him. Any second now, they'd turn around.

Joe held his breath, as if even that might give him away.

The seconds passed. The siren grew fainter.

He was safe.

Joe carefully sat up. He must have seemed like a madman just now.

Peter shifted the jeep into gear and drove off.

"How the heck did you find me?" Joe blurted.

"After our battle on the night of the first attack, I searched for you, but you were already gone. I realized that we'd been separated, but I trusted you'd find a way to Brimtown. Jesus himself had said that would be easy. I came ahead in the jeep but didn't see you, so I retreated to a quiet space and prayed for direction. This morning I felt led to drive the surrounding streets. I saw you exit the café and then take off in a hurry, and I pursued you from there."

"So," —Joe couldn't hide his skepticism— "all you had to do was pray?"

Peter raised an eyebrow. "Haven't you done the same?"

Joe recalled his own unanswered words to Jesus the night before, crouched shivering on the ground. Had Jesus heard him then? Did that possibly have some connection to . . .

No, he thought. *I prayed for help, and instead I found the Rook.*

"Well, you sure took long enough to find me," Joe snapped.

181

The apostle nodded gravely. "Don't think I was indifferent. From the moment we were separated, you and our mission have been foremost on my mind."

Joe instantly hated the way he said *our* mission. Had Peter been at the bridge with David? Had it been Peter's father who'd taken the moment away? Of course not. In fact, after all their time here, Peter hardly looked worse for the wear. If anything, he appeared to be quite rested. His gray beard was thick and clean, and his clothes were unsoiled. Joe, on the other hand, had literally been through Hell. Patchy stubble covered his face, his hair was greasy and matted, his clothes were dirty and burned. Every inch of his body smelled of sweat, ash, and sulfur.

They drove on in silence for several minutes, Peter navigating the streets with confidence. Joe had no idea where they were going but honestly didn't care. He took solace just knowing it was uphill, away from the lake, away from the Bridge to Nowhere.

After about fifteen minutes, the jeep stopped at an outdoor bazaar, one that Joe recognized from his drive into the city. Covered stalls with various assortments of clothing and jewelry were packed tightly together, the paths between them narrow and crooked, as if the market were a scaled-down model of Brimtown itself. The small parking lot was full, but Peter created his own space at the end of a row and shut off the engine.

"What are we doing?" Joe asked.

"As it turns out, these shoes are about a half-size too small. They've been constricting my feet since we arrived. Not that I would've known when I picked them out. Back in my day, we all wore sandals."

Joe stared in disbelief. "You can't be serious."

"Also, if you haven't noticed, the back of your shirt is a little singed, right at the bottom there. I mean no offense, but perhaps you could join me and purchase another."

"You want to go shopping? Right now?"

"Leave your shield in the car. I don't foresee any danger here, and it's best not to draw the attention. Besides, you'll need to carry the bags." Without another word, Peter took out his pouch of coins and exited the vehicle.

"Wait," Joe called, following after him. "What is going on with you?"

But the apostle ignored him and strode into the marketplace.

The bazaar was busy without being crowded, a mixture of men and women bouncing impatiently from stall to stall or lingering in indecision. All manners of shirts, dresses, trousers, hats, sunglasses, scarves, and belt buckles lined the aisle, with designs about as drab and lifeless as the shoppers perusing them. Like at the café that morning, Joe quickly observed that each customer was alone—in fact, he and Peter stood out as the only pair walking together. Beyond this, though, there was little to catch his attention. Unlike how Joe might imagine a thriving marketplace, with eager vendors hawking their wares at full volume and half price, most of the sellers here appeared downright uninterested. They took little action to solicit a sale, responding only when a customer approached the booth of her own initiative, and even then speaking only when necessary to finalize the transaction. The result was a low, murmuring backdrop occasionally punctuated by car horns and shouts from the street, although these interruptions became less and less audible as Joe and Peter wound their way deeper into the market.

"Here we are," Peter said at last, approaching a rack of athletic shoes. "I do find these comfortable, although I need the right size . . . here it is. Do you prefer the gray or the black?" Peter held up one of each for Joe's consideration.

Perhaps, Joe supposed, *this is meant to be therapeutic*. Use everyday things to take his mind off the disappointment and pain. His only brother had rejected Heaven and was suddenly allied to the father who'd abandoned them. On top of that, Joe was wanted by the

Brimtown police, and, as far as he knew, he and Peter had no way out of Hell unless Jesus himself came down to get them—that is, assuming he could forgive their colossal failure to complete the mission. Well, no problem. Joe could forget about all of that and enjoy a shopping spree with St. Peter to buy a new pair of Nikes. Sure.

But then it hit him. He hadn't actually told Peter about what had happened at the bridge, had he? How would Peter know if Joe hadn't told him?

Now everyone has played you for a fool. The voice echoed in his head.

"I'll take the black ones then," Peter said, counting out the coins while the bored shopkeeper stuffed the shoes into a box. "And do the socks come with it, or what's your price for two? Excellent . . . yes, those will do nicely. Thank you, sir."

"You already know, don't you?"

Peter looked at Joe and regarded him for a moment. "Know what?"

"You know exactly what I mean," Joe snapped. "Cut the crap." Joe silently cursed the fact he'd left his weapons in the car. Was suggesting that just another part of Peter's game? Yet even if this were all a giant pretense, it was Peter's turn to explain.

"I want to know right now what this is really about."

The apostle's jovial expression gradually faded to concern. He took the shopping bag and stepped away from the vendor, speaking in a low voice so that only Joe could hear.

"You're asking about David," Peter said. "Words aside, your whole being tells the story. I'm truly sorry, Joe."

"You're sorry?" Joe exclaimed. "Sorry for what? Sorry that you had to leave your mountaintop to come down here with me? Sorry that you had to slum it up in Brimtown instead of lounging back in Heaven? You've been two-faced this entire time, acting like you care about David when really you couldn't care less. This is all just a game to you, isn't it?"

"Joe, you misunderstand—"

"Do I?" Joe raised his voice, drawing the attention of some nearby shoppers. "Because I think I understand just fine. This whole time you've been talking at me and trying to teach me some kind of moral about God and Heaven and who knows what else, and all that just led up to leaving me alone with David and my father, and all for what? Is this just another one of your tests, like back in the armory? But what's the lesson now, Peter? Was I wrong for wanting this? Am I supposed to repent of trying to rescue my only brother?"

Peter gripped his shoulder to steady him, for Joe was trembling now. "Joe, if you'll allow me to explain—"

"Explain what?" Joe cried. "How you've been in on it since the very beginning? How you're all about the narrow road to life for some people but not for others? How you never cared about David in the first place? How you took part in leaving me down here when all I ever wanted was to rescue my brother? I assume that's why Jesus called you, his saint, his right-hand man, to make sure it all went off without a hitch. You know, I was so freaking amazed when I first met you. The real St. Peter. My bodyguard, my mentor. Or should I say, the man who abandons me in the middle of the night and leaves me alone to suffer?"

"Hear yourself, Joe. The demons have poisoned your mind."

Joe flung his arms out and stepped back, bumping into a rack of shoes, absolutely livid. "I'm thinking clearly for the first time since coming to this godforsaken place," he shouted. "You better start telling me everything, or I swear to you, I am walking away from all of this. I don't care where I go, as long as it's not here, as long as it's not with you. The games stop now, Peter. Tell me everything, or I swear to you, I'm gone."

A small audience had surrounded them now—even the shoe salesman was watching Joe's outburst with interest. Joe couldn't care less who saw him at this point, but Peter appeared to be bothered by it. He again reached for Joe's arm, but this time didn't touch him. He merely offered a hand.

"Walk with me, Joe. I assure you, the justice you seek will not be found on your own."

To be honest, Joe had expected more of an argument. He'd flung some serious accusations, but from what he could tell, Peter had taken no offense. Joe might as well have been screaming at a wall. Yet the apostle was neither stubborn nor defensive, nor did he ignore the charges. Instead, his posture was open and receptive, pacifying Joe with a soft glint in his eyes that could only be called compassion.

"Did you know?" Joe asked again, quieter this time. "Did you know about David? My father? All of this?"

Peter sighed. "You wish for me to confirm or deny the suspicions you hold, yet neither action will bring you peace. Your prejudice rules you. In this moment, you cannot see me clearly."

"Yeah?" Joe scoffed. "Try me."

Peter appeared to consider this before saying, "Walk with me, and I shall tell you a story."

The apostle turned and went ahead, and Joe at once saw he had a choice. His weapons were in the jeep—he could go back and leave Peter all alone for a change. Or . . .

Doubt me if you must, Peter had said, *but do not doubt the Holy Spirit inside you.*

This was the armory in Heaven all over again; this was Joe against the demons in the middle of the night. To go back was to find his own way. To go forward was to follow.

Not all is lost, Joe. Indeed, there is still much to be found.

Joe jogged to catch up, cautiously, as they pushed past the onlookers and continued ambling through the market.

"You know," Peter began, "I relate to your anger. Especially in my earlier years, I was quick to rage, blaming everyone around me for my circumstances. Anger itself is not the problem. True anger leads to justice, so long as we direct it at the proper cause."

A backhanded consolation if Joe had ever heard one.

"Is that your story?" he asked with more than a hint of sarcasm.

Peter laughed. "No, more a word to the wise."

"You sure have plenty of those."

"I have a good teacher."

Something about the way he said it made Joe clue in. "You mean Jesus."

Peter nodded. "I was younger than you when we first met. From the moment I first encountered Jesus by the Sea of Galilee, I was wholly devoted to him. I had never met a rabbi with his wit or knowledge, nor had I ever met anyone who so clearly challenged me to live for more than myself. I eventually accepted that he was the Messiah, the one the prophets had told of, who would come to change to the world. My personal ally and the hero who would save our people were one and the same. In my pride, I thought no one was closer to him than I was. Then, the night before he died, in front of all his other disciples, Jesus boldly predicted I'd deny him three times. Can you imagine? I'd never been so hurt as I was in that moment. After all we had been through together for years, my closest friend in the world thought I'd so readily disown him. I tell you, I would have died for him, and there, he questioned my love in front of everyone."

"But," Joe replied, "you did deny him, didn't you? Everyone knows that story."

Peter nodded solemnly.

"So God has used it. My sin stands as a reminder for all. But my point is this. I don't think Jesus said those words as a curse upon me. It wasn't that he meant for or caused me to renounce him in those final hours, as if he were spiteful after all our time together. No, I think because he knew me well, he knew that in the panic of that night, I would first protect myself. It's a complicated thing, but I believe he only wanted me to see what he already could, perhaps in the way a parent can guess a child's actions well before that child knows himself. He was right, of course. Once my eyes were opened, I was overcome by weeping and remorse. Shame covered me like a heavy blanket. And yet the Lord did not abandon me, even after his own death. After Jesus had resurrected, he appeared to me. He came to offer his forgiveness and to reinstate what I'd thought was surely lost."

"So are you saying he planned it all along?"

"I don't doubt he knew, but the choice was always mine. I was as responsible for my action as I was for my repentance. So, perhaps, it is with you, Joe. Jesus knew the choice you'd find in Brimtown, but now the choice is yours to make."

Now they were getting to the point. Joe's pulse quickened.

"What choice? David didn't give me much of a choice yesterday."

"I'm speaking not of David, Joe, but of you."

Joe, however, shook his head. "That's where you're wrong, Peter. I tried already, and it didn't go too well."

And from there Joe recounted the events at the bridge, from finding David, and the surprise of his excitement for his job, and the greater surprise of seeing his father, and the fight that followed. "And then, I . . . lost the salvation key. I should have told you that a lot sooner. I'm so sorry. I figured you'd know another way back. I mean, there has to be, right?"

Peter raised an eyebrow. "Was not the very purpose of this mission to give the key away? You gave it to David. Wasn't it then his to keep, and not yours?"

"I'm not sure what you're getting at."

"Salvation," Peter explained, "is not an object to be held, nor can it be so easily lost."

"But . . . Jesus said! He said we'd need the key to unlock the way back to Heaven."

"He said the locks are turned from the inside, and yet the doors could be opened at any moment. Do you suppose you're the only one to whom he gave a key?"

"You mean you got one too?"

"I mean everyone."

They reached an intersection, and the apostle turned down a row of jewelry vendors.

"I don't think I've asked you, Joe," Peter said, "but why is it so important for you to save your brother?"

A day ago, Joe would have said what he told Maya—David had always needed rescuing, and Joe had always been his brother. But, strangely, with his body aching and his hands empty and the thought of his shield tucked safely in the jeep, another answer came to mind.

"There's a part of me that thinks I deserve it, you know? To be in Heaven. But everything I've done down here has been a complete disaster, and the things that have gone right are the ones I can't take credit for. And I remember when those angels all looked me, back at the gate to the city, I thought for sure they'd say no. I thought maybe I was just scared or doubting myself, but really it was the opposite. That was the first time in a long time—maybe ever—that I'd really been honest with myself. My instincts were right. I didn't deserve to be there. But Jesus took me anyway. And this was such a stupid idea to think I could come here and fix anything, but Jesus said yes anyway. Even though he already knew. About my dad, about David, about all of it. I thought coming here was just about saving David, but it's bigger than that. I see that now."

Peter nodded. "Then our work here is not yet finished. In all things, God works for the good of those who love him."

As they wandered, one of the jewelry displays caught Joe's attention, and he stopped to examine it. The female shopkeeper glanced up from her magazine without saying hello and soon lost interest as Joe browsed the rack of diamond pendants. Or, more accurately, the faux-diamond pendants—Joe was no expert, but even he could see they were imitations. He held one of the gold chains in his fingers, feeling its texture. He thought of Maya—how could he not? He'd been preoccupied with his conversation with Peter and thinking about David, but she'd never fully left his mind. As the necklace reminded Joe of her story outside the Rook's warehouse, he suddenly understood why losing that diamond had mattered so much to Maya. Although she'd certainly been coerced, ultimately her prized possession was neither taken nor damaged nor forgotten nor misplaced.

The hardest way to lose something, Joe thought, *is to choose to give it up.*

Peter joined him at the counter and peered at the selection of rings inside a glass case.

"An uninspired collection, I must say." He glanced over at Joe. "Am I correct that you were never married?"

Joe blushed at the unexpected question and quickly dropped the necklace, as if to hide the evidence of his thoughts. "Um, yes. You are correct."

"Did you know that I was?"

Joe had never thought to ask. Yet it must have been so. Here was the strong and mighty apostle, speaking gently with affection.

"I was the luckiest fisherman in Galilee," Peter said with a wink. "She was a lovely woman, a captivating beauty, full of godly character. All of Capernaum called her Amana because she possessed such great faith. She gave all her concerns to the Lord and trusted him with her life. She reasoned with me beyond my impulses and encouraged me in my deepest disappointments, staying with me even as I journeyed out for the sake of the gospel."

"She sounds great," was all Joe could think to say.

"I know of the custom in your time," Peter continued. "A marriage is arranged simply by extending a ring and bending a knee. When I lived, it was not so easy. As soon as I was ready and of age, my father set about to find a bride for me. Her father also entered into the negotiation, and still then we were required to agree upon a *ketubah*, a covenant outlining my obligations and the terms of the marriage. Then a long betrothal followed, in which we were promised but set apart. I worked tirelessly and awaited my father's final approval. And only when I had gathered the full bride price and prepared a home could I go to her to consummate the marriage and hold a feast to celebrate."

"Wow. So the whole thing was planned out for you, then?"

"You misunderstand. The marriage negotiations were my want and not my necessity, for truly no other woman had so caught my eye. The arrangement, however, required her approval as well as mine. The bride had to consent, you see, lest the contract be null and void. It was not enough that my father and I had chosen her. She also had to choose me."

Joe nodded. "That makes sense, right? She should have a choice, shouldn't she?"

"Ah, yes," Peter replied, "but you can imagine a young man's agony. How many good and strong men have known a woman's scorn? Could I even count high enough to number my own faults and imperfections? Weren't there others who came from better families with higher standing or who could carry more weight on their shoulders or who could better sing and play the lyre? Yet I dared to think she would desire me at all. No, it was the riskiest thing imaginable to make an offer of any kind, for what was an offer other than a proposal to be refused? How much easier would it have been for us to simply wed on my command, regardless of her hesitations, intentions, or concerns? Or if that were beyond me, then surely my father could have issued such a decree, powerful as he was. But any wise man sees the folly. Love is a gift and not a shackle. As it is given, so it must also be received."

Joe considered this. "Well, it was, wasn't it? Your wife loved you back."

Peter nodded. "I have shared this for your benefit—so now hear the lesson. In the same way, it goes with God. The contract has been arranged, and the bride price has been paid. Why else if not for love did Jesus go to the cross? But there remains a gift to be accepted. The world spins its lies and offers false hopes and fleeting glories, but the truth is as simple as this—the Lord of Heaven has made his proposal."

A dramatic pause. "And now?" Joe asked.

"Now he waits for his beloved to say yes."

Joe took it all in, carefully, sensing all the while that some core element was shifting inside of him. It was an epiphany less of understanding and more of mystery. To his surprise, he found that even to describe it was an act of romance. His heart opened as a flower to the sun.

"So what you're saying, then, is that this great, epic adventure with swords and shields and demon fires was all along just...a love story?"

Peter smiled. "Who says a love story can't be adventurous?"

Joe idly fingered the necklace, recounting the events since he'd left the café that morning, feeling lost and utterly hopeless. It'd been hours, but the gray sky above them was far from dark. They still had time.

"I have an idea," Joe said, "but it's a little risky."

Peter raised an eyebrow. "And what's that?"

"First," Joe replied, "we're going to need some help."

SIXTEEN
SECOND CHANCES

AS THEY APPROACHED the house, Brody was outside keeping watch. Like a one-man welcoming party, he held his sentry position without flinching while the jeep coasted along the dusty road. The same military man as ever, he stood with his shotgun slung over his back and binoculars in his hands, the same ones that Joe had borrowed to scan the desert on the first morning after the attack. Had it really been only two days?

The vehicle came to a stop, and Joe was the first to hop out.

"Long time, no see," he offered.

Brody turned his head to the side and spat. "You got some nerve coming back here."

Joe swallowed hard. Not a great start, and he knew better than to think the tough-guy bit was just an act.

"Yeah. Good to see you too." Nodding toward the driver's side, he added, "This is Peter. He's the one I told you guys about."

No acknowledgment, no handshake—Brody's face was as blank as the desert around them. The dark circles under his eyes spoke of a restless night, but Joe sensed something beyond the fatigue. Small impulses betrayed the soldier's discipline—a slight tremble of the lip, a quick flare of the nostrils. This was a bomb set to go off at any moment.

Best get straight to the point, Joe thought.

"Is Maya here?"

Brody stepped forward, blocking his way.

"You're lucky she is. Otherwise I might've gunned you down on sight. But hey," —he smirked —"boss's orders."

"Right. Hey, Brody, it seems like there's some tension here, and I just—"

Joe spun hard before he even realized he'd been punched. Uppercut, straight to the jaw. A small miracle his teeth didn't spray across the ground. He stumbled back and nearly fell over, instinctively lifting his hand to feel the throbbing bone beneath the raw and stinging flesh. His head was dizzy. He tasted blood.

"You know," —Brody cracked his knuckles as if to say the first one was just a warm-up—"I tried to tell Maya about you. Something about it all seemed a little too convenient. Our great savior, coming to us in the middle of the night. The man with a magical key. That's not how the world works though, is it? You know, we've run into a good number of losers and outcasts over the past couple years, but none of them even came close to screwing us like you did."

Joe spat on the ground and tried to recover his wits. "What are you talking about?"

"The demons," Brody snapped. "That was you."

"What, at the warehouse? That was an ambush. They surprised all of us."

"Here's the thing, though. Not all of us were supposed to have a demon sword. For all I know, you attracted them in the first place, just like I thought you might. Maya should've never taken me off the job. If I'd been in there sooner, we might've salvaged something out of that mess. Maybe we'd have kept a bigger haul. Maybe Charlie would still be able to walk." Brody stepped to the side, like a predator circling before the kill.

"Look, you can't possibly think I'm responsible for—"

Too late—Brody dove in for the takedown, grabbing Joe's leg and ripping it from under him to throw him to the dirt. It was a total mismatch, and they both knew it, like a schoolyard bully and his helpless victim. If Brody had felt like it, Joe would be lights out already.

From his position on the ground, Joe groaned and looked to Peter. "Are you going to help or just stand there?"

The apostle watched with interest but not concern, despite Joe nearly losing his jawbone a second ago. He could have easily jumped Brody from behind—and was strong enough to do it—but he stayed put.

"I will not repay insult with insult, and neither must you. On the contrary, give a blessing. This is yours to resolve, Joe. See the conflict for what it is."

Unbelievable. Joe muttered a curse. Of all times for a lesson.

Brody, for his part, ignored Peter completely. "So when Maya said you might still be coming back," he continued, "you have to understand my surprise."

Joe slowly got to his feet. "I didn't come here to fight you, Brody."

"Well then, consider it a bonus."

Brody lurched forward again, but this time Joe saw it coming. His shield was still in the jeep, but he was familiar enough with the motions. He raised his left arm and blocked the hit, feeling the sting of bone against bone. The impact shook him, but he maintained his footing. Brody countered with his free arm, but Joe stepped back, surprising both of them with his agility and leaving his attacker off balance. Joe swung his leg to seize the advantage, this time knocking Brody for the takedown. The soldier fell forward onto his knee but recovered into a roll, springing back to his feet and turning just as Joe drew the sword from his waist, leveling its point at Brody's sweat-covered face. One lurch forward and the tip would slice his neck.

At the end of the blade, Brody flashed a mocking smile. "I dare you."

Give a blessing, Peter had said. Now Joe understood.

"We're on the same team, Brody," Joe replied, voice as level as his sword.

"Yeah, and what team is that?"

"Against the demons. Against the Rook. Look," —Joe lowered his weapon, slowly—"I'm truly sorry for what happened yesterday, and I'm sorry for leaving you guys like that. It was no way to thank you after how you helped me. And if you're mad enough to throw me to the ground, that makes sense. You have every right to be. I can't say I didn't play some part in what happened at the warehouse, and so if you're angry, I get why you'd want to take it out on me. But I'm not the enemy, Brody. You're obviously strong and disciplined, and you're good at what you do. I see your loyalty to this team, and I know you care about protecting them and doing what's right. So maybe I broke your trust back in Brimtown, or maybe I never had it to begin with. But right now, we're in a battle that's bigger than either one of us, and I wouldn't be here if I didn't need your help."

For the first time, Brody's hard exterior showed a crack. His shoulders relaxed just slightly, and his arms dropped to his sides.

"Nice speech," he grunted.

"I might have practiced in the car."

Brody almost smiled. "You're tougher than I remember, Joe." He stole a glance at Peter, too, acknowledging the apostle's presence for the first time. "What happened while you were gone?"

"Let's just say I saw things from a different perspective."

"Yeah," Brody said. "Join the club."

Joe opened his mouth to ask what that meant, but a noise from the front of the house caught his attention. He turned and looked up just as the screen door swung open, and Maya stepped out. She had a blanket wrapped over her shoulders and, like Brody, looked as if she'd been up all night. Her green eyes met Joe's stare impassively, without a single ounce of surprise or elation: On the drive over, Joe had imagined just about every scenario of their reunion, from her startled disbelief and relieved embrace to an angry outburst that he'd dared to leave in the first place. But Maya's sad, almost indifferent reaction to his return caught him off guard. Did she just now notice he'd arrived, or had she been watching the whole time?

"Come in," she said flatly.

Every cell in Joe's body tensed at once.

The first shock was the obvious one. Since he'd last been there, the living room had become a makeshift hospital. The blinds were down and the sofa bed pulled out. The end table supported a heap of discarded cold packs, painkillers, and various ointments and creams, each tube curled tight to show it'd been squeezed to the limit. There was only one patient.

Charlie.

Seeing him alive was a shock all on its own. And he was *alive*, or conscious, or aware, or whatever the heck a person was whose living soul hadn't completely perished into the fathomless void of Hell. Joe could see this as clearly as he had seen life on Earth.

The second shock, however, was Charlie's physical condition. Joe had last seen him sprinting for his life in the warehouse inferno, and now Charlie was bedridden with thick bandages covering every piece of skin, save for his eyes and mouth. Charlie's whole body was wrapped with whatever they could find—a few gauze dressings as well as towels, shirts, and even strips of a bed sheet, like a low-budget mummy costume, although with all the gravity and alarm of a victim in the ICU.

"Joe's here," Maya announced.

Charlie made an effort to lift an arm, either to wave hello or flick him off. Joe couldn't quite tell with the bandages in the way, but he had a decent guess.

Joe shifted uncomfortably. Was this really his doing? No. It'd been a horrible, tragic accident. Not even an accident—they'd been deliberately attacked! But it hardly seemed that way now. It seemed like everyone blamed him. Joe struggled to keep eye contact. His stomach hadn't felt so tight since David . . .

No. Eyes shut, and a sudden image: The lake of fire swirled in a tempest.

Stay focused, he thought. *Remember why you're here.*

"Charlie," Joe stammered at last, "I . . . I'm so sorry. Is there anything I can do?"

Maya answered for him. "Demon-fire burns are difficult to treat. We got him home and did what we could—Ethel and I have been sleeping in shifts so someone's always down here. But we don't really have the proper supplies for something on this scale. I know of a few doctors in Brimtown who might have a solution, but talking to them could be costly."

Joe perked up. "What do you need? We have plenty of money. If there's some way to help, I'd be glad to pay for it. It's the least I could do." How ironic would it be to heal Charlie's burns from the Rook's own coffers? Perfect. Joe was already reaching for the coins.

Maya, however, glared in annoyance. "That's not what I meant. The Rook knew we were coming last time, and anyone I talk to could be working for him. It's too risky to go back while he knows we're here. I can't trust anyone, and I'm not sure we can survive another trap."

Meanwhile, Peter, who'd been observing in the background since entering the house, finally stepped forward.

"May I have a word with him?"

Maya raised an inquisitive eyebrow, and Joe suddenly remembered his manners.

"Right. Maya, this is Peter. Peter, Maya. You've both heard about each other."

"He needs to rest," Maya said, referring to Charlie.

"And he will," the apostle replied, "but perhaps not as you imagine." Peter approached and knelt beside the bed. He unhooked

198

his sword and laid it on the floor before rolling up the sleeves of his sweater and putting both hands over Charlie.

"I see a great willpower in your spirit. You fight, believing that you can be healed, and I believe the same."

Joe glanced at Maya to judge her reaction, but she remained inscrutable. At least for now.

Peter continued, "Demon fire sears not the flesh, but the spirit. Your essence is burned by lies and deceit. For that, I'm afraid, there is no balm in Brimtown. No gold I have can buy a cure, for the cure does not exist in a vial or jar. But I have something else. The God of Abraham, Isaac, and Jacob has glorified his servant and raised him from the dead so that by his name you may be strong. May I place my hands on you?" To Joe's surprise, Charlie gave a faint nod.

Peter pulled back a bandage on Charlie's arm, revealing black and purple skin, slimy with pus and ooze. Joe looked away, squeamish.

"Hey," Maya barked. "Don't unwrap that."

"Trust me," Peter replied, calm and collected as ever, "these wounds must be brought into the light in order to heal—not by my own power, but by the power of Christ within me." He continued removing the bandage strips, running his fingers along the charred and ugly flesh.

"Stop!" Maya yelled. "What are you doing?"

She stepped forward to pull Peter away, but halted as Charlie made a noise. In a pain-filled yet perfectly audible moan, he said, "It's okay." Joe was shocked as anyone. Either Charlie was so desperate for a cure that he was willing to try anything, or he was sincerely interested in the apostle's words, but either way his message was clear. He wanted Peter to stay.

Dumbfounded, and perhaps a little embarrassed, Maya nodded and reluctantly motioned for Peter to proceed. She looked on for a few minutes, tapping her foot with either nerves or annoyance, until finally she couldn't take it anymore. Without a word, she retreated to the kitchen. Joe hesitated, then followed.

"Is everything okay?" he asked. A stupid question, he knew.

Maya paced restlessly, eventually deciding to fill a kettle and set it to boil for tea.

"I told you already, I'm really not a religious type, that's all."

"Yeah, right. Actually, I meant to apologize for that. The last time we talked, I might've gotten a little carried away. I'm sorry if I upset you."

She waved her hand dismissively. "It's fine. You and your friend can believe whatever. I'm not here to judge. But this healing prayer thing he's got going on in there, that's just . . ."

Joe waited, but the sentence never finished.

"That's just what?"

Maya leaned back against the counter. "I just don't think you should give a person false hope, that's all." She sighed, then looked at Joe. "Do you need some ice, by the way? I saw you and Brody get into it out front. He's got some anger issues from time to time—I wouldn't take it personally. Anyway, I've got some in the freezer still that was supposed to be for Charlie."

Joe felt his jaw, wondering if it was swollen already. Maya removed the ice pack and wrapped it in a towel before handing it over.

"Thanks."

"No problem."

They stood in awkward silence, staring at different points in the room. The air felt dry and stiff. Apparently people never opened their windows in Hell. Joe looked around for the fan that had been there the last time he was in the kitchen, but someone had moved it. Maybe to the living room for Charlie—that would make sense.

"So," Maya began, "how'd it go finding your brother?"

Joe straightened up, instantly on alert. How did she know about David? Had she followed him? Was she spying on him the whole time? The Rook's sinister voice came like a whisper in his ear, full of insinuations.

Maya blinked. "You told me about him, remember? At the warehouse?"

Oh. Of course. Joe blushed. She must have seen the question on his face.

"Yeah, I remember."

"So?" She crossed her arms and waited. Joe readjusted the icepack.

"Well, I found him. But it was, uh, a little different than I expected. We didn't get a chance to leave right away, but I'm hoping to go back and do that soon."

Maya raised an eyebrow. "You mean leave for Heaven?"

"Yes."

She gave a knowing smile, like a parent to a child. Joe caught on but wasn't fazed: He still had the trump card.

"Well," Maya said, "I'm glad you're back with us."

To think, twenty minutes ago Joe had longed to hear those words. The heart could be such a fickle beast.

Now, he decided, *is as good a time as any.*

"Actually, Maya, I'm not back just to join the crew. I need your help."

"Oh?"

"I met the Rook," Joe said. "In person. Last night."

Maya's eyes widened. So much for the conspiracy—clearly, this was news to her.

"He found me," Joe continued, and he recounted their conversation with as much detail as he could recall. "So I can see how he tricked you. And why you hate him so much."

"You're a fool for accepting his gifts. Now you're in debt to him too."

Joe, however, shook his head. "I'm not afraid of him, Maya. Maybe I was when everything was still unknown, you know, before I found David or lost the salvation key—yeah, I didn't tell you about that yet—but now that I've been at the bottom and know what I'm up against, I'm not afraid of it. And with Peter back, and you, I'm not alone."

She considered him for a long moment. "So what are you going to do?"

"Go back to Brimtown. I need to find David again, and then this time we *are* going home. But it's not just about David anymore. I mean, it's David, you, Charlie, all those people at the bridge, even my father—no one should have to suffer like this, living in constant fear of the demons and being tricked and cheated and lied to. I thought I came here just for David, but now I want to take everyone out. All of Brimtown if they'll come. I mean, can you imagine? No more demons, no more hopelessness, no more people feeling alone. We have to expose the Rook for who he is and end all of this. And with God's help, it's possible, Maya. I know it is."

"Quite the plan," she remarked. "Save the whole world at once, huh?"

"Not by myself. We're gonna need a team to pull this off, to round everyone up, because he's got people on his side too that we'll have to—"

"Joe," she interrupted.

"I mean, now's the chance! We can do it!"

Maya scoffed. "You don't get it, do you? Do you really think that you're the only one who's plotted to stop the evil in this place? The demons at the warehouse, the Rook at the café? That's the tip of the iceberg. I've been to more places than I can remember, trying to do good, and all the treasures I've given back to people haven't mattered one bit. Nothing changes, Joe. Nothing ever changes. You have no idea what powers you're up against. You're naive at best and delusional at worst. The rulers of Hell can do things you can't even imagine."

202

"Their power is nothing compared to God's."

"They control the land and everything in it."

"God made the land and set his people free."

"Ugh," Maya groaned in exasperation. "There is no God, Joe! The sooner you figure that out, the better off you'll be. This is it, okay? This is the end of all things, right here. And we can fight for as long as we're able and resist as much as we want, but then someday it all turns to dust. Religion is words and feelings, Joe, but reality is the dirt on your shoes and the burns on Charlie's skin. And the sooner you cope with that, the better chance you'll have at maintaining some kind of sanity. They will take your mind if you let them, all before you even realize it."

The teapot sounded and rattled. Maya shut off the heat and grabbed a mug from the cupboard, angrily slamming the cabinet door.

"What proof could I give you?" Joe asked quietly.

"None that exists."

Maya dunked the tea bag and took the cup in both hands. She looked down for a long moment, as if trying to decide what to say next. Joe stood silently and prayed.

Let her see, Lord Jesus. Let her see that you're real.

"I'm going upstairs," Maya said. "I'll send Ethel down to keep you company." She took her mug and brushed past Joe toward the entryway, her green eyes tired and cross.

But she never left the room. Instead, her path was blocked.

There in the doorframe stood Charlie, his chest bare and a towel around his waist. Every bandage had been removed, revealing his skin completely healed. Not a scratch. As if he'd just exited a pool of bathwater, every inch of his body was glistening and clean. Every scar and mark had vanished. Every scorch and burn had been made new. Not one singe remained upon his body.

"Maya," Charlie said. "How sweet. Did you make that tea for me?"

The mug fell from her hands and shattered on the floor.

SEVENTEEN
THE SWORD OF THE SPIRIT

THEY SET OUT THE following morning. After sharing dinner together and celebrating the miraculous healing the night before, the team had quickly agreed to Joe's mission. Charlie declared he'd never fear a demon again, and Ethel tossed her cigarettes into the garbage, claiming that all the hope and excitement had squashed her cravings, perhaps for good. Even Brody shared a laugh. They'd all seen firsthand what damage the demons could do and how fear of them ruled the land, but for the first time ever, they felt convinced they actually could do something about it. They were going to strike at evil itself.

Only Maya had appeared to hold any reservations, but once Joe explained the details of his plan and she made a call to one of her contacts, she slowly came around. Joe interpreted her unusually quiet demeanor to be lingering shock from seeing Charlie cured. After denying the existence of God her whole life, she'd just seen real, undeniable evidence for the power of the Holy Spirit. It'd be a lot to take in for anyone. Joe had no room for *I told you so*; he felt only elation that she was finally coming around to see the truth. Maybe she'd come with them to Heaven after all.

Maybe they all will, he hoped. Maya, Charlie, Ethel, Brody, David . . . perhaps even his father. It was a tall order, but who could stop the power of God?

"Alright," Joe said as the van rolled over a bump on its way into Brimtown, bouncing its occupants, "let me review a few things." Ethel drove with lead in her boots, and Brody rode shotgun while the other four sat in the back.

"There are essentially two parts to the mission. Part one, we rescue my brother. He's not exactly happy with me right now, and I'll owe him a big apology when we see him. But we'll need him to come with us. I'll have Peter with me, so hopefully he'll be able to win David over if he has any lingering doubts."

"The word of God does not return to him empty," Peter added, "but will achieve the purpose for which he sent it."

Joe nodded, then continued. "I thought we'd have to do a prison break, but instead we got lucky. They're being tried today. Maya made a call last night to an old associate and confirmed that both David and my father are appearing at the courthouse near City Hall. The charges are trumped-up and frankly ridiculous, but we're expecting a guilty verdict nonetheless. Our best chance to extract them is before they're carted back to jail.

"Maya will be inside checking the court schedule. Once she finds out what room they're in, she'll signal us in the lobby. Charlie, I need you to find the electrical room and cut the main power. There could be security, so you'll have Brody as backup."

"The brains and the brawn right there," Charlie remarked. "I think we'll be able to find a light switch."

"Peter and I will use the power outage as a diversion to grab David and my father." It was still hard for Joe to include that last part, but what was the alternative? Leaving him behind would be no better than what Bill Platt himself had done to Joe, and Joe intended to be better. Joe had been forgiven. Now it was his turn to forgive.

"Finally, the rendezvous point will be out here with Ethel. We all load into the back and drive over to the steps of City Hall. That's where we begin part two. I lost the salvation key on the day we were attacked, but, based on what Peter tells me, with a little faith, we should be able to open a way back to Heaven."

"If you confess with your mouth that Jesus is Lord and believe in your heart that God raised him from the dead, you will be saved," the apostle quoted.

"So what," Maya asked skeptically, "we all just hold hands and pray?"

Joe shrugged. "Actually, that's the gist of it. Us, David, my father, and anyone else who wants to join. That's the reason we're going to City Hall. I saw from the posters that there's a revival going on there today"—he left out the part about his impersonating Isaac Washington at the bridge because at this point, it hardly seemed relevant—"so if there are others in Brimtown who are interested in Heaven, they're likely to be there. It's the most strategic point to spread the message. We can't force anyone to join us, but the goal is to save as many as we can."

"Question," said Charlie. "I'm all for a ticket out of here, but what makes you think the demons will just sit back and watch while we make our little holy powwow? If they attacked during daylight at the warehouse, what's stopping them from pouncing today at City Hall?"

"It's a risk we're taking," Joe acknowledged. "And given our plan, I think it's safe to count on at least some demonic resistance. But now that we know what we're up against, I'm confident our weapons will hold. If any of them come near me, I'll be playing for keeps."

The van jumped a curb as Ethel took a hard right. They were in Brimtown proper now—minutes away from the downtown courthouse.

"One other thing," Maya added, her expression resolute. "I don't know what you're imagining that I do once we're inside, but I'm coming with you when you enter the courtroom."

Joe had already thought about it, and he knew he couldn't be too careful. He remembered all too well what happened to Charlie last time, and if worse came to worst, he and Peter couldn't fit David, his father, and Maya all under their shields.

He swallowed and made his reply. "I don't know, Maya. We can't be entirely sure what we're up against. If it's anything like the warehouse . . ."

She scowled with offense. "Don't you dare give me that it's-too-dangerous macho crap. I'm not some damsel in distress. You might have some special powers over the demons, but I remind you that this is still my crew you're working with. I can handle myself just fine, and I've robbed enough places to know how to find my way out in the dark. You might need help getting David and your father out of there, especially if the demons do show up. Going in blind is all the more reason to need me. There's no way I'm sitting this one out."

Joe glanced at Peter, but the apostle simply raised his eyebrows. His message was clear. *Your operation, your call to make.*

Charlie leaned over to whisper, "I've learned it's best not to argue. Honestly, I've known mules less stubborn."

Joe sighed. Against his instinct, he knew it made sense to bring her. Personal risks aside, it would help to have another set of eyes and ears. On the upside, he reasoned, she did battle the system for a living. It was hard to find someone more anti-Hell than Maya.

"Alright then," he agreed, "we'll go together."

"Good," she replied, her curt response not hiding her satisfaction. She turned to look out the window, avoiding Joe's gaze. He studied her for a moment, noting how her green eyes shone with expectation. There was some fulfillment there, some deep emotion stirring up in her soul. Joe had been looking for it last night but hadn't quite seen it. Now, on the streets of Brimtown, he finally caught a glimpse. If he hadn't known any better, he might even have called it hope.

We're coming for you, David, he thought. *We're coming for you soon.*

Traffic was worse than usual due to the revival—who knew Isaac Washington would draw such a crowd? While it might be good for their endgame of gathering converts, it certainly slowed the operation on the front end. Joe anxiously hoped they wouldn't miss the hearing. Ethel pulled up in front of the courthouse, and the rest of the crew hopped out. Ascending the steps with his head down and his shield tight against his side, Joe did his best to keep a low profile while still carrying his weapons. They passed lawyers toting files of loose papers and journalists with spiral-bound notepads, a few of whom stole a quick glance, but none who bothered to ask them questions.

Inside, the courthouse boasted lofty ceilings and neoclassical columns, accompanied by murmuring attorneys and footsteps echoing on the marble floor. The whole place had a faded grandeur of sorts, looking as if it had once been magnificent but now had lost its shine. The security officer at the front desk appeared more than a little suspicious of Joe and Peter's weaponry, but Maya allayed her worries with some smooth talking—and, Joe noticed, a fat handful of coins. Up a few more steps to the main concourse, and just like that, they were in.

Maya visited the clerk's office and returned with a sticky note. "Room 1616, second floor," she reported. "It looks like theirs is the first case up. Is Charlie in position?"

Joe nodded. "They came in right behind us." He glanced over his shoulder and gave a nearly imperceptible nod to his counterparts. Signal sent and received.

"Alright then," Maya said. "Let's do this."

They took the stairs then moved quickly down a windowless corridor. White tile, soft lighting, thick mahogany doors marking the entrances to each of the various courtrooms. Except for the occasional aide passing through, the hallway was empty. Joe found room 1616—a "court in session" sign hung from the door handles— and leaned in to listen. No luck. He couldn't hear a peep through the solid wood. Well, they'd know soon enough. Any minute now, the lights would go off and they'd charge inside, using the diversion to find David and make for the nearest exit. Joe tried to relax, but he had the anxious butterflies of a person about to jump off a high dive. Or maybe a cliff, overlooking a waterfall.

This is it, he thought. *Today we return to Heaven.*

Peter sat on a bench across the hall and prayed quietly. "Your kingdom come, your will be done . . ."

Maya paced, acting even more nervous than Joe felt.

"Are you ready for this?" he asked her.

She glanced over her shoulder down the hall. "I guess we'll see."

"Remember, get in, get out. We're saving the conversation part until we find a place to talk. Kind of like when you first found me." He smiled at the memory, but Maya looked away.

"Yeah, sounds good."

She must still be rattled from the warehouse, Joe decided. Who could blame her? After such a disastrous operation and the stinging reminder of the one who'd hurt her so much, it made sense why Maya wasn't thrilled to be back in action so soon. With any luck, though, this would be the last heist any of them would ever need to run.

Joe tapped his foot and counted to sixty. Then counted to sixty again.

C'mon, Charlie, he thought. *Let's get this show on the road.*

Finally, it happened.

The hallway went dark, and surprised cries sounded from downstairs. Now or never—Joe flung open the courtroom doors. He ran inside with his shield up and hand on his sword hilt, scanning the room for some sign of David. Maya followed right on his heels. They had to charge up front, grab their guys, get back to the hallway, and then . . .

He stopped. Something was wrong.

Something was very wrong.

Strips of emergency lights on the floor provided faint illumination, enough to tell that neither David nor his father was anywhere in the room. In fact, no one was. The courtroom stood completely empty.

"What in the world?" Joe spun around. "Maya! Are you sure you got the right room?"

But her back was to him as she pulled the doors shut, just as bright red flashes erupted in the hallway. Joe instantly recognized the demon fire.

She bolted the doors. "They're out there."

"That was fast," Joe said, drawing his sword. Then, realizing it, he asked, "Where's Peter?"

"We can't wait for him," Maya replied, her voice trembling with fear. "We have to keep going." Tremors rattled the door frame, and Joe could distinctly hear the apostle's booming invocations from the hallway, battling the forces of evil. Alone.

"Open the door!" Joe cried. "We have to help him."

"No. We have a mission."

"Maya, look around you. There's no one here!"

"Just look harder," came her frantic response.

"What? What are you talking about? What's going on?"

No answer. No eye contact. The next voice was hauntingly familiar.

"How wonderful to see you again, Joe Platt."

Joe whirled back to face the front of the courtroom. A menacing figure had appeared on the bench, dressed in black robes, his face obscured in shadow.

The Rook.

The empty room, the demon fire, his feeling of panic and dread . . . Joe should have guessed.

"What did you do?" he spat. "Where's my brother?"

"Always a little slow on the uptake, aren't you, Joe? I mean, really, did you actually think David was here this morning, just twiddling his thumbs until his big, strong brother could come save the day? And my goodness, all the tactics and secrecy! A daring rescue under the cloak of darkness? Why, who needs a SWAT team when they've got Joe Platt and his mighty sword?"

Joe approached the bench with all the ferocity he could muster. "Where is David?" he repeated.

"David? Why, he's at work, I should think. It turned out that the whole scuffle by the bridge was all just a big misunderstanding, all cleared up at the station. Apologies accepted, charges dropped, no real harm done. Just something about an imposter spreading false allegations. You wouldn't happen to know anything about that now, would you?"

Joe stiffened. This was a trick, wasn't it? It had to be.

"I'm surprised," the Rook continued. "With such wonderful news, you'd think David would want to tell his brother before anyone. Unless, of course, there's a reason he didn't call . . ."

"Shut up! No more lies."

"Oh, come now. Let's be rational. You haven't spoken to David since the bridge. For all you know, he's there right now, just as I've said. Think about it, Joe. Who did talk to you? Who was it that directed you to this courthouse? Who was it that sent you upstairs to this very room? Or after all your time in Hell, are you really still so blinded to the truth?"

Joe turned around slowly to find Maya staring sheepishly at her feet.

Maya. No—she'd been helping him. She'd called ahead and gathered information and . . . locked the door. As much as Joe wanted to deny it, the evidence was right in front of him.

"Maya," Joe stammered, "tell me he's lying."

"Yes, tell us," the Rook mocked. "Tell us who you called for all those mysterious contacts in the city. Or tell us who owns that nice little safe house where you all spent the night. No, Maya, I must commend you. You've played your part beautifully, and at last, you shall be rewarded."

Joe grabbed a wooden railing to steady himself. He swore the room was spinning.

Then the Rook climbed down from the bench and strolled toward the center of the room. "Give me a chance, Joe, and you'll see I'm quite the benefactor."

Maya, however, found her voice: "But you lied. You never said anything about Charlie getting hurt."

"Oh, collateral damage, my dear, as they say. Do accept my sincerest apology. Although, I might add, he appears much better now. I just ran into him downstairs not five minutes ago, along with your other friend Brody." Now to Joe, he whispered, "Or did you still think that they were the ones who turned out the lights?"

Joe had had enough. He drew his sword, and the Rook recoiled, but only a step. Joe pulsed with anger. "I don't know what you want, but you're not getting it. I came for David. Now where is he?"

"Actually, I was hoping we could talk about you. I came to offer an opportunity. Despite your obvious nearsightedness and distressingly poor judgment of character, I do admire your tenacity. There's a place for men like you in my operation. Heaven's loss is my gain."

"Screw you."

"You have such a bright future in Hell, my boy, and with a proper mentor . . ."

Joe raised his sword. "Last warning. Tell me where David is, or I'll cut you in half."

The Rook folded his hands as if to pray. "How it pains me to see you in such an immovable stance. But my dear Joe, if anyone's offering an ultimatum, it's me."

A colossal blast sounded like an explosion from under the floorboards, and suddenly the room blazed with demon fire. Blinded, Joe covered his eyes. Over the roaring inferno, he heard that venomous hissing, and soon those horrible vultures came swooping down from the ceiling. Joe ducked under his shield and slashed his sword wildly, spinning, cutting, jabbing, driving back the beasts as they lunged for his neck. He tried to go for the Rook, but he'd already disappeared, although Joe could still hear his voice. Joe spun to look for him, but he couldn't keep his focus. The demons were everywhere, and he had no choice but to fight.

With each slash of his sword, the fire intensified, and soon in the center of the courtroom was a dance on all sides. A bird dove for his face, and Joe reached up to slice its talons. A snake bit at his feet, and Joe impaled it through the head. Yet for every demon he slayed, two more appeared. His opponents were endless, and the heat was suffocating.

You failed, tempted the whisper. *They tricked you, and you fell for the lie.*

"No!" Joe shouted, remembering his battle cries from before. "The Lord is my strength!"

Another demon slashed, its warm pus oozing out onto his hands. Another whisper, this time louder in his ear.

"You're on your own, Joe."

Only Joe realized the voice wasn't a demon whisper at all, but Peter! The apostle's voice sounded at once both near and far off, like an echo in a cave. Was he still outside the courtroom? Yes, he must be beyond the walls.

"It's time you learn," Peter called. "You brought this upon yourself."

Another creature crashed hard against Joe's shield, and he came to his senses. It wasn't Peter. It couldn't be.

"You should have listened to me," said his mother, suddenly there in front of him, a silhouette walking among the flames. "You can't change this, Joe. Now I've lost two sons instead of one, and it's all your fault."

"No!" he shouted, but no sound escaped. His throat was as dry as the desert of Hell.

You're selfish, snarling voices jeered from all sides. *Arrogant. Unwilling to see the truth.*

Tongues of fire shot toward him like arrows, one finding its mark on the back of his right hand. The burn caused Joe to lose his grip on his sword, sending the weapon clattering to the floor as he cried out in pain. Instantly, the demons seized their opportunity to disarm him. Three more of those vultures swept low and dragged the blade deeper into the flames, out of Joe's grasp and away from his sight. It was all too much. No matter how he tried, Joe couldn't win.

Another apparition—Bill Platt, his father, standing before him in the flesh. His bright orange construction vest matched the fire, and his eyes were dark with disappointment.

"Do you know why I left?" he whispered. "All those years ago?"

Joe's hand throbbed in agony. It was all he could do just to stand.

"It wasn't because of me, Joe. It wasn't because of your mother."

For once in my life, David had said, *I didn't need you to rescue me.*

"Do you know why I really left, Joe?"

At last, Joe dropped his shield and collapsed to his knees. There was nowhere to hide from the answer he already knew.

"It all stops if you want it to," the Rook said calmly. "All the guilt. All the shame. You don't owe it to anyone, Joe. Think about yourself now. Renounce your God and be free."

No, Joe thought, and a new wave of fury surged up toward the Rook. Joe crawled toward the sound of the voice, moving in a frenzied delirium, ready to choke him if he had to.

"Help me, Lord Jesus," he panted through the smoke, the words renewing some of his energy. Joe repeated the phrase, watching the flames shrink back at each mention of the name. He rose slowly to his feet to face his accuser.

"He can't hear you," taunted the Rook, who seemed to be everywhere and nowhere at once. "And he wouldn't save you if he could. You're completely alone, Joe Platt."

"Help me, Lord Jesus."

"Your God rejected you. He left you to die. Now I welcome you with open arms."

There. Joe could see the form of the Rook, outlined in the flames to his left. He could jump from here. A quick leap, and both hands around his throat. Joe tensed his body, preparing for the lunge.

"End the suffering, Joe. Only say the word and—"

The Rook convulsed as a sword point pierced him from behind. Someone else had beaten Joe to it. Instantly, the whole room dimmed. Or perhaps the sword itself grew in brightness. Its white-hot intensity dazzled like a guiding star. Howls of demonic agony reverberated off the walls, and the Rook himself collapsed to his knees.

Peter must have broken in, for real this time. He must have won his battle outside and come to their rescue.

But then Joe looked up and saw who held the blade.

Maya twisted the hilt and rammed the sword in further, its sharp edge cutting between joint and marrow. She pulled back on the Rook's collar and moved the weapon in deeper still, penetrating to the bottom of his dark and twisted soul, judging the very thoughts and attitudes of his foul and wicked heart. The sword glowed brighter each time she pushed it deeper, and her wild eyes reflected that righteous luminescence.

"Our contract is over," Maya declared. "Today, I am free."

Then she ripped the blade out with a strength beyond herself, and the Rook unleashed a frightful and deafening wail. Veins and sinews burned upon contact with the air, the great cavity in his chest growing out like a cancer. His bony hands clutched his wound as if to stop it from spreading, but it was no use. From the inside out, the Rook's body crumbled like ash, falling to the courtroom floor and dissolving into a million fractured pieces.

It was over. The Rook was no more.

The lights came on. The wooden benches around them were charred, and the air reeked of sulfur, but otherwise they were alone. The danger had passed.

Maya dropped the sword to the ground, still heaving from the effort. "I'm so sorry, Joe," she began. "I wanted to warn you—please believe me. But he said that . . ."

Unable to finish, she fell to her knees and sobbed. Long, aching moans of pent-up emotion. Maya, betrayer and rescuer both. But her free and honest tears left no doubt that her deception was over. Whatever the Rook had done to sway her, it had clearly lost its hold. Joe couldn't help but think of Sahil, the man who'd finally been able to walk on the golden streets of Heaven after decades of paralysis. The tone was darker, and the atmosphere heavier, but he could tell that Maya's experience was similar in kind. Some invisible shackles had dissolved along with the Rook. Her oppression had finally reached its end.

At last, Joe thought, *the captive is free.*

He sat beside her, offering neither a hand nor words. Joe sensed he should be celebrating the moment, but he couldn't. Not yet. In the wake of his own personal battle with the Rook, he felt a pang of sadness return. Despite their victory, they'd still missed their main objective. They'd come for David, but they still hadn't found him. Was he even in the building at all?

It had seemed obvious to Joe that his brother would choose Heaven over prison. Wouldn't anyone choose to escape a cell? But what if the Rook had told the truth and David wasn't in jail at all, but back at the job he loved? Would he really give that up for the promise of a Heaven he'd never seen? Joe looked around at the room still smoldering from the roar of demon fire.

Either way, he realized, *David's imprisoned. The difference is whether he knows it or not.*

But if Joe hadn't convinced him to leave the bridge the first time, what could possibly be different now? Despite their triumph here, if they couldn't save David, would the whole mission have been for nothing?

Joe closed his eyes. Wisdom nudged an answer in his direction, but he felt unready to take it. He couldn't know for sure—not until they'd exhausted all their options.

Suddenly, a forceful kick burst open the doors to the courtroom, and Peter rushed in. Joe carefully stood up to greet him. The apostle's shirt bore some singe marks, but all in all, he'd survived the attack quite well. Naturally, he wanted to know everything, and Joe did his best to bring him up to speed on their encounter with the Rook.

When he finished, Peter looked to Maya, a curious expression on his face.

"Sister," he said, "rise and tell me what happened."

Maya collected herself as best as she could. With a heavy sigh, she explained, "Everything I told Joe before was true. I wanted nothing to do with the Rook after I left Brimtown. But it was harder than I thought. We were always on the run, and no matter how much good we did, it never felt like enough. A few weeks ago, the Rook found me alone one night, right after a job had gone horribly in Dumah. I was feeling pretty low, and I think he knew it. I should've known better after all I'd been through, but out of nowhere, he offered to return my necklace. I had thought I might never have a chance to get it back. It all sounded so simple. I just had to follow his instructions and bring Joe to Brimtown. The Rook provided a safe house under a false name and the plans to enter his own facility and rob it—all part of the cover—and then that night you showed up exactly how he said you would. I swear, no one else was in on it. But nothing went as he said at the warehouse. There was no money in the safe, and then what happened to Charlie . . . I thought I'd just been lied to again, but then he called me that same night and said you'd be back, that I just had to maintain the part. But I swear, I never thought that . . ."

Peter, however, raised his hand to cut her off. "No, Maya. I hear your story and share your pain, but your journey here is not what I meant. Tell us what happened with the sword."

She blinked. "Joe's sword?"

"The very one you used to slay the Rook."

"I . . . I don't know," she said. "After the demons dragged it out of the way, it was right by my feet, and I just realized that I had to pick a side. The Rook's only ever lied to me. And after seeing you heal Charlie and Joe fight back from that onslaught just now . . . well, I just figured if there really is a God, and if Jesus is real, then that's the side I want to be on."

Peter smiled wide. "Blessed are those who thirst for righteousness. Truly I tell you, a greater battle has already been fought—and won."

Maya's eyes widened. "Does that mean the Rook is gone for good?"

"The creature you spoke with is destroyed and will never return," Peter explained. "But he was merely a branch and not the true root of evil. The Rook was one of many who serves the real prince of this world. But take heart. I sense that the end of all these things is near."

"We should hurry then," said Joe. "I came here for a reason. There's no way we can leave without finding David first."

"We should still meet up with the others," Maya pointed out. "They might be waiting for us. We can figure out where to go from there."

"Alright then. Let's go." Joe located his shield and brushed the ash off his clothes. Every muscle ached, but he couldn't stop now. They were so close. So close to the end.

"Do you want your sword back?" Maya asked, motioning to it on the ground.

Strangely, Joe hadn't even thought about it. He looked first to his weapon, and then to Maya. "I . . . I don't know. I feel like I owe you one."

"I mean, it is yours."

"Well, technically, it belongs to Jesus. I just have it on loan." Joe considered it for a moment. Something had transformed when she stabbed the Rook, both in Maya and in himself. A few hours ago, he was hesitant to even let her come along, but now . . .

He unbuckled his sheath and handed it over. "Why don't you hold on to it for me? After all, like Peter said, I have a feeling you might still need it."

EIGHTEEN
THE LAKE OF FIRE

APPARENTLY, STABBING THE Rook had unraveled whatever daytime détente had previously existed between the demons and the people of Brimtown. Minutes after Joe and the others exited the courthouse—with Charlie and Brody back in tow—the gray sky took on a foreboding green tint, reminding Joe of tornado weather in his native Midwest. With no time to dwell on it, they found Ethel idling the van at the base of the steps and quickly piled in. They still needed to find David before opening a way back to Heaven, and Joe had a sinking feeling that time was running out. Some final cosmic hourglass had already been turned.

The van raced down the street to reach City Hall, where presently Isaac Washington's spiritual revival was well underway. Roadblocks cordoned off the main avenue as people crowded around food tents and so-called pardon vendors—Joe could see the neon banners offering absolution à la carte, even featuring discounts for those with no criminal records or decent credit scores. A platform with a podium and sound equipment had been constructed at the front of the expo, presumably where Reverend Washington himself was set to give the keynote. Taken all at once, the scene was much like a carnival—lively, colorful, fake. There must have been hundreds of people there, all roped into the swindle.

You can't buy what's already been freely given, Joe thought. Especially not from a booth on the side of the road. It incensed Joe to know that such a con existed, even more so that he'd pretended to be part of it. No, this time around, he would only speak the truth.

The van rocked as Ethel plowed through a barricade. She drove like a character in a racing game, dodging around pedestrians and food carts, swerving around those pardon vendors and the throngs of eager patrons waiting to buy their remission. Joe stared out at their faces. Men, women, old, young—some even younger than him. They stood with expectant eyes and skin marked by sorrow, like refugees fleeing their war-torn homes with dreams of a better life. These were wandering souls, searching for purpose and satisfaction, drifting across this desert landscape with only memories of joy, assuming they'd ever known it at all. Yet Joe could still see the small glimmers of hope, those daring beliefs that something, anything, could ease their present doubts and heal their deep afflictions. They asked for respite but needed love. They longed for Heaven although they'd all but forgotten its name.

And wasn't this the real mission? Maybe Jesus had known it all along. Joe had come for David, but there were countless millions in Hell just like him. Millions upon millions upon millions, all tired, lost, and alone.

By the grace of God, Joe knew, *am I not forever among them.*

Joe's attention snapped back to the present as the van skidded to a halt. They'd stopped in front of a colossal bar tent proudly bearing the label "Jacob's Well." The crowd here was denser than before, with dozens of customers packed tight on all sides. People climbed over each other and shouted their drink requests into the chaos, each demand for service more angry than the last. Joe watched as a heavyset woman finally received her order, only to trip and spill the drink in front of her. The dry ground swallowed it quickly, leaving her more frustrated than before and with no option but to push back into the mob and try again.

"Run 'em over," Brody said flatly.

"Might have to, unless they get the idea." Ethel blasted the horn but to no avail. Most people ignored her, although those who might have wanted to move really couldn't. With more tents on both sides and the crowd as thick as it was, there was simply nowhere to go.

"I've never seen this many people at once," Charlie remarked. "At least not in Hell, that is. This preacher man must do quite the show."

"Back it up," Joe said. "We'll have to go around."

But she didn't have the chance. At that exact moment, the whole sky ignited.

Lightning—*lightning*, in this gray, monotonous, weatherless world—tore across the atmosphere as if to fracture the heavens themselves. Electric tendrils shot out in impossible webs—transfixing, shocking, brilliant, and then gone as suddenly as they'd appeared. And with the flash came that sudden, tremendous explosion, booming thunder on all sides, causing Joe to instinctively crouch and duck his head. Every soul in Brimtown stopped. Sales paused with money on the counter, voices halted abruptly mid-sentence, and even Ethel moved her foot from the pedal and kept the van at a standstill.

Then, quite literally, all Hell broke loose.

People shrieked in terror as more lightning shot across the sky, their screams overpowered by the roaring thunder. The crowd was still too dense to move, but this time they tried, clawing and pulling each other to the ground in a riotous melee. Bodies slammed against the van so hard Joe thought the windows would break. Ethel came to her senses and threw the van into reverse, trying to navigate the panic.

More thunder, but this time not from the sky. The ground shook in violent tremors, rocking the van, collapsing some vendor stalls, rattling City Hall itself. As the storm intensified, however, the earthquake became the least of their concerns. Even inside the van, Joe felt a growing despondency, like a changing pressure in the atmosphere, aching him to the bones. He could see it out the window. The dirt moved of its own accord, swirling up with dark and malicious intent. Particles coalesced midair, forming spots then masses then clouds then legs with torsos and misshapen heads. On all sides now were black spirits with solid form and substance, heavy chains draping from their shoulders and gaunt faces marked by famine and disease.

Demons, no doubt about it.

Charlie gulped. "You know, I've got a really bad feeling about this."

In the front seat, Brody loaded his shotgun with salt shells. Peter wrapped his hand around the hilt of his sword, and Joe saw Maya do the same.

The demons turned, stared, wrapped skeletal fingers around their rusted irons, and attacked.

Like swarms of bees, the nearest demons jumped on the van, smashing the windshield with bony fists and slashing the tires with their chains. Brody cocked his shotgun and blasted one right in the face—the shot having all the effect of a water balloon. Soon they were reaching inside the vehicle like a horde of zombies, their eyes burning and their mouths hissing threats. Joe threw open the door and charged with his shield, crashing into the first demon he saw. The creature flew back onto the ground, flailing about for a moment before combusting into flames. Joe knocked two more off the front of the van as Brody continued cracking shots, determined as ever although the salt made little difference.

Peter and Maya were out now, slashing their swords and pushing the demons into retreat. Joe noticed how their attackers ignored the dozens of other people fleeing in all directions. The demons turned all their focus to the van, and Joe had seen enough to know why. Indeed, the fact of being their sole target was what gave him courage.

They're afraid, he knew. *They're afraid of what we can do.*

Lightning flashed in the brightest streak yet, and with it the sky itself burst open. Balls of light hurtled toward them like small meteors, and the demons howled at the sight. At first, Joe thought this was another attack like the one they'd faced at the warehouse, but as those fiery spheres approached, Joe saw they weren't meteors at all.

"Angels," he gasped.

The seraphim—those six-winged creatures who'd greeted him at the gates of Heaven—descended, now enveloped in light. Each one held a long sword covered in white flames. In a ferocious wave, they reached the ground and slashed the demons to dust, scattering the particles with beats of their mighty wings. A single angel could have defeated the multitude all on his own, and yet here were a dozen. The angels' voices carried louder than the thunder, a resounding battle cry of force and conviction. "Holy, holy, holy, is the Lord Almighty!"

The demons had no time to cower and no way to fight back. The terrifying creatures from only moments before were gone in an instant, leaving only wisps of smoke in their place.

"Well, check that out," remarked Charlie. "I think I'll take one of those swords, if anyone's got an extra."

"Who are you?" asked Maya, gaping at those heavenly beings.

"We are seraphim," they said together, "and you are warriors in the great battle. Blessed child, it was your show of faith that opened the door for us. Go now to prepare for the banquet of God that will end the reign of the beast."

From behind the crumpled tents and scattered debris, a few residents of Brimtown dared to peek out. The earthquake had stopped, the sky had calmed, and these glowing arrivals drew a reverent fascination. People had fled from the demons, but to the angels they cautiously returned.

Feeling more confident than ever, Joe reasserted their mission. "We have to find David." Aware of the smashed-in van behind him, Joe looked at the angels. "Can you take us to him?"

The dozen seraphim all faced him in a single motion, using their wings to hover just off the ground. Joe flitted his eyes from one to the next, awaiting their response.

"We have come to sing and gather those willing to join the song. Your journey is not yet finished. What remains of it is yours to make."

Not exactly what he wanted to hear. Joe swallowed. "So I have to go on alone?"

"Not alone," Peter declared. "I am with you."

"Me too," Maya added. "I led us into this mess today, and now I want to see it through. Besides, I know a shortcut to the lake from here."

Peter, who'd disappeared their second night in Hell. Maya, who'd betrayed them to the Rook. To think, there was no one else Joe wanted to go with him now.

In Christ, he believed, *everything can be made new.*

"Alright then," Joe said. "The three of us will go. The rest of you stay back with the angels and try to gather as many people as you can. They know what they've seen, and perhaps now they'll be more willing than ever to reject the hold of this place. Just like we talked about, we'll bring David and my father back here, and then we'll all go to Heaven together."

"What do we tell them?" Charlie wondered.

Joe grinned. "Tell them the truth."

True to her word, Maya's shortcut took them directly to the lake of fire. They reached a small jetty with six or seven boats tied up at the dock. The place was empty—presumably everyone had fled during the lightning—and the lake crackled and churned its noxious swell. The great bridge itself loomed a few miles down the coastline, marking their finish line in this crazy race through Hell.

"It'll be faster to take a boat," Maya said. "These ones all have motors."

"Who's going to drive it?" Joe asked.

At that, Peter looked up. "Times change, but a fisherman never loses his instinct."

Maya untied the rope, and the three of them climbed in. Peter yanked the starter and steered them out into the molten sulfur. The engine had surprising horsepower, allowing them to cut through the waves with ease. The sizzle against the boat's hull made Joe plenty nervous, but thankfully their constant motion kept the smell to a minimum.

"I feel like it's all ending now," Maya said. "In one day, more good has happened than in the seven years I've been here. I feel lighter, you know? Like it's all going to be okay."

Joe smiled. "Yeah. I know the feeling."

David. His father. Maya and her crew. They'd all be together soon, leaving this hopeless place behind forever. Joe looked out on the lake, soaking in one last view as his souvenir.

"Hey, Maya," he said after a moment. "Are there fish out here?"

She wrinkled her brow. "None that I've ever seen. Why?"

"I don't know. Do you see that dark spot over there? It kind of looks like a whale or something. What do you think that is?"

Peter had seen it too and eased up on the throttle. The spot in question resembled an oil spill, a shadowy coloration just below the surface. At first, Joe thought it was merely bouncing with the waves, but he soon realized its movements followed some conscious direction. A new sense of foreboding filled the boat, worse than when the demons had gathered outside of City Hall. Joe had never felt so vulnerable as he did out on that fiery sea. Now they could all agree that whatever it was, it was coming toward them. Fast.

The shape broke through the surface with reptilian scales, a deep and violent red like the fire from which it came. Every type of demon Joe had seen thus far paled in comparison to this hideous monster. It had the form of a dragon, but with ten horns and seven heads, each covered with a golden crown. The beast towered over them, colossal and petrifying, its fangs yellowed and its body scarred with the marks of some ancient evil. The dragon hissed and twisted its seven heads, weaving them in and out like a gigantic nest of snakes.

And they were trapped. On a boat, unable to move, unable to swim, alone in the middle of a lake of fire. Those vulture-demons and even the Rook were harmless bugs compared to this beast. All Joe's confidence in their weapons remained on the shore. One look at this creature and he knew this was a battle they simply couldn't win.

The dragon lurched forward, spitting flames from all of its mouths, jets of fire racing toward them from seven different directions. They reacted immediately, but their shields couldn't block it all. The blasts charred the boat's edges and listed them far to one side, inches from capsizing. Catching them, however, was the monster itself, lifting its tail to hold the vessel, then rocking it back to throw them all to the floor. They were completely helpless, unable to reach its necks with their swords and having no other weapon on the boat—and Joe sensed the creature knew it. The dragon toyed with them, mocking their efforts, prolonging their certain demise.

Or so it seemed. But then the sky brightened again as with the lightning storm before, only this time it kept its glow. Joe removed his shield and looked up, seeing the heavens themselves come open. Light came down over the lake—pure light, not like the glow of the fiery waves—and the sea itself appeared to suspend its motion. The dragon relented, lifting its heads in unison and clearly distracted by the happenings in the sky. Joe watched as a new creature emerged, a white horse, standing in midair. The horse shone with glorious splendor, and on its back sat a rider Joe already knew.

In Heaven, Jesus had been unremarkable in appearance, a beloved and gentle teacher full of wisdom and kindness. But not anymore. This Jesus was a king in all his majesty, powerful and dignified, dressed in a crimson robe and adorned with a series of crowns. His eyes blazed with righteous anger that even Joe could see from below, and his gleaming sword was one to strike fear into nations. On his robe was emblazoned, "King of Kings" and "Lord of Lords." This was Jesus, faithful and true. This was Jesus, the living

Word of God. Joe had been knocked from his feet in the boat. Now he rose to his knees in worship.

At their darkest hour, Jesus had come.

The great dragon took the offensive, launching into the air with a push of its mighty wings and spraying fire toward the rider. Jesus took charge and engaged his enemy, deflecting the flames with turns of his sword and sending each in a different direction, like a display of fireworks in the sky. And now behind Jesus rode a heavenly army, scores of riders atop white horses and dressed in fine linen. They moved out in flanks to face the beast on all sides, repelling its fire with weapons of their own. High above the lake, they waged a war of darkness and light, of deceit and truth, an epic conflict the size of worlds.

"Hurry," Peter said. "We won't stay afloat."

Joe pulled his eyes away from the battle in the sky and quickly realized the same thing. The bottom of their boat had cracked under the dragon's attack, and now trickles of lava were seeping in through the hull. Joe clambered to his feet to get away from the danger, but it was only a temporary fix. In a matter of minutes, they'd sink.

"Can you still drive it," Maya asked, "and take us to shore?" But one look at the motor's blackened remains told them all they needed to know. The dragon had fried it beyond repair, and now the only place the boat was going was straight down to the bottom.

"We'll have to cross the lake without it," Peter said. "There's no other way."

"What, do you mean, like swim?" Maya replied. "You can't swim in this. It's liquid fire."

"Agreed. We must cross over it."

"So you mean walk on water. That's impossible."

"With men, yes," the apostle declared. "But with God, all things are possible. Trust me, I've done it before."

Maya gaped, incredulous. "Are you insane? First of all, this is not a normal lake. This will burn you alive. Second, even I know that story! Jesus called you out onto the water, and then as soon as the wind picked up, you fell in. This isn't some prayer you say while swinging your sword against the demons. This will destroy you."

"I see no difference," Peter replied. "I had little faith then, but look now at the battle above us. One is the dragon, who intends for us to sink and perish, and one is Christ our Lord. What matters is not some word or perfect invocation. What matters is the heart. Though one may be overpowered, two can defend themselves. A cord of three strands is not quickly broken."

Joe could already smell the rubber burning on his shoes. The boat had a puddle of lava now, and it would only get worse. There was no way to fix the leak. If they stayed, he'd be a human torch in minutes. If they took Peter's plan and left the boat, well…not exactly stellar options. Stay and melt or walk by faith.

These are always my options, he realized. *Lake of fire or not.*

"Okay," Joe agreed. "Let's do it. I was just attacked by a seven-headed dragon, so walking on fire won't be the strangest thing I've done today."

"No," Maya cried. "Let's think about this. If we can just patch the leak . . ."

"Maya," Joe said, "you told me that you were never one to play by the rules, so don't start now. You've wanted to stop evil ever since you got here, but you're not the one who has to do it. Look up! That battle, that fight in the sky, that's for all of us. You said you know what side you want to be on, so be on this side now. Trust Jesus."

Maya looked at Joe, then to Peter, then to the sky, then back to the lake.

"Alright," she said softly. "Let's do it."

The three of them joined hands, and Peter led them in prayer. "Lord, it is you who tell us not to be afraid. Help us now to walk upon the flames."

Then, carefully and still with arms linked, they stepped over the edge of the boat. Some part of Joe still wanted to panic, but he felt

Peter on his right and Maya on his left, and their presence gave him courage. He lowered his first foot. A wind carried the sulfur smell stronger than ever, and waves of fire lapped up against their shoes, but Joe's leg did not sink. And with another step, they left the boat entirely, now having both feet on the lake and their eyes locked on the horizon. With each new step, the waves came higher, as if they'd enraged the lake by denying it its pleasure. But each time the flames did not burn, and with every step, they gained confidence. They increased to a jog, and now they ran, taking long strides to cover the final mile to the bridge, step after step after step, hearts beating, bodies sweating, feet still not sinking no matter how the currents moved. At last they came ashore at the same dirt-covered peninsula with picnic tables and a view of the bridge where Joe had first spoken with David and lost the salvation key. They climbed up on dry land after the whole length of their journey, still in awe of the miracle.

A few bridge workers acknowledged them with a head nod or dumbfounded stare, but most of the crew had their eyes on the sky. They'd halted construction while the epic battle unfolded out over the lake, all the builders just standing there open-mouthed and silent. Joe and his companions turned to view it with them—the rider and his army and the dragon with seven heads desperately trying to stay alive. The beast had lasted for quite a while, but it was clear that Jesus and his cavalry held the advantage. The dragon's flames grew weaker with every breath, and Jesus showed no signs of fatigue. At last, with a final triumphant slash of his sword, Jesus knocked the dragon to its side. It spun, disoriented, in the air, and then angels rushed forth from the heavens and surrounded it with thick and heavy chains. They flew in circles, trapping the beast, wrapping it tightly so its wings couldn't fly. The dragon's seven heads all screamed in protest, but this time no flames escaped. Perhaps the chains choked it, or perhaps it had finally exhausted its fuel. Either way, the battle was over. The angels lifted the dragon together and swung it up high before hurling it down into the fiery lake of burning sulfur. The resounding splash could be heard from the shore.

NINETEEN
CHOICE AND CONSEQUENCE

DAVID WAS UP ON the bridge when Joe found him, leaning against a guardrail and staring out across the lake. He wore his vest and hardhat and had a lunch box open at his feet, as if he were just taking a break on a regular day at the job. If he saw Joe coming, he didn't acknowledge him. Not until he'd walked all the way up and joined him at the railing. Peter and Maya stood at a respectful distance on the opposite side of the bridge to give the brothers some space—and pray for them.

"I knew it was you," David said coolly, still looking out at the lake. "When I saw you running across the flames, headed straight toward us. Most people were watching the dragon, but I was watching you."

Joe folded his hands and stared out at the spot on the horizon where Jesus and his army had disappeared. They'd gone away from the bridge after the dragon's defeat, riding with haste across the sky. Joe had no idea where they were going, but he knew with certainty they'd circle back soon, as sure as his feeling on Earth that the sun would rise again each morning.

"Everyone up here was talking," David continued. "They said they'd heard legends of the beast. They said he rules all of Hell from down there, that the bridge itself is his project, that demons in every city take their orders directly from him. The King of the Abyss. The way they were saying it, it didn't really make sense. It's like they all

233

wanted him to lose and were rooting against him, but at the same time they all thought it'd never happen, like the battle itself was a big waste of time. They said you can never kill him, no matter what anyone does, and that even after today, he'll be back just the same as before. They said it so calmly, like they weren't even afraid. Just certain, like they were telling me how best to do my job."

"What about you?" Joe asked. "Were you afraid?"

David turned to face him with sunken eyes and skin paler than usual.

"I'm still standing here, right?"

A small boat motored out from under the bridge, a crew of workers assessing the structures for needed repairs. The great battle had been over for less than an hour, and already they were back to business as usual. As if nothing had changed at all.

"I want to apologize," Joe said at last. "I should probably start with that."

David raised an eyebrow. "Oh yeah? For which part? Getting me arrested? Lying about me? Almost costing me my job by telling my supervisors I'm some kind of thief?"

Joe swallowed. "Yeah. All of that. But there's more, though. I'm sorry for thinking I could just come down here and save you, easy as that, when really it was never in my power to do so—not my own power, anyway."

"What are you talking about, Joe?"

"I thought it was my fault you'd ended up here, and I wanted to fix this problem I caused and be the hero, to rescue you and release this burden I felt. I really did want to help you, David, but in the most selfish way possible, if that even makes sense."

"It doesn't."

Joe forced a laugh. "You know, most people want good for the people they care about. They want good things to happen to them and to keep away the bad. There are times when it's even okay to force good things on someone, even if he doesn't want it or know how to ask for it, like teaching a lesson or saving a life, because the good is just that level of important. If I'm being honest, there's a part of me that wishes I could just take you to Heaven like those policemen took you to jail the other night, throw you in a car and be done with it. I think I would, if that were possible. But that's not how Jesus works."

David held his gaze, listening but skeptical, not quite willing to go along with it.

"You know," David said after a moment. "I thought about what you said. When you asked what's the point of building this thing, and I said I was drawn to the challenge."

"I remember."

"You called it impossible, and I just . . . I just didn't want to agree. But then two nights ago, I was sitting there in handcuffs while they tried to figure out if they were charging me or not, and you know what I realized? Not a single thing has changed. I couldn't do anything right at home, and I can't do anything right here. And Dad—you know what he told me when we first met down here? He said he wanted to pick up where we left off. Just like that. I mean, I wasn't even in school yet, you know? He's acting like nothing changed in twenty years of not seeing him, like we can just start over at square one. But then maybe he's right. Maybe nothing did change. Life still sucks like it used to—it's just as impossible as it was before. I didn't want to say you were right, Joe, but you were. The bridge, Hell . . . everything here is pointless."

"I know," Joe replied softly. "That's why he came."

"Who?"

And, as if in answer to this question, they heard voices behind them, whispers and gasps at the sight of the army returning in the sky. Joe and David turned around and recognized the triumphant king and the sweeping host behind him, singing songs of the angels and declaring their arrival. Those white stallions numbered enough to block the sun—if such a celestial body had existed in Hell. Instead, on that dull and colorless sky, the heavenly steeds rode forth with dazzling life, forming the eclipse in reverse—light blotting out darkness, the sun crossing over the shadow.

Jesus rode his horse down onto the bridge, alighting directly in front of Joe. His crimson robe hung royally from his shoulders, and his outer crown richly displayed those same gemstones Joe had seen embedded in the city walls of Heaven. But all the wonder at his garments faded with the first look into his eyes.

In Heaven, those eyes had shone with compassion, gentleness, and love. And this love hadn't left, but now added to it was some ardent spirit, like the blazing fire of the lake below. These eyes burned for justice and truth, wanting to stamp out enemies and move with righteous anger. This was fierce and jealous love, the kind fueled at the simplest provocation and wisely feared by any who knew its strength. And just as before, these eyes saw Joe, saw beyond every pretense and beneath every mask, saw in him and through him and around him, saw the exact size and contour of his very soul. And such was their assessment. They saw in Joe the object of their love, the focus of their fierce and jealous desire.

"Truly I tell you, unless a kernel of wheat falls to the ground and dies, it remains only a single seed." Jesus leaned forward and placed his hand on Joe's shoulder. "Well done, my good and faithful servant."

Joe started to reply but then stopped. He felt that disarming effect he'd known in Heaven. He sensed the relief that soon all would be well.

Sitting up, Jesus addressed the crowd.

"The time has not yet come for Heaven and Earth to pass away. A day is coming when the dragon, that ancient serpent, will again be free and deceive the nations, and after his final defeat, there shall be a new Heaven and a new Earth. And on that day, woe to them who call evil good and good evil. But see now, the Kingdom of God is among you. My father has prepared a wedding feast for his son, and the church is his bride. All are invited, but many will ignore the invitation and go their own ways. Here I have a horse for every man or woman who wishes to ride, although I shall not stable them here. We'll ride together, and we'll ride at once. Come, leave all your possessions and follow me."

A row of white horses with empty saddles came alongside him, waiting for new riders to step up and claim them. This must have been the last stop in a full tour of Hell, for Joe saw mounts already filled behind those that were empty, men and women from every corner of Hell who'd made the decision to go with Jesus. To his joy, he saw his companions riding first among them, and now they addressed the crowd with words of encouragement.

"By his power, I was healed," said Charlie. "And my fear of the demons is gone."

"I used to mind my own business and preferred others do the same," said Ethel. "But with him, I know I'm never alone."

Even Brody chimed in. "I've seen what horrors Hell can do to a person, and I've seen how my own weapons compare to his. If Jesus is fighting, I'm on his side."

Peter climbed up onto a horse, and Joe soon followed, leaving his brother awestruck beside the railing. A handful of others joined them, tossing their hardhats on the ground and readily hooking their feet into the stirrups.

But for each one who stepped forward, dozens more stayed back. It was more than hesitation. They jeered and scoffed at the message. Joe heard their complaints from all sides. Who was this man who demanded they leave a good paying job and the cars and the houses they'd worked so hard to earn? Who could blindly pledge their allegiance to him with no terms or contract or written guarantee? Sure, it'd been enjoyable to watch the fight, but they still had work to do and their own mouths to feed.

The more superstitious added their own concerns. Perhaps they'd all been wrong to cheer from the shore, for was it really wise to betray the dragon who commanded every demon? Would not the chains around him soon melt in the lake, and would he not then return with a fury unlike any they'd ever seen? Repentance, then, was owed to the beast and not to this newcomer, for surely no horseman could defeat such a creature. For others, the matter was even more simple. It was a fine enough offer and maybe even one that made sense, but they lacked the right feeling or knew this wasn't the right time. Maybe tomorrow, or next year, or if a battle ever came again. They were simply not the type to join in such adventures on a whim.

"Won't he do something to convince them?" Joe whispered to Peter. "Jesus could give some display of his power. He could crush the bridge with a wave of his hand. Then they'd come with us. Once they saw that, they'd have no excuse."

But Peter shook his head. "He possesses the power and even the right, but our king is no tyrant. Remember, the bridegroom awaits his bride. True love relinquished the keys at the moment of creation. He opened the door—it's they who lock him out."

Distressed, Joe scanned the crowd of unwilling faces. They looked upon God incarnate and still chose their tired routines. And for years and years before this, others had chosen the same. How many had worked on this exact same spot and slaved away until their souls had crumbled apart? How many had heard some hope or goodness and rejected it with ease? For surely if Jesus hadn't come or if Joe hadn't spoken of him, the very rocks would cry out. Denying him was like denying the sun! And yet they chose. Since the dawn of time, how many millions of salvation keys had been thrown into the lake?

Not all, however, had completely walked away. Some stayed frozen in indecision, there to watch but not quite to join. First among this group—Joe felt his heart sink—was Maya. What was she doing? After all they'd been through, why wasn't she coming? Yet there she was, standing near Jesus but with both feet firmly on the ground. She had her eyes on her feet and the Sword of the Spirit extended out to him hilt first, offering back the weapon.

"This is yours," she said in a voice soft and trembling. But Jesus didn't take it. He kept both hands on the reins and his eyes on her face.

"Will you not still wield it?" he asked. "It is my gift to give."

"But after all I've done," Maya said, still looking at her feet, "I can't keep this anymore. Someone else should have it. I'm not worthy. I worked for the Rook and followed his every bidding. I stood by while he tortured and lied. I betrayed my only friends and served the demons I hate, all for myself. Please. Just take it and leave."

In response, Jesus dismounted and approached her at equal height.

"My child, my grace is sufficient for you." He reached out and placed a hand on her shoulder. "Don't you know? You say you served the Rook, but when you took the sword to slay him, it was your faith that let me in. You've always held the key. Now you've turned the lock."

At this, she dared to look up. "But why? Why would you come for me?"

Jesus gently moved his hand, and Joe saw him take hold of the golden chain dangling from her neck, the one recovered from the warehouse and still missing a pendant.

"Know this," Jesus said. "You are worth far more than diamonds."

Then he removed his hand, and there on the necklace rested a new crystal, sparkling with a light of its own. Joe had seen the fake pendants in the market and real diamonds on Earth, but this one outshone them all. Maya tenderly pressed her fingers against the diamond, as if not quite believing the stone was real. But it was. What she gave up—what was taken from her—and what she'd given everything to earn back, had now been freely given. And at last, comprehending the beauty of the gift, she threw out her arms and embraced the one who made all things new.

Another voice called out from the crowd, and this time Joe recognized his father. He'd seen the commotion from the shore and had charged out onto the bridge to meet them.

"What's going on?" Bill Platt demanded. "David, what are you doing up here? I thought you were working receiving. And is that Joe? What in the—why are you riding a horse?"

"Well," Joe began, "I can explain."

"Oh, like you let me explain?" Bill shot back. "Because what I seem to remember is you chewing my head off right before calling the police on both me and David, all while I was trying to make you feel at home. No, I don't want to hear a word about whatever this is. Now come down. I wasn't around much when you were growing up, but I'll still protect my sons. And right now, all I see you doing is ripping this family apart."

Joe's blood boiled. *If I ever felt protected,* he thought, *it certainly wasn't by you.*

Joe looked up and took a deep breath, saving his silent retort. His father probably deserved every harsh word Joe had for him, but that wasn't the path he wanted to take.

"Our family knows what it's like to be ripped apart," Joe said after a moment, "but this isn't the kind of rip we can fix. Don't you see? That's why Jesus came. We were all ripped from him, and he wants to mend the tear."

"C'mon, Joe," Bill spat. "Don't tell me you're buying this whole city-in-the-sky bullcrap. Life's hard work, son. Nobody's gonna fix your problems for you."

Joe gripped the reins and looked at both his father and David with pleading eyes. "I'm going home now, and I want you to come with me. I want you both to come."

Bill considered this for a long moment. The bridge grew silent as the whole crowd—those riders on the horses and those construction workers who hadn't yet walked away—waited to hear his reply. His shoulders sagged, his earlier rage and hostility now replaced with a cloak of sadness and a faraway look in his eyes that spoke of regret.

"Do you know why I left all those years ago?" he asked softly.

Unseen, an arrow slipped through Joe's armor, its tip laced with poison. From both sides, the lake of fire shot up to entrap him, enclosing him now like those dark walls of the courtroom. The flames moved in from all sides, surrounding him, choking him, filling his ears with the mocking voice of the Rook.

Never good enough. Banished. Rejected. He wouldn't save you if he could.

Do you know why I left, repeated the voice, *all those years ago?*

Joe's lips quivered with his response. He couldn't dare say it. But he knew. Wasn't it David his father had come up here to see? Wasn't it David who had restored some form of relationship and Joe who'd held on to their differences? Had he really been the reason that . . .

His thoughts were cut off. Now, another voice, squashing the first, this time belonging to Jesus. The Rook's words had been whispers, but Jesus spoke with volume and authority.

"You are blameless in my sight."

But what about in his? Joe thought.

"I chose you before the creation of the world, Joe. You don't decide what you're worth, and neither does he."

He abandoned me.

"And so I came to save you."

The voices shrank back, and Joe realized they had been in his head and no one else's. Through eyes welling with tears, he sat up and addressed his father.

"My war is not with you," Joe said. "It's against the demons and the lies. You left, and now I forgive you. I forgive you . . . Dad."

Bill Platt stared up with bewilderment in his eyes, the look of a man who'd been ready for a punch and had instead received a hug. Joe kept his gaze locked on his father's face.

Bill's next words were unsteady. "I left because of me, Joe. That's all there is to it. I have a tendency and, well, I don't know why that'd change now. You wanna talk about forgiveness, that's fine. But it's not yours I need. A man's gotta first forgive himself."

And such were his final words. Bill Platt turned and lowered his head, then walked away from his sons and all the riders on horseback, trudging alone along the length of the bridge, all the way back to his old existence on the shore.

"Come," Jesus said, now for all to hear. "It's time for us to ride."

"Wait!" David shouted. "What about Dad? You can't just leave him. What will happen to him?"

Jesus replied, "I am lord to whoever calls my name. No one who knocks at my door will be refused, but neither will I force the weary traveler inside."

"But don't you care?" David demanded. "Aren't you sad to see him go?"

"Immensely. There is no greater loss I know. There are many things which can make a man happy, but he cries only at losing what he loves. Blessed, then, are those who weep for others."

"But," David stammered, looking from Joe to Jesus and back to the shore, "how can you ask me to choose? How can you ask me to choose between you and him?"

"Don't you see," Joe said, "I'm not! It finally makes sense to me. I came here to save you, David, but Jesus already did that. So I can listen to the demons and creatures like the Rook, stumbling around lost and alone, or I can trust that Jesus has a better way. I'm choosing him over me, David. That's the choice."

Joe sighed, looking out at the riders on the bridge, the lake of fire, his only brother standing between them. He knew he had only a moment, but he dismounted from his horse.

"I can't," David whispered, his body shaking, his eyes not daring to make contact. "I can't leave Dad."

"Dad left us," Joe replied. "You saw him go just now."

"You're one to talk," David huffed, taking a step back against the railing. "If it's that important to you, why didn't you just let me go too? Why'd you even bother coming back?"

Joe's whole body swelled with emotion. He held out his hands and looked to Jesus for support. Joe had come back, hadn't he? He'd left Heaven, been shot at, burned, abandoned, betrayed, frozen, and starved nearly to a second death. He'd been impatient, prideful, and naive. He'd been wrong, and others had paid the price. He'd risked everything to come here, and what did he have in return? *Salvation,*

Peter had said, *is not an object to be held, nor can it be so easily lost.* Why had he bothered? Why had he bothered at all?

"Because I love you," Joe said. "But there's someone who loves you more."

David understood at once—and looked away.

"So that's it, then?" he said. "You'll leave me too?"

Joe let his silence be the answer as tears welled up in his eyes.

"The time has come," Jesus announced. "We must go." Placing a hand on Joe's shoulder, he added in a whisper, "What a loveless world it would be if there were no pain in goodbyes."

Joe nodded to his brother one last time before mounting his horse. The whole bridge maintained a mournful silence, and even Jesus reached down to David as if to pay his respects. Joe thought he heard something fall from Jesus' robe, but he didn't dare look back. He wasn't sure if he could bear it.

And so the horses took to the air. Jesus first, then Peter and Maya and all the rest—a solemn procession up and away from the fiery swell. Joe was the last to leave, and truly nothing had been so difficult in all of his life. For even in trading shadows for light, chains for freedom, misery for joy, there remained a price to pay. What was new life without the old one dying first?

The hardest way to lose something, he knew, *is to choose to give it up.*

The army flew high above Brimtown, soaring over gray buildings and crooked streets. They wheeled in circles around City Hall. The revival had continued after the demon attack, and Joe could see Isaac Washington on stage and hear his voice pumping through the speakers.

"Do today's events not prove the necessity of our work?" he bellowed. "Yet who among you who purchased a pardon felt the sting of demon chains? No, it's plain to see they only targeted those who sinned by disturbing the peace, those who spoke their allegiance to that false prophet in the sky. My friends, there's a reason the demons left us alone . . ."

243

But Joe was already leaving the city, galloping out over the gray and lifeless desert. As they sailed upward, his burned and tattered clothes transformed into a clean linen robe like the one he'd first worn in Heaven, and all of his small cuts and bruises fell away like dirt in the shower. With each passing moment, Joe had the impression of landmarks below shrinking in the natural way one expects to see while ascending, until he realized that he wasn't going higher so much as he was growing. As if all of Hell had been a miniature playset and by some magic he'd shrunk down to explore it. For surely his size now belonged to his true self, brandishing his shield alongside his lord and savior, more than a conqueror through Jesus who loved him.

"Why'd you do it?" Joe asked. "Why'd you send me . . . for this?"

Jesus smiled. "The man who blamed himself for his brother's decisions is not the man who rides alongside me now."

"But you knew, didn't you? You knew you'd come here after me anyway and be the one to save the day. You knew David . . . why did you send me?"

"Look around you, Joe, at all the brothers and sisters who've joined us. All your stories are connected. You had your journey. They had theirs."

"But you could have come sooner! Some of these people were in Hell for years."

Jesus leaned back on his mount, displaying the fullness of his crimson robe.

"Do not some find love at first sight while others cross paths a hundred times before finally joining hands? Yet show me two lovers who would not say love found them at just the right time, that their stories have served to make them who they are. This is your story, Joe, and I've come at just the right time. Could it not also be so for others?"

"Will it always be like this?" Joe asked. "I still feel sad, even though I'm with you."

"The heart," Jesus replied, "is never silent. The lover chooses to listen."

"But it's a heavy weight to bear, isn't it? To care for everyone all the time?"

"You forget that you are man, and I am God. I saw the creation of the world and everything in it. I am the Alpha and the Omega, the Beginning and the End. A day is coming when God's dwelling place will be among his people. The old order will pass and every tear be wiped away. To the thirsty, I give water from the spring of life. Those who are victorious will inherit all this, and everything below will again be made new."

As they flew, Jesus reached out and rested his hand on Joe. Immediately, Joe felt his pain ease, like a hefty backpack finally off his shoulders after a long hike through the mountains. Although the weight itself hadn't changed an ounce, Joe no longer felt the pressure. He was free, not because the burden was less, but because Jesus had taken it from him.

"So we just go back now?"

Jesus grinned. "We, and anyone else who joins us."

"Right. Peter, Maya, and everyone else. I didn't forget about them."

"Nor did I. But the shepherd calls his friends and neighbors to rejoice when the lost sheep returns home."

Joe cocked his head in confusion. "What are you talking about?"

Jesus nodded, and Joe followed his gaze back down toward Hell. Suddenly the strangest sight caught his attention. There was another flying horse, one like his but not with their company, racing toward them at breakneck speed.

Its rider wore a bright orange construction vest.

"David!" Joe gasped. He pulled the reins of his own horse and sped down to meet his brother, crying and laughing and shouting all at the same time.

"David!" he called again.

Joe's brother pulled back on the reins and brought his horse to a halt midair. "That was wild. I can't believe how fast this guy flies."

"But," Joe stammered, "what are you doing here? I thought you were staying behind."

"Me too," David explained. "That is, until right before you took off, when I saw this fall out of Jesus' robe." He held up an exact replica of the salvation key, perhaps the very same one that he'd kicked into the lake.

"I remembered you showed it to me earlier, but it wasn't really yours, was it? It was his all along. Jesus gave it to me, and even after I tossed it, he gave it to me again."

Joe smiled. "The locks are turned from the inside and can be opened at any moment."

"I knew you came for me, Joe," David said, "but I didn't really think he did. Not with his giant army and that whole fight with the dragon and his speech and everything else. Why would a big guy like that come for a little guy like me? But then he gave this key to me, again, and I realized he did come for me after all. So I picked it up, and then all of a sudden this horse came down from the sky and, well, I guess I just made up my mind."

Joe raised an eyebrow. "So you're really coming, then? No more job at the bridge? No more Brimtown?"

David shrugged. "You were right about one thing. I wasn't getting anywhere on my own down there. Besides, I figured anyone with flying horses can't be all bad."

"So you have no idea what you're getting into."

Now it was David's turn to smile. "That's what makes it an adventure."

And so the angels surrounded them, and all the other riders on horseback, and their king in crown and crimson robe, and together they rejoiced.

TWENTY
ALL THAT IS

HIGH UP IN THE MOUNTAINS, far beyond the tree line and deep into the alpine tundra, they hiked across a rolling meadow. Pockets of remaining snow hid among depressions in the ground while elsewhere grass and lichen gave color to the landscape, giving the impression of spring after a long and bitter winter. They made their trek in a sort of reverent calm, speaking only when needed, Joe gasping at each new magnificent view and at times compelled to hum a song of praise. Up ahead, a wide pool reflected the craggy peaks in perfect stillness, and the cloudless sky appeared painted on the heavens.

"I've never felt so peaceful," he said as they neared their destination. "Is this why you bring people here alone?"

Jesus held out his arms, as if to touch the mountains on either side. He wore his usual white again and was without his many crowns. He was every bit as sovereign, though, king over every living creature down to the smallest blade of grass.

"They all belong to his pen," Jesus said, "and a good shepherd knows each of his sheep by name."

Joe nodded, accustomed by now to Jesus' way of responding to his questions, although the full meaning of it still eluded him. He admitted, however, that there was a certain specialness to this journey that hadn't belonged to the army's triumphant departure from Hell. The great walled city below was full of conversation and activity on its golden pathways and in its open squares, always with new arrivals and sounds of angels' trumpets. But up here, they'd found a private world. They stepped from rock to rock in moments of sacred intimacy, forging a new path as part of some secret adventure that belonged only to them. The whole experience was a kind of romance, an exciting, mysterious chase through uncharted lands and quiet pastures, skirting boulders and jumping streams, Joe's sense of wonder as fresh as the air he breathed.

At last, Jesus stopped. They had reached their final summit—a steep gradient leading up to a wide plateau, from the top of which Joe imagined one could behold the entire realm. From his current angle, he couldn't yet see the throne, and Joe suspected this fact was by design. He would have to take each hand- and foothold on faith, climbing steadily with all of his mind and soul and strength, the encounter reaching its zenith only as he crested the top of the mountain.

"I feel like Moses on Mt. Sinai," Joe remarked. "Minus the burning bush." He drew level with Jesus and shot him a glance. "Should I be nervous?"

"Who may ascend the Mountain of the Lord and stand in his holy place? But take heart, I have made your hands clean. Consider now with whom you are conversing—the Father and I are one."

Joe nodded, although still feeling a bit unsatisfied. Wanting to explore and perhaps to delay the final leg of their journey, Joe wandered off for a moment and tried to collect his thoughts. A lifetime had happened since he arrived in Heaven. How much he knew now that he hadn't known then. How many places he'd been and people he'd met and battles he'd fought. And all of it was merely the prologue. How much would he still discover and learn? What parts of his story were still yet to be told?

He came upon a patch of snow resting in the shadows and tested it with his feet. He'd done this many times already since they'd first reached the snowline, but it never got old. Touching snow must have been one of the strangest things in all of Heaven. Joe's bare toes sensed the cold exactly as they would have on Earth, but only now with joyous connotation. Instead of chill or threat of frostbite, Joe felt a gentle icy tickle dance across his skin.

After several minutes, Jesus said, "I have something for you. A gift."

Joe almost laughed. Another gift? What else could he possibly need? What else could he even receive? Jesus had already given him true life.

But Jesus insisted, and presently Joe came near him once again. They sat together on a wide boulder, their snow-colored robes upon the rock blending them into the landscape. Joe found his posture naturally curious and alert, figuring there must be some significance to the timing of this present. For his part, Jesus had the eager look of a parent anticipating his child's reaction on Christmas morning. He held his arms out with hands folded and, after a dramatic pause, opened his fists to reveal a stone.

"Take it," Jesus urged. "It's yours."

It was a white stone, resembling one Joe might find at the bottom of a river, made smooth and flat by the constant flow of water. He took the stone and examined its polished surface. On both sides were patterns of little black lines that reminded him of ancient runes. In fact—he noticed upon closer examination—the lines were indeed symbols of some sort, being uniform in size and intentionally carved into the center of the rock. Joe figured it must be some kind of language or code, but he didn't have the slightest guess as to its meaning.

"What is it?" he asked.

Jesus leaned back against the boulder and stared up at the precipice before them.

"Tell me, Joe, what makes a name?"

"A name?" He shrugged. "It's just what people call you, I guess."

"So it serves only to distinguish one from another?"

"Um . . . I don't know. I guess it depends on the name."

"True, there are many types. Begin with the titles, epithets, designations, and ranks. Consider the doctor, the champion, the general, the king. Or what of the graduate or recipient of every award, granted the name by some merit or right? Think of the childhood nickname, the measured honorific, the spouse's sweet terms of endearment. What supplies the truest affirmations? What belongs to the worst of all insults and slurs? Compare the assistant and the colleague, the acquaintance and the friend, the mistress and the wife, the boy and the man. They are more than mere monikers, are they not? Does not a name suggest both who you are and who you are expected to be?"

Joe ran his thumb along the white stone, feeling the ridges of the carving. "But most of the things you said, those can change, or not matter after a while."

"Right you are. But a true name speaks not of erroneous presumption or some mutable state of being. A true name speaks only of reality itself—who you're becoming and who someday you'll be when all things are redeemed."

Joe looked out across the landscape and saw rocks scattered in every direction, all shapes and sizes and patterns in a way he hadn't quite noticed before. He'd heard no two snowflakes were identical, and surely the stone in his hand was also one of a kind.

"Does everyone have one, then? A true name?"

"Everyone in all creation," Jesus said. "They are all fearfully and wonderfully made."

"So how do people find their true names when we've all got other ones to start with?"

"Don't you know that a name is given, not found? A stranger must ask for it. A friend knows it. A father gives it."

"So this," Joe said, holding up the stone, "is my true name? Written on here? But I don't know how to read it. I can't even pronounce it."

"And so I will teach you to say it. Indeed, you'll find the sound of it is not so foreign after all, not to the innermost parts of your heart.

Your talents, gifts, and deepest-felt desires have been hints and previews, a foretelling of who you're created to be. For even new creation is not a metamorphosis in full. Consider the sapling that grows to be a mighty oak—a tree becoming more of the tree it was made to be. Only God says I am who I am. The rest are still becoming."

Joe recalled his mother's words from his first day in Heaven. *Even the trees here grow and bear fruit. Why should we not do the same?*

"When I first got here," Joe confessed, "I didn't want to eat any of the apples in the grove. I thought it was a test or something. I didn't want to fail. But I only ever could fail, right? I thought I was rescuing David, but I never stood a chance in Brimtown without you."

"When you were a child, you reasoned like a child. You knew in part, but soon you shall know fully, just as you are fully known. For as long as you love, love never fails."

"I've learned a lot about love," Joe said. "But I'm still not sure I know what it is."

"Not a what," Jesus replied, "but a who. It is love who gives you your name."

He hopped down from the boulder and beckoned Joe to follow.

"Come. We have journeyed this far, and now you are ready."

"Ready for what?" Joe asked, although he already knew.

"To ascend the mountain," Jesus said, "and behold the face of God."

Maryann Warren reclined back in her armchair, the book she'd meant to read untouched on the table beside her and her cup of coffee now cold and half-finished. The Christmas tree glowed in the corner of the room, plugged in more for the sake of her company and tradition, not because she felt at all in the mood for it. There must have been plenty of people in the world who had it worse than her— no food or shelter or clean clothes to wear—although giving thanks tonight was nothing more than hollow platitude. It'd been enough to lose her daughter, but now her grandsons too? And all of them so suddenly, all without a diagnosis or warning or goodbye.

She hadn't told this to anyone, not even to George, but at the funeral, she'd found herself wishing that she were there inside a casket instead of them, and not in the way that people so casually blurted "it should have been me" in a state of guilt-stricken grief. No, hers was a dark and desperate longing to depart from this world and all its meaningless tragedy. And why not? Her own day was not far off to be lifted by the pallbearers and carried down the aisle, hands folded and finally laid to rest. Surely it'd come sooner than she expected, even if later than she wanted. She'd never felt so exhausted, not ever in seventy years.

"You alright, Mom?" asked Russ, poking his head into the room. She looked up at him, her lifeline, her one remaining joy. He'd done so much for them these past two weeks, driving up as soon as he'd heard and helping make arrangements for the funeral. They'd canceled their family trip to Breckenridge and all come up to spend the week, handling all of the calls and cooking and cleaning without a single complaint, even staying in when she'd decided not to go to service. She'd never missed it as far as she could remember, but tonight of all nights she just couldn't bring herself to go. Not this year. Not with her wounds so fresh. This was no season of joy.

"Oh, I'm just resting," she said, looking at Russ.

He gave an empathetic nod. "Okay. We're all going to be in the backyard if you feel up to coming out later. It's a little chilly, but a beautiful night."

His gentle encouragement, same as always, prodding her out of the chair but not demanding she stand. But it hardly mattered. He might as well have asked her to climb a thousand steps.

"Maybe in a bit, Russ."

She closed her eyes but found no sleep. A full two weeks after the fact now, and the house still rang loud with echoes of the boys, not of recent years when David was out on his own and Joe had his job in Detroit, but a peeling back of all the layers of their time growing up, their voices and shouts and those racecars they'd loved zipping through the halls and their laughter following close behind. Especially in those hard few years after they took custody, George used to be the one to say it. *I'm not thankful for how we got 'em, but I'm thankful that they're here.* They'd had their share of struggles—she'd be the first to admit it—but somehow it had all turned out. She couldn't use the front door without remembering Joe's nervous excitement while he stood by his suitcase and waited to leave for computer camp, or when David had stopped to hug her as he was leaving the house on the day he finally graduated. Yes, it had all turned out in the end. She'd been so proud of them both.

"I'm not thankful for how you left us," Maryann whispered, "but I'm so thankful you were here."

The doorbell rang, startling her from the memories.

"Now who would that be," she wondered aloud, "on Christmas Eve?"

A neighbor? A well-intentioned friend who'd missed her at church and had thought to stop by? God forbid carolers. She shrank back in her chair, willing the visitor to go away, grateful the blinds were shut in the living room window so no one could spy her at home.

But the bell persisted, and soon George hurried down the entry hall to pacify the visitor. He turned the deadbolt and swung the door open. Maryann waited to hear a voice, to receive some kind of clue as to the identity of their late-night caller, but none came.

"George," she called, curiosity finally winning out, "who is it?"

"Come here for a minute," he replied. "You have to see this."

She sighed and reluctantly climbed out of her chair. Maryann had been married long enough to know he'd keep her in suspense all night if he had to, until at last she came to the door.

"Who is it?" she repeated, pulling her sweater against the cold and moving around the door to see out across the threshold.

But there was no one there. The street was deserted save for a few parked cars, and the sidewalks were empty in front of the brightly lit homes. Whoever it'd been must have made a mad dash away from the doorstep, but, strangely, there were no footprints in the snow. She might have thought she were going mad hearing things, until she looked down.

On the step was a single bouquet of flowers.

George crouched low to collect them, lifting them up into the porch light. As a lifelong gardener, Maryann immediately noticed the diversity of blooms. They were wildflowers of every sort. Sunflowers and roses and marigolds and zinnias—twenty, thirty different varieties, all individually selected and trimmed. Each stem was fresh and colorful, as if they'd just come from the florist, because certainly no one could pick these in winter. They'd had plenty of flowers at the funeral, but this single bunch was more lively and bright than any of them.

"There's a note," George said.

She found the card attached to the bouquet with a small piece of twine. No name—just a short, handwritten message. She cleared her throat and read aloud.

"He died for us so that, whether we are awake or asleep, we may live together with him." Below the note was a reference: "1 Thessalonians 5:10."

"Who do you suppose brought this?" George asked.

"I don't know," she said. "There's no name." Although she did have some idea, the kind of instinctual gut feeling that only a mother develops with regard to her own. She had a suspicion, but it was the stuff of books and movies, something far too outlandish to say.

Instead, she asked, "Do you think they're at peace, George?"

"Oh, I do," he replied, knowing exactly what she meant.

"I can't help but think how it won't be long before we're up there too," she said. "I wish I knew what to do with the time we have left."

He reached over and squeezed her hand. "We've got some work to do yet. I feel it."

They stood in silence and looked at the sky, and for the first time, Maryann noticed how perfectly clear it was. Russ had been right. It was a beautiful night. The brilliance of the stars defied the usual suburban light pollution, creating a vast and sparkling array. Even up at the cottage on Duck Lake she'd rarely seen it like this. These were the same constellations that had hung in the sky for all of human history and well before that, light shining in the darkness.

And somehow as she gazed up at the stars, she forgot the cold, and the numbness drained from her limbs. For there was purpose in her grief, and time for it too, but the story itself did not end in death. She knew this with certainty, like how she knew spring would follow winter, although they had several months to wait.

"Do you have the radio on?" George asked. "I think I hear music."

"No," she replied, "but I hear it too." And she did—soft but distinct, the jubilant sound of trumpets drifting down from the stars. "It's faint, but it's there."

"Where's it coming from then?"

"From Heaven, I think," she said without hesitation, as if it were the most natural thing in the world—and indeed, perhaps it was.

"I think we're hearing Heaven's song."

And so they listened. There on the front step, with the door still open behind them, they joined hands and looked to the sky. And together they basked in the glory of the God who came down, standing free in his kingdom and alive in the wonders of his love.

Made in the USA
Lexington, KY
09 June 2017